BLACKPOOL

D0262444

THE LITTLE DOG
LAUGHED

THE LITTLE DOG LAUGHED

BY

LEONARD MERRICK

HODDER AND STOUGHTON
LIMITED   LONDON
ST. PAUL'S HOUSE
WARWICK SQUARE
E.C.
4

01076061

155928

PRINTED IN GREAT BRITAIN
FOR HODDER AND STOUGHTON, LIMITED,
BY RICHARD CLAY & SONS, LIMITED,
BUNGAY, SUFFOLK.

CONTENTS

GALOPIN'S circle was not squeamish, but its eyebrows rose when he announced that he meant to marry Lulu.   Lulu had been for six years what newspapers in England would have described as his " friend " if they had had occasion to refer to her.   They might have added that she was famous for the many friends she had made before she knew him.   One or two of his intimates were moved to remind Galopin of her experiences of friendship—in an abbreviated list, their time being valuable.   The lessee of the Comédie Moderne was biographical for a quarter of an hour, and Jaccottet, the gifted author of the most improper farces in Paris, spoke very gravely indeed.   He said :

" When I urge you to reconsider your intention, my dear colleague, I assure you I am not influenced by personal considerations.   Certainly your marriage might imperil my peace, but believe me it's for your own sake that I say ' don't.' "

" *Comment?* " interposed Galopin, his bald

head askew. " My marriage with Lulu might imperil your peace ? How do you work that out ? "

" But naturally ! Your Lulu and my Yvette have been chums for half their lives, n'est-ce-pas ? If, in your defiance of decorum, you make Lulu your wife, Yvette also may develop an itch for matrimony. For that matter, all the women we know may be wanting the men to marry them— there is no limit to the evil you may create. You would, of course, be acting in a most egotistical way; but, I repeat, my counsel is dictated solely by your own interests."

" Ah, but listen ! " exclaimed Galopin. " You horrify one by the philistinism of your views. I discover you to be bourgeois, positively bour- geois; I no longer recognise you. I have always thought you had the sincerest liking for Lulu."

" You were not mistaken. I find Lulu charm- ing. She is intelligent, and jolly, and she has a good heart. I dine in no home with more pleasure than in yours. Ah yes, your arrangement with Lulu is perfect as it stands. But when you talk of wedding ceremonies—Mon Dieu ! That is another pair of shoes."

" What does one seek in marriage ? " shouted Galopin. " It is companionship, n'est-ce-pas ?

Above all, companionship ? Very well. I have found the best companion of my life in Lulu. My affections have never wavered from her since we came together. I do not romance, it is a fact. My virtue has been impregnable. There might be something in what you say if I were twenty years younger—but I should know myself by this time ! I am not a boy. Remember I am forty-three."

"That's true," said Jaccottet, who knew he was forty-eight.

"I am a writer—I am above restrictions. Vice is at once my pastime and my inspiration. From the sewers I derive my daily bread. To share my interests, to be congenial, my wife must be emancipated. Lulu is, to the finger-tips, bo-hemian, she is a ' good fellow '; I can take her anywhere—I do not speak of the show places. If you had seen her with me the other night in the rue Aubry-le-Boucher ! To the manner born. And, mind you, there are more bottles broken across heads in the rue Aubry-le-Boucher than in all the rest of Paris. For us intellectuals it is essential to wallow in the mire—life must hold no secrets from us. Do you suggest my marrying some unsophisticated miss, if there is any left now, whose idea of seeing life is to look at the spectre of the Place Pigalle ?   If I go to supper in the Place Pigalle now, I wear mourning."

" Your outlook seems no wider than a wedding ring, my dear Roland.   It is within the scope of human endeavour not to marry at all," said Jaccottet.

" I owe it to Lulu !   I do not forget her constancy during that year I was so hard up.   An angel of devotion and economy.   She walked with a string bag for miles every morning to find the lowest prices.   Lulu, who has had the most fantastic luxury in her time !   In Russia she was like Royalty.   There were ninety-eight domestics in the palace."

" Too many ! "

" I do not boast—I have her word.   Nothing was too superb for him to lavish on her.   He was at her feet.   Not only he.   If you knew half the frantic things men have done for her !   I am not bragging when I say it—Lulu's career has been effulgent.   And this winter, when I had pneumonia !   Her devotion was sublime.   No words can say.   She has more than deserved the step I take.   But I have never had a hint from her—not a hint.   She was stupefied when I told her my intention, she could scarcely believe her ears. She is veritably in ecstasies; her delight and pride are touching to see. During my convalescence last month I felt I must buy her something very handsome when I was up again, but a gift commensurate with all she had done for me would have been terribly expensive. And this hasn't cost anything at all."

"Not yet," said Jaccottet.

Galopin did not exaggerate Lulu's joy. Nor should the uncharitable think she was so much elated because, being but slightly his junior, and having lost her figure and gained a double chin, she put a reduced value on herself. Far from it. Parisians view the years of the opposite sex generously—off the stage; a woman of charm is found young for decades; and a man of intellect doesn't begin to look old till he falls to bits. Her elation was of the purest brand; she was to soar to the dizzy heights of respectability. Her head reeled in contemplating the sensational ascent. The gushing congratulations of the ladies at her next at home were delicious to her. There was a note of jealousy in their gush, and an air of superiority in her wreathed smiles.

Alone at last with her confidante Yvette, she said censoriously, "Blanche gets more loose-tongued every day. That wasn't at all a nice story that she told."

"We have been hearing it for months," yawned Yvette, surprised. "It is time she got a new one."

"It was much too free. And I don't like the way she goes on—her affairs are too unsettled; before you are familiar with the name of one man, it is another! Blanche, you know, was never of our world."

"We are used to her. Our world? I have not recognised it for years, my dear. Wherever one goes, one runs against some nondescript from no-man's-land, or some upstart from the mud. The deterioration since the war is frightful, of course. I always say I may see my servant emptying the slops in the morning, and supping at the next table to me at night. All the same, Blanche isn't a bad sort—she is all right in her way."

"I don't say she's not—in her way; but I complain that she has no moral sense. Blanche is one of the people I shan't be able to keep up."

"What? You don't mean to drop her?" cried Yvette. "Ah, no, you can't do that, after all this time!"

"It will be compulsory. As a married woman I must draw the line. Blanche is not the only one I shan't be able to receive afterwards."

"Avec ça!" sneered Yvette.

"My position will forbid. It will be due to Roland that I live up to what he does for me. He pays me the supremest honour, n'est-ce-pas?"

"It is showy," allowed Yvette, who had no prospect of such aggrandisement herself.

"Showy?"

"It is very nice to look at—it makes a good display. I am entranced at the news, my dear, because you are so bucked about it, but—I know I may speak frankly, dear—what is there in it, boiled down? You do not figure to yourself that because he marries you the upper classes are going to flock to leave their cards? Your life will be just what it is now."

"Aha! You will see," returned Lulu loftily. "I shall make a lot of changes, as I tell you."

"You mean you will make a lot of enemies. There is nothing difficult about that. What I say is, you will get no solid advantage out of it. But why should we argue, my dear friend? It is all a matter of taste. To me contracts for love have no attraction. Personally, I find them a little—er—sordid. But then I am a sentimentalist!"

She departed, after an exchange of kisses on both cheeks; and Lulu raged, "How she envies me! What a spiteful cat!" And Yvette fumed, "Elle en a du toupet! What a pompous pig!"

Her epithet was false.   Lulu was not a pig—
she was the victim of noble emotions.   She was
ardently, overwhelmingly grateful to Galopin,
and her meritorious desire was to prove worthy
of her preferment.   Almost she wished he
were in low waters again, that she might repeat
her acts of heroism with the string bag.   But
his latest brain-wave, *Accroche Ton Cœur*, was
crowding the theatre, and they were dining or
supping at every auspicious place in Paris, from
the Chinese restaurant that had newly opened in
the Latin quarter to moribund Montmartre,
inclusive of holes around the Halles.

On their wedding day they dined in the rue
Fontaine.   Trees and the moon, or a high-grade
hotel would have chimed better with her exultation, but it was the wrong weather for tables in the
open air, and high-grade hotels bored Galopin
very much.   He was voluble and gay at dinner.
" Here's to us, old girl ! "   From time to time
he patted her arm affectionately.   He knew his
gift of marriage had meant a lot to her, and he
was on capital terms with himself.   But he was
at sea when he held out his cigarette case and she
shook her head.

" What ?   They are the same as your own,"
he urged.

" I shall not smoke any more," she told him.
Even then he didn't follow her. " What do
you mean ? Why not ? "

" Because ! " she said, with a tender smile.

For a moment he was dumbfounded. " Thou
art daft ! It isn't true ? "

" But yes," she said. " I shall not smoke any
more now we are married. I shall train myself
to do without it."

" But why ? What for ? What is the idea ?
Go on, take one ! Don't be absurd."

" No," she said ; " it isn't refined for women
to smoke. The right women do not do it."

" What an illusion ! Where do you get it
from ? You are behind the times, ma chère !
In the best society women smoke now."

" Not all," she insisted ; " not the most
correct."

" But listen ! You astound me. Manners
have changed, voyons. Not only in Paris. In
London, I hear, it is sensational. Things that
used to be audacious for cocottes are now customary among young English girls of good
family. I am told one sees them sprawling in the
best hotels with their flash cigarette-holders stuck
in their painted mouths—and taking their cock-
tails, and looking like grues."

"Perhaps," she said. "But I do not wish to look like a grue. I may be too particular, but I should feel ashamed. Now put your case back, for I shan't touch it, and order the liqueurs. For me, crème de menthe."

"Are you sure it is refined enough?" asked Galopin, chuckling.

"Shut up, you villain," she laughed; and she was going to throw her napkin at him, but remembered that that wouldn't be refined.

It may have been her refusal of a cigarette that moderated his suggestions that evening. They went simply to see the end of the revue at the Perchoir, so tiny but so bold, and sauntered from it into the Canari afterwards. The star of the moment at the Concert Mayol came in by and by and greeted them. She was with Rose Biot, who had written *Carols to Cocaine*, a young, cadaverous blonde, not ill-featured. The poetess's hair was trimmed like a man's, and she had a monocle in her eye. Galopin had not spoken to her before, and he regarded her with interest; to her esoteric knowledge of the under-world an elderly realist was said to owe the boom of shocking Paris with his recent novel. At Galopin's solicitation the newcomers joined them at their table, but Rose Biot proved very disappointing. The monocle and her right eye permanently attached, she drank his champagne till four o'clock without making a remark, and answered laconically in lifeless tones when she was addressed.

"Morbleu! that was a poor investment," he growled as soon as he and Lulu were in a taxi.

"But what in the world made you ask them to sit down?" burst forth Lulu. "To plaster such people on me was not chic."

"*Comment donc?*" he asked, startled.

"It was not the thing to do! It was an indignity," she cried, her voice breaking between anger and a sob.

"Quelle blague! What are you talking about?" His amazement was open-mouthed. "I don't understand. Such people? It isn't a month ago that you were dying to meet her."

"A month ago!" retorted Lulu passionately. "A month ago is not to-day. I am your wife now."

He thought he was going to say something vehement, but as the full import of her words overwhelmed him, his voice died in his throat. The bridegroom sat, faint with horror, staring at a black future of respectability.

. . . . . .

B

Lulu pursued the narrow way bravely. To refrain from smoking was a hard struggle; and she missed more than cigarettes. For one thing, she missed popularity. Though she had intentionally affronted but five ladies during the first six weeks, other ladies, broader-minded, regarded her act as a reflection on their own salons, and the affront had spread. Even Yvette had gradually faded from view. The narrow way was thorny, but the consciousness of virtue supported Lulu. It supported her despite the fact that her righteousness lacked her Roland's approval. She found Galopin distressingly blind to the beauty of her conduct, ungratefully opposed to it. Galopin had often moaned the French for " damn it," with reference to her new idea of a sprightly night out.

More than once his remonstrance was more prolix—and then she answered, " Little man, thou hast been bien gentil. If I do not repeat it every day, I remember it all the time. It is not merely for my own sake that I comport myself with more reserve now, but for thine also. I should be thankless if I did not. It is thy due that thy wife should be esteemed."

" But, hell !   I find it dull," groaned Galopin.

" At the start," said Lulu encouragingly.

" The first steps are a little irksome for thee. Soon thou wilt accustom thyself to a tranquil life, chéri. I am not sure but what we should be wise to quit Paris and make our home in the country. It would be very agreeable. Thou wouldst have a garden, and thy poultry, and no doubt we should make nice friends among the neighbours."

" Ah, I beseech thee ! " cried Galopin wildly. " Not much ! We grow mossy enough in Paris."

And when three or four months had passed, there was occasion for him to expostulate more firmly. He had asked Jaccottet to bring Yvette to dinner, and Jaccottet, with a wealth of gesture, had professed to have no evening free. " Ah, it is futile to discuss ! " he said, when pressed to be explicit. " If you insist, I am surprised by the invitation."

" What ? "

" Surprised."

" Why ? "

" Because we no longer have the honour of being visited by your wife."

" Hein ? She does not go to you ? " gasped Galopin.

" You were unaware ? "

" Completely. What's wrong ? Yvette and she have quarrelled ? "

" Pah ! Do I concern myself with the quarrels
of women ? At that I should mock. It is not
that there was a quarrel. No. It appears that
madame Galopin has adopted towards Yvette a
certain attitude—I cannot pretend to elucidate it—
which has conveyed to her—as you drag the facts
from me—that her society was not congenial.
Well——"

" You appal me," said Galopin. " But I
assure you, I have not the shadow of a doubt that
Yvette is mistaken. You know how easily——"

" Oui. Yvette endeavoured to close her eyes
for a long while, but at last she was compelled to
recognise she was unwelcome. Accordingly——"

" I am positive——"

" As for me, I make no criticism. It is a
matter——"

" Lulu's affection for Yvette is so intense——"

" Oui. My wish is to say nothing about it.
But as you wring the truth from my reluctant lips,
I am constrained to own I do not go to dinner at
an apartment where Yvette has been insulted."

" Insulted ? My dear friend, I am absolutely
convinced——"

" And since you coerce me into candour, I may
add that her case is not unique. Insults rain on
everybody. It is a deluge."

"I shall have to talk to Lulu," stuttered Galopin. "But as regards Yvette, I would bet you a thousand to one——"

"Oui. In the interests of Yvette it is not worth your while to disturb madame Galopin. The affair is finished. But as you importune me for my views, I must tell you honestly that the position you are placed in is ludicrous. And it will soon be solitary. Ere long the exalted society of madame Galopin will be the only society left to you."

Galopin betook himself to a café, and sat immersed in thought. The last words were still loud to him, louder than anything else in the city of dreadful noises. He heard the words above the blasts of a myriad vehicles, hooting, screaming, roaring, bellowing on every note of torture; the crashing thunders of the trams, bungling and bounding on their insurgent course. The hour had come for him to speak solemnly to his wife!

He said to her, "My darling, in matrimony there are responsibilities. There are mutual obligations. I do not misjudge your heart—I know it is pure gold—but I perceive with pain that your head is turned by vanities that are beneath your truer nature. It is the love I bear you that prompts me to appeal to you. In your feverish cravings for respectability you have lost sight of the things that matter—the vital things, my dear one, on which domestic happiness is built. I seek in vain now the Lulu who was so near to me in the noonday of our union, and on our bridal morn."

" Ah zut ! " she cried. " Yvette was looking for trouble—I didn't do anything at all."

" I am not thinking solely of Yvette," continued her husband earnestly. " I think of the rue Aubry-le-Boucher and the joyous companionship of yore. I think of the bright evenings in our home, and the homes of others before the poison of respectability had warped your mind. But it is not too late. All hope is not yet lost. With resolution you may again be normal. Pull up while there still is time ! Each day's delay will make recovery harder. The poison will soak into your very bones. You will grow more bourgeoise than the bourgeoisie. An effort now may save you. Courage, courage, and you will retrieve your fall ! "

But the best he could do was to persuade her to patch it up with Yvette. And, the reconciliation being hollow, he did not find it make matters any livelier.

.   .   .   .   .   .

As the months went by, there was born in

Lulu a doubt that she strove to stifle. Her
husband's depression she had viewed with gallant confidence, but at his sudden gaiety of late
her mind misgave her. She recognised, with a
pang, how frequent were his " business appoint-
ments." And when he surprised her by a
piece of jewellery, without an anniversary to
explain it, self-delusion was impossible.

It was doubly mortifying that Yvette chanced
to be present when the conscience offering came.
Yet its coming renewed their intimacy. They
were alone. " It is ravishing, it is exquisite, what
perfect taste ! " enthused Yvette—and the look
on her face made Lulu's eyes fill. " Ah, don't
do that, imbecile ! " cried Yvette, putting out her
arms.

" You know I have been devoted to him,"
quavered Lulu, clinging to her.

" According to your own ideas. But—well, I
can only say it has amazed me ! "

" What ? "

" Your rotten judgment. Your experience has
gone for nothing; towards your husband you
have behaved like an ingénue. I shall never
understand it. I don't want to rub it in, old
dear, but astonishment has kept me awake at
night. If you had never seen a man before, you

couldn't have shown more tragic innocence.
Roland, who is as bad as they make 'em, who
married you because you were a kindred spirit—
you rewarded him by emulating the principal of
a young ladies' seminary. You, who used to
know a bit ! The result was certain. No one
is surprised—except perhaps that it is Rose Biot,
with her legs like a wish-bone."

" She ? They talk ? "

" Zut ! In a month it will be ancient history.
In your place I should not worry about the talk,
but I should be more prudent for the future,
especially as you love him. Anyway, a per-
centage on his presents to others wouldn't be
good enough. You have been dismally proper
for a man to whom propriety is nauseous. Alors,
be yourself again ! "

Lulu sat brooding, with her chin sunk. " You
are right," she muttered. " There is nothing for
me to say. I meant well—the defence of a fool.
Well, finished ! " She rose. " I win him back.
You'll see. All Paris shall see. Her little hour
when I was asleep ! Need *I* fear *her ?* Ha ha !
She may whistle her dirty head off for him now;
I laugh at her, the salope. I regain my own !
I am still *I.*"

Galopin, who came in to dinner, and was to

meet Rose Biot at nine o'clock, was glad to find the surprise had been such a success. His wife sparkled with pleasure. She had made a toilette in honour of the gift, and there was champagne on the table.

" Sapristi! we go the pace," he remarked. " It is the champagne we bought for festivals, too ! Do you know what it cost, that wine ? "

" It is a festival to-night," she said gaily; " I celebrate my jewel. If you had seen me ! I thought it must be some mistake when the packet came. It was adorable of you, vieux chéri. You have the art of doing a pretty thing with chic. That was always a knack you had. I remember when we first met, I said—Take some more spinach ! "

" What did you say when we first met ? "

" A trifle. Not worth repeating."

" But tell me ! " urged Galopin.

" It was nothing; I remember saying, ' He is a gentleman who has the rarest quality in men— tact.' Apropos of—I forget. But I am paying you compliments ! That isn't judicious. Fill up your glass."

" Yes, I have tact," assented Galopin, beaming. " It is instinctive—I haven't to think. It is a fine wine, hein ? It was worth the price. But do not figure to yourself that men are less tactful than women. Quite the reverse."

" Ah, my dear friend ! " she protested radiantly. " It is well known."

" That is to say, it is a parrot phrase. Mais, mon Dieu ! In my life I have met far fewer tactful women than tactful men. Of a truth, women, as a sex, are astonishingly tactless. For a single instance : at every spa, the progress of every invalid is retarded hourly by women who tell him, with condolence, how exceedingly sick he looks. Of all nations. I do not doubt that if I were sick in Zululand, my friends among the black ladies would delay my recovery by sighing over me that I looked paler every day."

" It is a fact," she acknowledged, with the air of one staggered by revelation. " You have a way of putting things ! "

Galopin's loquacity at dinner interested him so much that he had sipped half his coffee before he noticed that she was smoking a cigarette.

" *Comment ?* You smoke ! " he exclaimed.

Her expression was discomfited. " Apparently."

" You go back to it ? "

" I don't think I want to tell you."

" Tell me what ? "

"Ah, this has been very nice—don't spoil it!" she pouted.

"Spoil it? But how?"

"You'd chaff me."

"I should chaff you because you smoke a cigarette?"

"There's more to it than that," she murmured, her glance half humorous, half contrite.

"Ah?"

"Yes. Everything. I've been a fool. I've been having a bad time. I own up; I've missed the fun. Horribly! I've given in."

She waited, smiling. Her heart sickened more in every second of his silence as she waited smiling.

He didn't speak.

"I have had enough of it—I've done with the idiocy. My nature wins. How patient you've been! You'll have nothing to be patient with in future—I want all the excitement I can get."

"You are quite right, my dear," said Galopin, looking at his watch. "Why bore yourself? Pick up your friends again. It will be much jollier for you."

Heroically there was still assurance in her tones, but the arduous smile was only on her lips now; in her avid eyes was dread. "Voilà. You've got it! I might have known. We're alike, we two. I pant to begin—to make up for lost time. Why not to-night? Leave it to *me* to plan the programme! It shall be hot stuff. If you knew how often thoughts have come to me in the dullness! I'm crazy to live again—I can't start too soon. Roland, to-night!"

"Unfortunately," sighed Galopin, "I must see Michel this evening about an alteration in the last act, and I fear we shall be at work till late. I should be going already. It's a nuisance."

"Ah, business is business," she said lightly.

"Shall we ring up Yvette and ask if she is free to go to a theatre with you?"

"N-no. After all, I'm not sure I want to go out. I think my head begins to ache a little."

"Perhaps it's the cigarettes. When one isn't used——"

"Perhaps," she said.

"In fact, now you have broken yourself of the habit, it might be a mistake to resume it. . . . Well, good-night, chérie. Sleep well."

"Good-night, chéri," she answered, still smiling.

She sat alone, gazing at the door.

"How queer a world," wailed Lulu, her face flopping to the table; "I never suffered for my sins—but I get it in the neck for being good!"

" ' P o m p o u s firemen, a century old, are growing in the park, and stables run about in them,' " said the young man.

" No, monsieur. ' Stately fir trees, of that age, are growing there, and squirrels run about in them,' " replied the professor, with a frown.

The scene was a compartment in the De Boo Institute of Languages, in Paris. It contained a blackboard, two chairs, and a narrow table, at which the professor and the student sat facing each other. The professor had beauty, and wore a becoming dress.

" I feared I must be mistaken," faltered the young man, who was taking his first lesson there. " My understanding of French is very slight."

" You speak it, however, with surprising ease in moments," observed the professor dryly.

" You do not flatter me, mademoiselle ? Ah, that is very encouraging ! I have a great ambition to speak French well. Do you know, it appears to me that I understand better when you converse with me than when you read phrases from the book."

" I have noticed it," she said.

" Indeed, if you would be so good as to converse all the time, I feel, somehow, I should advance more speedily."

" Conversation is against the rules. I have been remiss already. You will find all the other professors keep strictly to the text."

" Other professors ? *Comment donc ?* " stammered the student, paling. " It will not be always you who instruct me ? "

" By no means. I may not see you again for a week."

" Ah, but listen ! " he expostulated. " I am here solely because I had heard such great accounts of your ability. I am most averse from having other professors fobbed off on me. When I paid for the tickets I mentioned your name with the utmost emphasis. Do not let me down, I beg."

" The arrangements are not made by me, monsieur—they are made by the Director; I do not know, from day to day, which pupils he may send to me." She recited from the dismal book again. " Tell me, in your own language, what that means."

The young man growled in English, which, strangely enough, he spoke with a marked

French accent, " It means that you have a cousin in Antwerp."

" It means that the cover of the cushion is inside out," rejoined mademoiselle Rousseau sharply. She regarded him with grave dissatisfaction. " I must request you to be serious."

" Serious ? I am tragic ! " he declared. " I desire a heart-to-heart talk with the Director. May I entreat you to do me the kindness to send for him ? "

" You can ask for him, in the office, when the lesson concludes, monsieur; or you can speak to the Inspector, if you wish—it is the time for him to come round. But I warn you that I think it will be useless. To assign to the student a different professor daily is a feature of the system."

" The feature does not commend itself to me. Mon Dieu ! I part with a high fee for a mere half-hour a day, and then I am told I have squandered the cash. It is not amusing. Between ourselves, I cannot afford the lessons; it was an act of terrible extravagance for me to indulge in the six tickets I have taken."

" Your present fluency might lead one to think they were superfluous," remarked the lady. And as the door was opened by a gentleman in a dirty collar, with a pencil behind his ear, she added in more scholastic tones, " ' The little birds are singing in the boughs.' Continue, monsieur."

But the pupil disobeyed her flagrantly.

"Monsieur the Inspector?" he inquired, springing to his feet. And with a volubility that took the other aback, he went on, "Monsieur, I receive strangely disagreeable news; I learn that I have enrolled myself as student here under a false impression—that I may not count on my education being constantly conducted by mademoiselle Rousseau. It is a shock of the first magnitude. My intentions are earnest; I am no temporary trifler—I propose to continue my studies for at least a year. Two years! Perhaps much longer! I am bent on acquiring a thorough knowledge of French. I protest strongly against being tossed from hand to hand. In such a fashion I could make no progress."

"Permettez, monsieur. We vary the professors in order to accustom the pupils to the inflections of different voices."

"The voice of mademoiselle contents me."

"It is by such means we achieve our rapid results," pleaded the Inspector, his arms outspread. " I repeat that the arrangement is to the pupils' advantage."

" Still more to the advantage of the Institute, hein ? They won't get on too fast, and there is small risk of their chumming up with a professor and being taught by him outside at half the price. Alors, I have, so far, purchased no more than six tickets, fortunately. I appear to have wasted a trivial sum; it is of no consequence—but to waste thirty precious minutes each day would be a disaster that I shudder to contemplate. I beg you will be so amiable as to inform monsieur de Boo of my attitude forthwith, and to apprise him that if his system forbids him to assure me that my tuition shall be undertaken by mademoiselle Rousseau solely, invariably, and without any ' regrettable mischance, for which he offers a thousand apologies,' I indignantly make the Institute a present of the five tickets remaining to me, and betake myself to an institute where the system meets my views."

" I go to speak to monsieur de Boo," said the Inspector, dazed by the flood of French the Englishman had been pouring on him.

During the foregoing colloquy the lady had maintained an air of sedate detachment, though at the young man's phrase a " trivial sum," and his cunning bait of paying fees for years, something like an incipient smile had twitched her lips.

c

Now, in the momentous interval, she gazed demurely at the blackboard, while the young man, tremulous with hope, gazed at the lady.

Within a few minutes the Inspector returned to say that the imperious pupil's point was conceded.

" Hurrah ! Always my professor ! " crowed the pupil as soon as they were alone again. And, conscious that the rapture might not be mutual, " You do not object to taking me five times more ? " he queried anxiously.

" I am not sure but what I do," said she.

" Ah, woe ! You find me so unintelligent ? "

" In one respect."

" I shall struggle against it with all my force. Name it, I pray."

" I find it unintelligent of you to suppose you could pass for an Englishman. I myself pronounce English better than you—and, when you forget to pretend, you talk French as well as I. As a professor I have no liking for jokes at my expense."

" Jokes ? Ah, be just ! " he cried. " I avow that I am French; I avow that I appear culpable towards you—but hear my defence before you condemn me ! I shall tell you all, and then you will realise——"

At that moment there was the commanding

clangour of an electric bell, succeeded by the clatter of feet—and, picking up the book, and her belongings, the lady made for the door.

"The half-hour has expired, monsieur," she stated, bowing. "All change. Good-day."

No sooner had they taken their seats next morning than the young man cried, "Now for it! You behold me racked with apprehension, mademoiselle. Yesterday I would have sworn my explanation must win your pardon, but this morning I tremble. Suspense makes cowards of us all. Besides, you have done your hair more severely."

"I usually do it as it is," she said with dignity.

"I felt more fortitude when it was fluffier." He continued in emotional tones, "My name is Casimir Blanc. By predilection I am a playwright; by necessity I am a notary's clerk. My berth is in Sotteville, and I came to Paris last week, on my annual vacation. Scarcely had I arrived when my project of visiting the Louvre led me to an auto-bus—— My prologue is not tedious?"

"But as an apology it is obscure," said the professor, examining her appearance in the mirror of her vanity bag.

"Ah, I was designing the apology for the climax, but I will begin where you will! I apologise with contrition, with humility, and on my knees. It led me to an auto-bus, in which sat a lady whose face inspired me with such overwhelming admiration that I was borne, spellbound, beyond my objective. Only when she descended did I awake to the fact. I got out almost at the same instant, intending to walk back—and then, as I stood gazing after her, it was revealed to me that the Louvre would prove a wash-out and its immortal masterpieces bore me stiff. I realised that all my being was consumed by one devouring need—to know the lady."

Mademoiselle Rousseau's fingers strayed abstractedly to her hair. Doubtless by accident, a tendril escaped control.

"As I instinctively followed her, the apparent hopelessness of my position filled me with despair. The most far-fetched fancies crossed my mind. I thought how delicious it would be to see her greeted by a mutual friend; I craved a chance to snatch her from destruction amid the traffic; I prayed she might enter a crémerie for refreshment and find she was short of money when the time came to pay the bill. She proceeded swiftly, and the sidewalk was so populous that I was in constant danger of losing sight of her. Presently, however, the crowd thinned, and I kept her graceful figure well in view until, just after we passed the Tour Saint Jacques, she suddenly swerved and vanished."

" Pardon, monsieur," murmured the professor, glancing at her watch, " but the Inspector will be round directly, and it would look more businesslike if you opened your note-book."

" Does that fellow come in every day, interrupting ? " exclaimed Casimir, aggrieved.

" Every day at a quarter to eleven, monsieur."

" Then they will have to let me have my lesson earlier; half an hour is short measure at the best, God knows ! She vanished," he repeated, " and I was only just able to descry the spot. I gained it in six strides—but there was no sign of her. I saw only a decaying courtyard, fast-shut doors, and a hint of stairs. Blankly surveying a long list of the tenants' names and trades, I wondered whether she dwelt there, or had entered *in re* transport, mother-of-pearl buttons, or lessons in languages. The next moment I heard someone tapping at a window behind me—and thanks be ! there was a concierge. She asked sourly what I wanted.

"I said, ' A lady just came in. You saw her ? '

" ' Since I am not blind.'

" ' You know where she went ? '

" ' Yes.'

"I put my hand in my pocket—and the rest was easy. Mademoiselle, duplicity was repugnant, but inevitable—it was my only means of making your acquaintance. I dissembled, but by reason of a power so mighty that I venture to think it extenuates my offence. Whether you, in your mercy, will concur is the supreme——"

Most inopportunely the Inspector appeared at this juncture and, with a glare of hate, Casimir made him a gracious bow.

The Inspector inquired, " The gentleman advances ? "

"The gentleman makes grave errors," said mademoiselle Rousseau.

"Persevere, monsieur," droned the Inspector. "Perseverance will accomplish all."

"I hope so, from my heart ! " said Casimir. And as the door closed, he launched into a long, eloquent address, of which the peroration was, " Have pity ! The homage that I felt when we were strangers is now vaster still; to my worship of your beauty is conjoined my reverence for your character. Even while your sternness has

cut me to the quick, the loftiness of your reproofs
has made me venerate you more. I am at your
feet. Do not tell me you possess the defect of
being unforgiving."

Her lips moved to speak, but before he could
conjecture the nature of what she was going to
say, the vicious din of the despotic bell sent her
flying to her next pupil—and her answer was
retarded till the morrow.

To prolong his pains, the disobliging dame at
the desk insisted that his further lessons must be
taken, not earlier, but considerably later, and by
the time the poor fellow reached the compartment
again his face was as white as the rose he carried.

He was encouraged to find his professor looking
much more cheerful; and when she accepted the
flower without demur, his relief was so intense
that gratitude compelled him to kiss her hand.

"What joy! If you knew the torments of
impatience I have suffered! It has seemed to me
as if this moment would never come."

"It nearly did not," she said. "Monsieur de
Boo was very close to revoking his favour to
you."

"And you pleaded for me?" asked Casimir
eagerly.

" No, the thought of the fees pleaded for you, monsieur. His mind is harassed, but his pocket has prevailed at present. Yet he is comfortably off, monsieur de Boo—he could afford to lose a pupil. If the Institute were mine I should count myself in clover."

" To teach foreigners all your days would hardly be enthralling."

" As the principal I should take good care to repose. By the by, what knotty points of grammar do you wish to examine in return for your outlay ? "

" My grammar is beyond reproach. The professorship is irksome, hein ? Is it lucrative ? "

" Far from it. Better than nothing, however. The first time I walked up these stairs—— Mais, ma foi, this is not a French lesson ! "

" It is infinitely more precious ; it is the privilege of seeing you take half an hour's relaxation from your labours. You were about to tell me something of your life."

" My life has been beset by perils," she said. " My face is my fortune, and to a young girl without means good looks are a mixed blessing ; they demand of her unsleeping shrewdness. My parents could provide me with nothing but education, and I was left unprotected at an early age."

" Your confidences flood me with pride and compassion," murmured Casimir.

" But I still think some grammar might be best for you," she said conscientiously.

As her suggestion was refused with vehemence, she continued, " Last year, when I was employed in the bureau of a little hotel here, a bewildered Englishwoman used to come to the desk and talk to me; she had been relieved to find someone in the place who really understood English. I told her that I had studied it at the boîte, and taken my bac—and when I explained that boîte was slang for college, and bac the short for a degree, her manner became quite cordial. The hotel was absolutely unsuited to her and, though it was not my business to do so, I recommended a pension de famille that pleased her well. I used to visit her there. It transpired that she kept a school in England. Enfin, when she had satisfied herself that my history was true she proposed that I should go to her, a few months later, as French preceptress."

" In my opinion——"

" The position was more becoming, and I consulted friends who knew England thoroughly. They said, ' The English are no worse than anybody else, except for their pretence of being much

better.' I went—and I found many things very
agreeable, though it was an effort to swallow the
vegetables. Unfortunately, one of the elder girls,
one Wavelet Jones, formed a strong attachment
for me. After she left she wrote me constantly,
and when her sister became affianced, I received
from madame Jones an offer of the tempting
post of companion to Wavelet. Alas, I accepted
it ! "

" You were unhappy ? "

" I was blissful. But my ease was fleeting.
Before I had been installed there long the fiancé
dined with them, and my discretion told me that
his remarks to me were too numerous. I was as
uninteresting in my replies as possible, but I
knew, all the same, that madame Jones was
regarding me with displeasure. His subsequent
visits increased her misgivings—and she soon told
me a preposterous yarn about Wavelet's being
suddenly required to stay for an indefinite period
with an aunt in America. ' To their deep regret,
they must lose me ' ! "

" Now who could have foreseen such a
disaster ? "

" It was not the worst," she sighed. She went
on speaking hurriedly, because there was a lot
to say. " I should have returned to France, but

by way of amends, madame Jones busied herself in procuring for me an engagement in the ménage of one Captain Upjohn-Pitblado, who had advertised for a young lady housekeeper at his castle in a remote region of which I had never heard till then. His wife, he wrote, was a semi-invalid, and his daughter too juvenile to superintend a staff of domestics. Figure yourself my dejection when, on reaching the wet, desolate spot late in the evening, I found the ' castle ' to be a very ordinary house, of dilapidated aspect, and learnt presently that the ' staff of domestics ' consisted of two villagers, who slept out !

" ' Is it, then, part of my duties to attend on madame Upjohn-Pitblado in the night, if she is indisposed ? ' I asked of the Captain, dismayed. He was an elderly individual with a jaunty bearing and a rakish eye.

" ' Oh, my wife is not so sick as all that ! Besides, she and my daughter are away at present,' he answered, quite at his ease.

" For a moment the disclosure held me breathless. Then I said firmly, ' Monsieur le Capitaine, I should have been informed of this before I came. The circumstances are not what I understood them to be, and I cannot consent to remain."

" ' Ah, quite as you please,' he exclaimed,

with a grand air; 'I should be the last person to detain a lady in my house against her will! You are at liberty to break your engagement when you like. To-morrow being Sunday, however, there is no train from here—and, as a matter of fact, a sister of mine will be arriving in a few days' time.'

"Well, there was no more to be said at the moment. Supper was served, and to some extent my constraint passed. He had travelled widely, and he exerted himself to divert me. Except that he drank champagne to excess, and whisky on top of it, I had no further fault to find with his behaviour that evening. As for me, I refused to drink anything but water, though I should have liked a glass of champagne very much.

"At the breakfast table next day, as he passed behind my chair, he kissed my neck."

"The scoundrel!" hissed Casimir, leaping with wrath.

"I rose and struck him across the face with my serviette."

"Well done!"

"At once I hurried, through the rain, to the chef de gare to make inquiries—but it proved a fact that there was no train before the morrow; and, to my consternation, the village was so

primitive that it did not boast a spare bed.   Quelle
horreur !   It was inevitable that I should pass
another night under that man's roof ! "

"My poor child," wailed Casimir, livid with
alarm.

" As his kiss had seared my neck very early in
the breakfast I had had little to eat, and, being
determined not to expose myself to danger in the
dining-room again, I endeavoured to take back
some bread to sustain me, in my room, during the
day.   But in England it is irreligious to supply
bread on Sunday—and by three o'clock my hunger
was extreme.   Its pangs drove me downstairs at
last, and the Captain, who had evidently counted
upon this, met me with a flow of fulsome excuses
which were in themselves offensive to my dignity.
Finding that these were powerless to induce me
to remain in the house, he claimed that his sister
was to be with us the very next evening.

" I said, ' Monsieur, even if it be true that you
have a sister, and even if it be true that she is
coming, I do not desire to know your family.'
And I collected some scraps in the kitchen.

" Never shall I forget the long Sunday in that
gaunt bedroom, sinister with forebodings, and
a mouse."   Modesty delayed her utterance.   " I
fear I can tell no more."

" I beseech you, speak ! " said Casimir hoarsely.

" Then . . . scarcely had I begun to disrobe when there was a rapping at my door, and the Captain urged me to admit him. ' I have something to say to you,' he called.

" I made no answer.

" He persisted with excitement. Evidently he had been at the bottles, for his tones were thick; but I gathered that he was telling me I did not understand him, and he was much grieved by my mistake.

" I replied at last, ' Monsieur, all that I have to say has been said, and I have retired for the night.'

" His next words sounded like ' I take a kindly interest in you, and want to come in and talk about it.'

" With all the authority I could summon I bade him begone.

" ' I must insist on seeing you,' he shouted. ' Your refusal is insulting.' He rattled the latch violently, and though I knew the key was turned, my heart stood still with fear. It was well founded. Since I would speak no more he strove to enter by force."

" I suffocate," gasped Casimir, who was trembling like a leaf.

" Ah, mon Dieu, mon Dieu ! The door heaved

ominously. I sought to barricade it, but the wardrobe was too large to move, and the washstand too small to serve. Now the door groaned, as in extremities. For an instant panic paralysed me. Then, rushing headlong to the window——"

" You escaped ? "

" I found it to be barred."

" Damnation ! "

" The house stood isolated—to shriek for aid was futile. I looked wildly for a weapon——"

" The poker ! " panted Casimir, on the verge of collapse.

" But there wasn't any. The door——"

At this frightful crisis, as sweat burst upon her lover's brow in beads, her narrative was checked by the mandate of the accursed bell—and for twenty-four hours he could scarcely breathe for terror.

" Good-morning. And—then ? " quavered Casimir, falling into the chair. The interval had made a wreck of him.

Mademoiselle Rousseau, on the contrary, seemed to be in high spirits. She said, " I was doubtful whether I should have an opportunity to tell you the rest; monsieur de Boo has complained again."

" The door ! " croaked Casimir. " The door ! "

" Ah, oui. The door defied the attack, and a moment later the Captain withdrew. His attack had been, perhaps, less puissant, or prolonged, than my agitation led me to suppose, for the door was fairly frail. I heard no more of him till I was departing on the morrow, when he tendered cringing apologies, which I haughtily rejected, and my railway fares, which I promptly took.

" I then returned to Paris—and the sight of it was sweet to me. I confess, though, that after my sojourn abroad, the humble quarters that I found seemed strange in some respects. A dinner-table spread with a red check cloth looked uninviting to me, and I did not re-accustom myself at once to napkins almost vast enough for sheets, and towels no larger than Englishmen's handkerchiefs. I commenced my search for employment without delay. I wished to avoid schools of languages because I knew that few of them paid their professors a fixed salary—and the search was long. And Paris had become very expensive; my savings melted fast, in spite of the exchange.

" One day I had to pawn this watch. On the way back I stopped to rest in the garden of the Tour Saint Jacques. I saw the gilt sky-sign of the De Boo Institute, and I reflected how very

much alike were the advertisements of all the
people who invited the guileless foreigner to learn
French without taking any trouble.   None of the
scores vaunted a method better than ' Rapid and
Unique.'   I perceived necessity for a still bolder
boast, and by way of distraction, I evolved a
nice one :

WHY NOT TALK FRENCH IN 48 HOURS ?
YOU WOULD FIND PARIS PLEASANTER.

" This seemed to me so much superior to all
the rest that I could not help feeling it should
be marketable—and I crossed the road and
requested an interview with monsieur de Boo.

" I was received by a portly, middle-aged
gentleman who approved my looks.   His countenance fell, however, when he discovered I
was not a prospective pupil.   He asked, ' What
then ? '

" I said, ' Monsieur, I have called to give you
the first offer of a great idea.   Our city teems
with foreigners who desire to talk French without
the labour of learning it——'

" ' Your idea is not new,' he said.

" I said, ' But I have invented a new announce-
ment.   If you find it attractive how much will
you pay me for the exclusive rights ? '

D

" ' Mademoiselle,' he said, ' I am addressing a charming lady, but obviously not a business woman. I will therefore be entirely frank with you. Your invention does not stimulate my curiosity, but you may exhibit it if you choose. In the improbable event of its having any value, we will talk terms when the Exhibition is open.'

" Alors, there was nothing else to do. He permitted me to sit at a desk, and I made the thing as striking as was practicable with pale mauve ink and our scratchy French pens.

" ' Behold,' I said.

" Quite clearly it was arresting. He gazed at it round-eyed. I proceeded to explain that forty-eight hours signified a lesson of half-an-hour's duration on ninety-six days—and he regarded me with interest.

" ' It is bright,' he acknowledged. ' You have a gift. I compliment you on this work. All my literary instinct applauds it. Nevertheless my commercial judgment turns it down. Not ten per cent. of the inquirers could be appeased when I broke the " ninety-six days " to them— and those whom I cajoled would insult me when the course was over.'

" ' But as they would not be able to talk French

you mightn't understand what they said,' I pleaded.

"He seemed to take increasing interest in me, if not in my advertisement. The conversation developed on very amiable lines, and he urged me to accept a position there as professor. When I had induced him to guarantee a minimum wage, which took a long time, I agreed to the suggestion gladly, and he said, ' I have made an exceptional arrangement with you; I ask you impressively to keep it to yourself.'

" ' You may depend upon my mentioning it to no one,' I assured him.

" ' Sapristi, I believe you ! ' he chuckled. ' You have a highly intelligent head. Your visit refreshes me so much that I regret I can make no offer for your invention.'

"I had not done badly, for all that, and I treated myself to a cup of chocolate and a brioche before I went home.

"I learnt from other ladies employed in the Institute that monsieur de Boo was a widower, prone to gallantry, and as he made many pretexts for summoning me to his office, it was not long before I found their assertion was correct. When I had been here a week he told me of the sadness of solitude, and the inadequacy of a school of languages to satisfy the secret yearnings of his heart. My reply depressed him; and he sent for me on the morrow to say he had passed a sleepless night.

"Often I was called to the office twice a day, and in a month's time I could not doubt his sincerity when he declared that my virtue was a bitter sorrow to him. Well, he was not youthful, and he was not handsome, but he was comparatively prosperous, and a girl without a *dot* must not expect everything in this world. I began to question if the circumstances, handled tactfully, might not yield an offer of marriage."

"*Comment?*" ejaculated Casimir. "I deny it! It is false. You do yourself a cruel injustice!"

"But he said no, his devotion would not stretch to such lengths as that. He said, 'My single experience of matrimony suffices for me. I adore you. I would die for you. I would commit almost any madness for you—but one must draw the line somewhere.'"

"The man is a fiend," moaned Casimir, mopping his brow.

"Yet it was plain that he was torn. His face, when I bowed to him serenely in the passage, was ever more entreating, and now I was called to the office to hear that he suffered from chronic insomnia."

"I shall liberate you from his persecution—it shall cease!" raved Casimir.

"Before long he was struggling so hard to resist my high-minded conditions that I was aware of a rising esteem for him—I had not divined that he possessed such force of character. When the struggle had endured for weeks, however, my esteem acquired a tinge of irritation. I am being candid with you. To see that his antipathy to wedlock might prove the winner was disquieting to me. You hold me mercenary, you condemn me, but the prices of provisions were going up every time the franc fell—and when the franc rose, the prices didn't come down; I saw that to marry the Institute was my only insurance. I am not mercenary in my heart—my heart was free. I had said to myself, from the beginning, 'It is not as if your affections were engaged elsewhere—you would be sacrificing no one who cares for you, no one for whom you care.' Then, on a sudden, only three days since—— Ah! Pardon, monsieur!"

"Devil smite that bell!" roared Casimir, stamping with frenzy as she fled.

.   .   .   .   .   .

Reaching the compartment, with a rush, for the fifth lesson, he was chagrined to be kept waiting. Five infuriating minutes passed while he stood straining to hear her footfall. He foresaw that she would be compelled to get up and go none the less promptly when the bell rang, and he cursed the unknown mishap that was stealing his minutes. . . . Now ten had gone ! Repeatedly he was at the point of flinging forth in quest of her, but always the thought that she might enter while he was away, squandering time, brought his frantic stride to a standstill.

His wrist shook fearfully as he attempted to consult his watch. Nearly a quarter of an hour ! . . . Seventeen minutes ! His knees failed him, and he sank into his chair, toying feverishly with the chalk for the blackboard. . . . Twenty-two now ! Ah, at last !

She appeared with a blithe smile upon her lips, but subduing it to an expression of concern, she said, " A thousand apologies, monsieur. I was detained by monsieur de Boo."

" Your last words," gasped Casimir, too impatient to say good-morning, " were ' Three days since.' My life hangs on that unfinished phrase. Continue ! "

" Monsieur, I cannot remain. I come to say

that monsieur de Boo has decided to withdraw his concession to you."

"I shall talk to him of legal measures," snorted Casimir, with a gesture of defiance; "I am not a notary's clerk for nothing! Continue, I supplicate."

"But he will assure you that other professors on the staff are equally capable."

"Continue!" clamoured Casimir. "'Three days since——' What happened 'three days since'?"

She said submissively, "A new influence arose."

"Ah, rapture!" He made to clasp her in his arms, transfigured. "In *you*—the dawn of love?"

"No, in *him*—the pangs of jealousy. You have been a thorn in his side. He has questioned me incessantly about the 'Frenchman who paid to learn French from me.' Well, you know, he was having a bad time already; when I found he had jealousy to contend with, too, I was pretty sure he would give in. I come to you from the scene of my betrothal! You have rendered me a service, monsieur, and I felt it was your due I should advise you that your attendance in future will yield not a glimpse of me."

The young man stood dumb, with heaving

breast. He drew the sixth ticket from his pocket, and tore it across, and threw the pieces to the ground. Not till then did he find voice to speak the words within him, words that she was never to forget. He said, " Before we part I shall say one thing, and one thing only——"

" Pardon, monsieur ! " she exclaimed. "Adieu —the bell ! "

LITTLE BIRDIE

A CHRISTMAS IDYLL

CHRISTMAS was nigh. In the old village church deft, reverent hands twined emblems of the season. On the Manor drive the carol-singers had assembled—a snow-clad group under the silver moon—with their message of peace and good-will. And behind the mullioned windows, lone in the Yule logs' glow, the Squire sat, grim, remorseless, steeling his heart against the child he had disowned.

To a footman who entered timorously the Squire said, " Go and 'oof them blighters out ! Tell that swine at the lodge, if 'e lets them come yowling 'ere again, I'll break 'is neck. D'y'ear ? "

The minion made a suitable reply, and the master of the Manor reverted to his occupation. Moodily gulping gin-and-water, he gazed into the past. This was it :

Two little boys—sons of shopkeepers in the same English townlet—bore the surnames of Penny and Rudge. Penny was slender; Rudge was brawny. Penny was refined and studious;

Rudge was common and a dunce. Penny developed an interest in anatomy, and was always messing about with bones in his spare time; Rudge grew more truculent every year, and derived his chief enjoyment from punching bigger boys' heads. The parson predicted that Penny would distinguish himself when he grew up, and that Rudge's parents would find him a sore trial.

The prediction was not fulfilled. Penny put his father to disastrous expense and became a medical man—and remained painfully obscure; Rudge showed promise as a money-maker from his seventeenth summer and became a pugilist—and won world-wide fame. It is, no doubt, another instance of our high civilisation which we hear so much about that a pugilist can win more wealth in five minutes by inflicting bodily suffering than a medical man can earn in a lifetime by assuaging it. Penny was never rewarded with more than a pittance for the science of relieving physical ills; Rudge was rewarded with a dazzling fortune for the science of inflicting all the physical ill that he could. After the war, when the stately homes of England were a drug in the market, Rudge, by then a widower, bought an estate in Sussex, and retired from the ring to a life of

affluent ease. As it happened, his domain was
in the vicinity of Penny's practice, and when the
indigent doctor trudged to his patients, he frequently had to flatten himself into a hedge to
avoid annihilation by the ex-pugilist's Rolls-
Royce.

People said of the Squire that he was hard—
hard in his nature, as well as in his frame—but
under his arrogance lurked tenderness for his
daughter. Though he was as keenly alive to the
value of money as any other pugilist, and had no
cause to set much store on education, he had
been lavish in the matter of school fees for Gloria.
The B.A.'s and M.A.'s who instructed her had
not taught her to speak her own language correctly, but the atrocities she committed on it
were no worse than those it suffered in the diction
of most English girls of the highest birth, and
she didn't put her knife in her mouth, and was
pretty. Rudge, as he was never tired of telling
her, "meant her to marry a nob." It was the
fly in his ointment that he had not been given a
knighthood, and all the mind that he possessed
was set upon having a lord for a son-in-law.

This cherished and worthy aim of his might
have been accomplished but for a boil on his
neck. It was an obstinate boil, and he sent for

the village doctor to lance it. Penny, who of course had marked Bill Rudge's illustrious career from afar, ventured to inform him that they had been acquainted in their boyhood; and the Squire, without a trace of condescension, as affably as if the doctor had been his social equal, replied, " Blimey ! What, you, young Penny ? Well, I never ! 'Ow you been doing ? "

" Oh, so-so," said Penny, trying to sound prosperous, " so-so ! "

" I remember the odds was five to one on *you* in them days," grinned the Squire. " You must come again. You must come in one evening. Bring the missis. 'Appy to see you."

" I've lost my wife," said Penny. " I'm alone now—my son isn't here."

" Oh, got a son, 'ave you ? 'E a doctor too ? "

" Oh dear, no ! No, I'm glad to say he didn't want to be. Harold is on the stage."

" What, an actor ? I suppose they've made 'im a knight," said Rudge morosely.

" A knight ? Harold ? Oh, Harold isn't a celebrity; he's only—er—— It's early days yet. He always had a strong bent for it—I think he's clever. Uphill work at the start, of course."

" Come in again," repeated Rudge. " Come in and smoke a cigar with me. Damn dull 'ole, ain't it? You'll be somebody to talk to. 'Ow long's this boil going to worry me?"

Thus the acquaintance was resumed. And some weeks later Harold Penny came down to stay with his father, and was presented at the Manor. To his surprise, he found Bill Rudge's daughter attractive—and the attraction was mutual. She asked him if he was keen on golf. He was a nice young fellow, though he had exaggerated ideas of the importance of the theatre —and the girl had charm, though she raved about revues, and didn't know who Shaw was. The links drew them daily. They had nothing in common, except youth, but that served. Harold told her of his ambition to play Hamlet, and though she thought it a strange, sad, dull desire, she tried to enter into it. He talked to her of the difficulties of his profession, and although it appeared that the best salary he had ever had was less than she paid for a hat, she was at the club-house again the next afternoon. On the day before his visit closed he made an unpremeditated confession of his love—and Gloria, who had long since decided he was to do it, promptly accepted him.

Gazing into the long-gone past this evening, the Squire did not, of course, review the love scene on the links, because he hadn't been present at it, but he re-lived furious scenes in the Manor after the news was broken to him. And he re-lived his defeat on the morning when he found that the girl had disappeared. It was the heaviest blow he had ever had.

" She's 'ad to pay for it," he growled now, nodding at his gin-and-water. " 'Er, and 'er 'Arold, and the 'anky-panky doctor too. Gord blast everybody," muttered the Squire, unconsciously misquoting Tiny Tim.

The carols had borne their message of peace and good-will elsewhere, but suddenly, in the deep silence, the bell of the hall-door pealed. The timorous footman reappeared, and said :

" Dr. Penny."

Before he could be refused admission, the intruder, caked in snow, walked briskly into the room.

" Forgot what I told you last time I spoke to you ? " roared the Squire, springing to his feet.

" No, Squire. But I've a message for you." He waited till the servant had withdrawn, and then went on : " Your daughter is down here— three miles off, in Redgate. She's been asking me about you—how you look, how you are. Squire, she loves you, in spite of everything—

she has felt it more than you know. She wants you to make it up with her. I promised her I'd speak to you—I said I'd do all I could."

For a second Rudge stood voiceless. Then he said hoarsely :

"Well, you done it—I've 'eard all I mean to 'ear. Out with you—quick ! "

"Squire ! " cried the doctor, "won't you be human ? Ten years is a long time. It wasn't a crime for them to be fond of each other—and they've been in tight corners, with no one to lend them a hand. *I* haven't been much use— I'm too poor myself."

"Pity you didn't think of that before you put 'im up to run away with her ! You thought you was being very clever, didn't you ? Well, you see, it didn't come off. All 'e got out of it was a wife and child to keep. *You* 'aven't done too well by it neither—I dessay it's cost you a bit more than you could afford; and I'd never 'ave you for my doctor, not if it was a matter of life and death and there wasn't another doctor in Sussex ! "

"Squire," exclaimed Penny, "I told you, at the time, I disapproved of the elopement."

"And *I* told *you* you was a liar. You was in the know. You 'elped my gal to go against me—you've 'elped to make me un'appy 'ere these ten years."

" There was no need for you to be unhappy. Your girl and Harold came to beg your forgiveness—and you showed them the door."

" And I'll do it again if they come back ! "

" And when she wrote to you, after Billy was born, you returned the letter to her, torn to bits. I don't know what she gave the boy your name for."

" *I* do. But 'e won't get a 'alfpenny."

" The infant didn't dictate the letter, anyway," said the doctor. " You'd think a lot of him if you saw him. A fine, manly little chap. He's down here too—she'd like to bring him with her, if you let her come. That's one of the things I was to say."

" You've 'ad my answer," said Rudge doggedly. " Tell her, what I meant then I mean now. I'm a man of my word."

" You're a foolish man," rejoined Penny; " a foolish, headstrong man. You're pulling your nose to spite your face, as the saying is. Good-night. If you should think better of it, they'll be at Redgate all the week. They're acting at the Plough Hall."

" What you mean by ' they ' ? " asked Rudge. " *She* ain't acting too ? "

" Oh yes. She's been acting a long time now
—every little helps. It's a poor sort of a show
they're in, but beggars can't be choosers. Don't
be afraid I shall trouble you any more."

" 'Ere, 'old on a minute," said the Squire.
" It's bitter cold outside; I don't like you, but
you can 'ave a drop of gin first."

" I'll drink with you when I can respect you,
Squire," said Penny curtly.

" Go to 'ell," replied the Squire, resuming
his seat.

But he could not resume his mood. The
message affected him more than he had shown.
And in the proud man's reverie the messenger's
last words re-echoed. Could it be true he wasn't
respected? It had been his inordinate self-esteem
that supported his obduracy. The intrusion had
been disturbing. Neither gin nor tobacco was
potent to efface it from his thoughts. The tidings
that his daughter was an actress, and performing
locally, offered an insidious temptation. Though
he was reluctant to pardon, he was weak enough
to want to look at her. . . . The Squire stared
into the dying embers, lost in thought.

On the following afternoon Mr. and Mrs.
Harold Penny sat in their sorry lodging at Red-

E

gate, eagerly awaiting news of the result. The statement that they had been in tight corners was not a flight of fancy. The earnest young Repertory actor, with views on Hamlet, was at present enacting the part of Eric Belvedere, in the lowliest company of " No Child to Call Her ' Mother.' " It was mortifying, but the tour provided a joint salary, of which the couple had been in urgent need. To Gloria fell the rôle of Eric's misjudged wife, who had no child to call her " mother " for a long while by reason of the villain's machinations. The child, Little Birdie, was represented by a pudding-faced brat in a grubby white frock and a wig of dangling curls.

" I think, darling," said Harold heavily, " we should have had a wire before this if your father had said yes. . . . What's become of Billy ? "

" I've let him go and look at the shop windows —I like to make Christmas time as merry for him as we can," sighed Gloria. " Yes, *I'm* beginning to lose hope too. What time is it now ? "

" Three o'clock. The guv'nor would have wired the first thing in the morning, I feel sure." He started. " Hark ! Someone's just rung. Look out of the window ! "

" You can't see the doorstep from the window," Gloria gasped. "Listen—it's a man's voice. . . . He's coming in! Oh, Harold, if it's Father!"

But it was only the manager of the company, in a state of perturbation.

"Oh, Mr. Bowser!" she said ruefully. "Is it you?"

"Looks rather like me. Any reason you should cry about it?" said Mr. Bowser. "Glad I've found you—I wasn't sure of your address. Well, we're in a nice mess at the show. That damn little girl's come to grief, falling out of a swing-boat. We can't play the piece without a Little Birdie."

They stared at him, dumb with dismay.

"Can't find a girl in Redgate and rehearse her between this and eight o'clock! There's just one thing to be done. Your boy's seen the piece often enough—we must put *him* on for the part for the rest of the week. It may be a bit of a tussle to get him into the frock, but the wig ought to do. I want you to run through the lines with him all the afternoon."

"He's out," answered the parents, hesitatingly.

"He *would* be!" Mr. Bowser replied. "Well, start rehearsing him as soon as he comes back. If *he* don't play Little Birdie to-night, we can't take the curtain up. Of course, he'll get paid. It'll be a bit extra for you."

" I don't think he'd like the idea," said Harold.

" *I* was just thinking the same thing," said Gloria. " I don't think he'd like it at all, playing a baby girl."

" My Gord," protested Mr. Bowser, " this drama wasn't created to feature your little boy ! He should be precious thankful to get such a chance."

" Here he is," said Gloria, as the door opened. And Billy, advancing brightly, said, " How do you do, Mr. Bowser ? Have you come to tea ? "

" Nice little lad," observed the manager. " Very nice gentlemanly manners. No, I haven't time to stay to tea. Come here, sonny. I've got a treat for you. I'm going to let you play Little Birdie to-night—because you've been a good boy, and it'll soon be Christmas. There ! What do you say to that ? "

" No thank you, Mr. Bowser," said Billy promptly.

" Let *me* talk to him," said Gloria. " Billy, we're in trouble at the show. Lottie has hurt herself, and we want *you* to be Little Birdie instead, to help us all—dad and Mr. Bowser and me."

" Oh, that's different," faltered Billy. " Do you think I *can*, mumsie ? Is she hurt much ? "

" I'm afraid I didn't ask, dear; I was too upset."

" It's me that's hurt most," said the manager; " but I'm told her face'll be a disgusting sight for weeks."

" Do you think I *can ?* " repeated Billy.

" Of course you can, my noble sportsman," said Mr. Bowser. " You'll make a hit in the part. Now, get to work with him, both of you. And bring him down early, so that we can run through the business with him on the stage, after he's been stuffed into the frock."

They were arduous hours that followed, though the part was not a long one. In the stress of the rehearsal, Gloria almost forgot her cares. The boy's abashment at impersonating a girl much his junior made progress slow. Twice, instead of lisping the line of Little Birdie, he burst forth, " Dash it ! I do feel such a fool."

" You won't say that on the stage, will you, old chap ? " asked Harold anxiously.

" No, dad, of course I shan't ! " scoffed Billy. " I shall *feel* a fool, but I'm not going to *be* one."

And at the hall he bore the ordeal bravely. His lips were tight set before the mirror of the dressing-room, as he viewed himself with dangling curls, in the grubby frock that was ludicrously short. And at one point of the performance, when somebody in the pit tittered at him, Gloria felt his body quiver in her arms. " You're doing it beautifully, darling," she told him under her breath, though that wasn't in her part, and wasn't true. It wasn't in his father's part to whisper, " You're a hero, Billy—by Jove, I'm proud of you ! "

There was general praise for him when the curtain fell. Mr. Bowser gave him an orange, and the Old Woman of the company affirmed that, " All joking aside, the boy showed talent." Billy felt better in the buzz of compliment.

What irked him most, after he had been lisping the infantile lines of Little Birdie for two or three nights, was the local notoriety he had obtained. People cast amused glances at him in the streets, and a tradesman's boy on a bicycle shrilled derision every time he passed him. Billy's eyes flashed. Fortunately, however, a new Little Birdie of the right sex had been acquired by now, and the indignity was almost over.

It was the relentless Squire's healthful practice

to take a daily walk, though the Rolls-Royce was not the only car in the garage, and several times during the week he had bent mechanical steps towards Redgate. But before he had covered half the distance, these steps in the right direction had always been restrained—and it wasn't till Saturday that he got there.

The little High Street was astir when he reached it, for the day was Christmas Eve. Under his bushy brows, his glances at the passers-by were keen. In the window of the Gallon Can he observed a playbill of Plough Hall, and paused to examine it. The name of Gloria Penny was not visible. He inferred correctly that for professional purposes she had adopted one. Scowling at the cast, the Squire questioned which of the Marjoribanks and Cholmondeleys in the list might be his child.

Even now he had not made up his mind to attend the performance. He wanted to view his daughter once again, without her knowledge, but if she or her husband saw him at the show, his presence would be taken as a sign of weakness —he'd be giving them a bit of satisfaction. He wished he knew the hall—perhaps it was big enough for him to look in for half an hour without any risk. He inquired of a loafer whereabouts it was—and proceeded, through purlieus, to survey it.

He proceeded ponderingly, but as he passed the public baths and washhouse, his meditations were suddenly deranged by a tumult of ecstatic cries. They held a note that woke sweet memories in the Squire's mind. Scenes long-forgotten came crowding to his mental view; he knew again the gladness of his childhood. Quickening his pace, he turned the corner, and saw a posse of vulgar urchins rejoicing at the spectacle of a fight.

The combatants were a small boy, and a boy much bigger; and, as the Squire instinctively stopped, the small boy delivered a blow with such admirable judgment that an exclamation of approval burst from the Squire's lips. This approval waxed fast to wonder. The little 'un fought with an élan that gave promise of a brilliant future, and his tactics were worthy of a far riper age. The attentions he paid to the taller boy's solar plexus, before concentrating upon his countenance, moved the retired champion to warm respect. Bill Rudge stood absorbed. In his mounting enthusiasm for what he saw, his personal affairs were forgotten; he was oblivious of all but the genius he had discovered. The qualities that he beheld stirred him to affection.

The heart of the master went out to the child—
and he wished that Heaven had given him such
a son.

"Boy," he said, in deep tones, when the other
lad had had enough, "you got a gift for it.
You got a great gift. What's your name?"

"Billy Penny," said the victor, putting on his
coat.

"Billy Penny?" panted the Squire. His
strong frame trembled. "'Penny,' did you say?
'Ere, is your mother's name Gloria?"

"Yes; do you know her? That cad boshed
me. He's been boshing me, from his bike, all
the week—calling me 'Little Birdie' and things."

No word, save the first, reached the man's
consciousness; his exultation sang so loud that
it deafened him to the rest. "Great 'Eavens, I
might ha' guessed it," breathed the Squire
devoutly—"'e gets it from *me*!" In the torrent
of his emotion his eyes were wet, and the icy
resentment he had nursed so long was melted
into tenderness. His voice shook as, mopping
the little visage with his handkerchief, he asked,
"Where's your diggings, kid?"

He bade his grandson lead him there.

Taking the child's hand in his, the Squire
walked rapidly towards the wistful hearth where
joy soon reigned supreme.

A s monsieur Poupon walked homeward in the rain one night, last October, his shoelace came undone. Its trailing incommoded him, and he stopped. He shut his umbrella, and having lodged it against a convenient door, bent over the lace to retie it. The next moment the door was torn open, and the wet umbrella fell against the knees of a young woman running out.

" Idiot ! " exclaimed the young woman.

Of course, those who know Poupon well have heard the story already. Only, Poupon tells it differently. He presents matters as they ought to have been. We take pride in stating that here, for the first time, the occurrence is recorded faithfully, without any exercise of the imagination.

The middle-aged person stooping over his left foot was a Parisian who, from youth downward, had desired nothing quite so ardently as to make conquests among the ladies. His star being adverse, Poupon was not handsome, or moneyed,

or even clever. Ladies had been unconscious
that socially he trod the earth. Only in his
official capacity did they note his existence, and
then they resented it. He was, officially, one of a
shabby trio in the foyer of the Théâtre Tronchet,
at whose obstructive rostrum playgoers had to
wait while their tickets were scrutinised and
scribbled on. Every evening he left his room
at the same hour, in the same second-hand dress
clothes, and traversed the same streets to his
humdrum job. Every night he left the theatre
at the same hour, and traversed the same streets
back to his ham sandwich and glass of beer.
For years he had been doing it, and no pleasing
adventure had befallen him on the way. For
long he had ceased to anticipate pleasing adventures. He walked anticipant of nothing but the
sandwich and the beer. And then, shortly before
midnight, as he trudged homeward in the rain,
last October, his shoelace came undone.

Rebuked as " idiot," Poupon raised his head
confused, and saw a comely domestic, in a state
of flurry. " Pardon," he said. And having
reverted to the lace, and picked up his umbrella,
he turned to go on. But before he could take
more than a single step, the girl's demeanour
underwent a startling change.

"O monsieur!" she cried joyfully. "I bring monsieur a message."

"A message?" echoed Poupon. "For *me*?"

"Yes, yes, monsieur. Madame begs monsieur to come in."

After a stare of astonishment, Poupon growled, "How dare you? Be off. If you are not very careful I shall report you to the police."

"Ah, monsieur misunderstands! I assure monsieur. Madame is a famous artiste. It is an affair of ceremony."

"An affair of ceremony? I am invited to it?"

"That's it, monsieur. A supper. Chic. Champagne. How fortunate monsieur is in evening dress! If monsieur will give himself the trouble to enter, madame will explain to him."

Poupon regarded her mutely. Supper and champagne? Had some woman observed and admired him—could the fair finger of romance be beckoning through the gloom for once? He swayed with indecision. "Alors," he said at last, "I will have a look. Lead on. If you try any tricks on me, you will suffer for it, I warn you. I am no country cousin in Paris for a week."

The girl led him briskly across a courtyard, through glass doors, and up a staircase that

threatened never to leave off. It was so dark
that only on the landings was he able to distinguish anything. On the fourth floor, the door
of a flat was ajar. " Entrez, monsieur," she
urged. And, with no little misgiving, Poupon
heard her shrill, " Madame, I have got one "—
and found himself blinking on the threshold of
a small salon, where a young lady and gentleman
stood, fashionably attired.

The lady sped to greet him, and Poupon saw
that she was of dazzling beauty. " Monsieur,"
she said excitedly, " I am grateful. Be seated, I
pray."

" Er—too amiable, madame," faltered Poupon,
sitting down.

" Monsieur," broke in the gentleman peremp-
torily, " the servant has made an error. I offer
you my apologies. I must request you to withdraw."

" Er—don't mention it, monsieur," faltered
Poupon, getting up.

" Stop," cried the lady, more imperatively still.
" You are here by my invitation, monsieur. I
entreat you, resume your seat."

" But this goes beyond all bounds," the young
man shouted. " It is the act of a lunatic. Control yourself for the love of heaven ! "

" Control myself ? " shrieked the lady, with
an hysterical laugh.   " I am not uncontrolled—I
am calmly resolute.   Do not imagine there will
be a supper party of thirteen persons because
you are fiend enough to leave me in the lurch
for nothing ! "

" For nothing ? "   Evidently the young man
had so many things to say upon that point that
they got jammed in his throat.   He beat his
shirt-front with clenched hands.   " Mon Dieu,
I do not know what you are made of !   Are you
absolutely without conscience ?   Have you no
glimmering perception that you treat my devotion
like a doormat ? "

At the edge of the chair, and encumbered by
his hat and umbrella, the scared Poupon gazed
from one assailant to the other.   He began to
make some excuse for his untoward reception
by this gentleman, who had manifestly suffered
deep wrong at her hands.   It was sad to learn
that the beautiful creature was so cruel.

" For nothing ? " groaned the gentleman.   He
paced the room turbulently.   " It is ' nothing,'
hein, that I waited for you in vain to-day for two
interminable hours ?   That I sat ordering one
cup of tea after another, from three o'clock to
five, with all the attendants sniggering at me in
their sleeves ?   I was a fool to come to-night at

all. But I was magnanimous, I wished to give you an opportunity to justify yourself—or at least to express remorse. And when I came what did I hear?"

"That my little one had fallen sick. And you didn't think that enough!"

"No."

"I feared for Aubrey's life—and you found it no reason that I should break an appointment at a tea-room!"

"No."

"And when you heard the crisis was passed, that my darling was spared to me, you hadn't the humanity to share my rejoicings!"

"No."

"No, monster, far from it! You said you would rather have a mongrel pup."

An exclamation of horror burst from Poupon. Aghast at the disclosure of the young man's turpitude, he felt all his sympathies now swing to the side of the suffering lady.

"You remarked, monsieur?" demanded the young man, with an intimidating scowl.

"I coughed," said Poupon.

"Never will I pardon you for that atrocity," vowed the lady, raising fervent eyes to the ceiling. "And because I complain of it you must refuse to sup. Maliciously you condemn us to be

thirteen. Half an hour before they are all due!
When there is no time for me to get anyone to
take your place. Even when you have watched
me ring up distractedly and fail. Well, you were
warned! I told you I would call in the first
man in dress clothes that passed the house."
She cast a careless glance at Poupon. "And
very nice, I am sure!"

"Madame," simpered Poupon, with a gratified
bow.

"Listen, monsieur," vociferated the young
man, "you are in the way here—you intrude.
Again I bid you go."

"Oh—er—well, certainly, of course—if you
put it like that," stammered Poupon, in fear of
being forcibly removed.

"Monsieur," said the lady in tones that
brooked no denial, "you are more than welcome.
Your presence is indispensable to me. I beseech
you to remain."

"Get up," roared the young man.

"Sit down," commanded the lady.

"Ah, it is insupportable!" the young man
yelled, with a gesture of frenzy. "Alors, I leave
—and we meet no more. All is over between
us. My compliments on my successor! It is
beneath me to pull his nose."

Poupon, happy to hear it, essayed an attitude of defiance not too provocative.

"I go. It is the end. Never shall I set eyes on you again. What will become of me? My career is in fragments. It is the end. And but yesterday you held me to your heart and pressed your lips to mine. It is the end. How hideous is youth—I shudder to guess how many years may lie before me. Ah, no! Fortunately there is always my revolver. It is the end. Adieu. Have you no word to speak before I die?"

"You took my watch to be cleaned. Where did you leave it?" she asked.

With a cry of torture beyond type to depict, the young man wrestled with his collar, and rushed wildly from the room. And during the next ten seconds it was plain that he expended all his remaining energies in slamming doors.

A brief silence occurred in the salon. After the clamour and confusion that had raged there, silence appeared a strange, uncanny thing to Poupon.

His hostess seemed to recognise that the circumstances had been informal, for she said now, "I fear you must find it odd, the maid neglecting to relieve you of your coat and things, monsieur?" And while he was being relieved of

F

them, she went on, "It was most remiss of you, Mathilde. Upon my word, I do not know which are more trying—lovers or servants."

"Oh, madame!" said the maid, wounded.

"Well, at all events, it was very thoughtless of you. Monsieur must think it a singular household, since the maid omits to remove his overcoat when he comes to supper. Ah, what I have borne to-day!" She clasped her head. "He has shattered me, that man. I am totally unnerved." And tumbling on the couch, she forthwith fainted—or made a very fair show of doing so.

"Madame, madame!" exclaimed the maid, in a whirlwind of solicitude. "Fan her, fan her, monsieur," she pleaded. "Slap her hands. I fly to fetch her smelling salts."

Poupon, much flustered, knelt on the floor, fanning and slapping alternately—and by dint of a little practice, doing both at the same time. The beauty's eyes reopened vaguely, and she asked, "Where am I?"

"I should assume, in a private asylum," thought Poupon. But he answered, "Lie still, lie still. Do not distress yourself." And, sustained by the fact that the young man wasn't present, he added stoutly, "I will protect you."

" You have done much," she breathed. " But I am beyond aid. All is dark. I am forsaken—alone."

" There is still your child," Poupon reminded her, moved.

" Who ? "

" Your little son—the Aubrey who has happily recovered."

" Ah, yes, I still have Aubrey. That is true. He is not my son. Aubrey is my white mouse. We are inseparable. I reproach myself fearfully for his illness. Truffles never did agree with him. What a world it is ! People will tell you I am capricious, but if you knew the tenderness I have wasted on that little beast ! "

" Aubrey ? "

" Edouard."

" Also a mouse ? "

" No, the gentleman you saw when you came in. He is very generous, but money is not everything. Don't you agree ? "

" Well—er—I am hardly in the position to judge. To speak the truth, I am not wealthy myself."

" No, you have not the aspect. Edouard has two—from London."

" Aspects ? "

"Dress suits. Ah, dear girl!" she broke off, as the maid returned. "Don't trouble—I feel better now. Mathilde is a blessing. More like a sister than a maid. N'est-ce-pas, Mathilde? I couldn't live without her. You must never marry, Mathilde. But I know you would not be so selfish. It must be nearly time my friends were all here. I wish they were in hell. No doubt I ought to be in bed. Well, I must not keep you from the kitchen, my lambkin. Don't forget to put candles down the stairs, and be sure the turtle soup is the right temperature."

At the reference to turtle soup, Poupon involuntarily smacked his lips. His stomach had begun to miss the sandwich and beer awaiting him in his bedroom, and he would have had no objection to some immediate nourishment on account.

"You see how domesticated I am," resumed the lady. "I could have entertained at an expensive restaurant, but I chose to give my party at home. I hope you do not think it heartless of me to give it now that Aubrey has been so ill? Of course, I should have put it off if his condition had not improved. I have simple tastes. He has never appreciated that. Between ourselves, he has not deserved such a devoted mistress."

" Aubrey ? "

" Edouard. You wouldn't believe what I have done for that man ! I have remained with him for nearly three years—and not altogether because I am too lazy to make changes. A very good thing it is over ! It isn't prudent for a girl to entrust her happiness to a man who would leave her to sit down thirteen to table. What do you say ? Imagine the consternation of my guests when they discovered it ! His character is not evil, but he has nerves. I cannot tolerate people with nerves. I like people to be reposeful. Your own disposition is reposeful, isn't it ? Is your wife happy with you ? What is your name ? Feel how hot my head is."

Poupon obeyed the behest with emotions. " My name——"

" And my hands are like ice. Perhaps it is brain fever. I ought to have a physician, instead of a party. I don't want a party. I want to keep quiet and go on listening to you. I hope you will often come and comfort me like this. I shall not forget what a kind friend you have been."

" Too much honoured. My name——"

" You must make the party go for me. *I* can find nothing to say to-night at all. I shall count on you to keep the ball rolling. Don't you think I am very brave, the way I stand being deserted ? "

Poupon got as far as " I——"

" Some girls would dope. Not *I*—I know too much. Why do girls love ? No man is worth it. How queer we should have met ! Where were you going ? If you had been passing five minutes sooner, Mathilde would not have seen you. Isn't that extraordinary ? She would have brought up some other man instead. I wonder what he would have been like. Tell me more about yourself. Perhaps he would have fallen in love with me—and I with him ? Wouldn't that have been quaint ? It would just have served Edouard right, if the stranger I had to fish up from the street had cut him out. Perhaps there would have been a duel. Edouard might have been killed. Ah, no, no, it is too frightful ! Edouard killed ! I can't bear it—I shall go out of my mind. What did you do with the salts ? Go on talking to me—it soothes me to hear you talk. You must not think me impolite for saying so little—I am not myself yet. Are you fond of fishing ? You must come and see me one day at my cottage in the country. It is called *Sweet Home*. It is an English name.

England is delicious, except for its climate, its cant, and its cookery. You shall confide more of your hopes and aims to me. I am deeply interested, and my life is an empty one. People want me to let my hair grow again, but what good would it do ? Do you think I ought to keep it as it is, or not ? "

" Your hair is superb. I——"

" You find it so ? It used to reach to my knees, but the weight was too much when I threw my head back, in my dances. It used to give me a headache every night. I think I have got one coming now. I am neglected. Something should be done."

" Are your hands warmer ? "

" I don't know," she moaned. " Feel."

Poupon's aspirations now were not wholly for his supper. Daring to press a kiss on the jewelled hands, he gasped, " Your hair is superb, and your eyes are superb, and you are superb too." And since her monologue was momentarily suspended, " I do not know what to make of it," he gasped on. " You make my brain swim. I am at your feet." Having no experience to encourage him, his heart was in his throat at the audacity of his doings.

Mercifully, she was not indignant. For a discomfiting moment, indeed, Poupon rather thought she was amused. Then she said, shaking her fair head :

" You don't mean it."

" Not mean it ? Mon Dieu ! "

" How can you be in love with me—you have hardly heard me speak ? "

Poupon, palpitating with self-approval, thought " Well, I never ! How I am going it ! It is like some scene on the stage. My word, I have fallen into clover ! " He maintained, " In all my life I have not seen a woman to compare with you. I am bewildered—I can't realise that not twenty minutes have passed since I entered. Already I am your slave. Er—isn't it odd ? I haven't yet heard your name."

" My name," replied the lady, " is Placide." She added, glancing at the clock, " And it is my fête day now ! "

" How I regret I was not carrying flowers ! All my felicitations and best wishes."

" That is why I am giving a supper-party. We celebrate my fête day in its first hour. Chic, hein ? Yes, it is droll. Twenty minutes ago we had never met—and now, what is there we have not told each other ? "

" My own name," said Poupon perseveringly, " is——"

" But do not talk to me of love, for I shall never trust a man again."

" Ah, but that is unworthy of your intellect ! Do not think that all men are of no account because Aubrey—that is to say, Edouard—was a sweep. You have sent me crazy. You would find me most congenial. I admit I am not opulent, but a girl of your exquisite sensibilities is not influenced solely by financial considerations, and it is a dead cert. my company would cheer you up no end. I shall talk brightly to you, when you pause; I shall obliterate that ruffian's base behaviour from your mind. I shall enrich you with new thoughts and joys. Ah, Placide, do not be pitiless ! Give me hope ! "

For once the lady was not prompt to speak. He bent nearer, breathless with suspense. She turned to make her answer. And then, maddeningly, the telephone bell rang.

She seemed to be swept from him on a hurricane.

" Allô, allô ! Mademoiselle who ? . . . Allô, Zouzou ! . . . Ah no, don't tell me *that* ! Yes, it does, it puts me out terrifically. . . . Just going to do what ? Have breakfast ? Well, have supper instead. . . . Not up ? Ah, it is the limit ! Enough, enough, enough ! You waste words, imbecile. I may forgive you on your deathbed."

She rose in a cyclone.

"One of them can't come. Again we are thirteen. They drive me demented. It is diabolical."

"Be calm, be calm," begged Poupon. "After all, it is not so important. Come back and——"

"What is to be done? It is fate, I see it is fate! If I raise another guest from the street, someone else will fall through. As fast as I catch one, another slips out. I cannot fight the devil—I am only a weak girl. Ha!" She saw light, and struck her brow. "You can save me! I am desolated to withdraw my invitation, but without you, all will be well—we shall be only twelve. I implore your pardon. Be gracious. Go."

"*Comment?*" croaked Poupon, dumbfounded.

"It is fate. I regret." She darted to the bell.

"But—but—— Believe me, thirteen is not so ominous. You attach too much significance to it. Most frolicsome parties of thirteen——"

"You can go to them. Nothing would induce me, nothing in the world! You cannot make objections. Chivalry forbids. Tell me your name, that I may treasure it."

"I—I—Ah, mon Dieu!" wailed Poupon.

" If your superstition is so insuperable, if you insist, I—I—— Of course, what can I say? But it is a dreadful sacrifice you ask, it is an heroic sacrifice. It is the greatest sacrifice I could possibly make." And, indeed, by this time, the thought of a copious supper appealed to him no less strongly than did the lady. " Enfin, you command, and I submit. My name is——"

" You have a gallant nature," responded Placide, in a burst of gratitude. She added urgently, as Mathilde appeared, " The gentleman's coat and hat ! " And, constrained to find a couple of francs for Mathilde's inescapable palm—his foretaste of turtle soup and tenderness a vanished dream—the chagrined Poupon began to feel his way down the black staircase, where no candles had been put yet.

" That individual has given me a tip of two francs," complained Mathilde, in deep disgust. " What has gone wrong ? "

" Mademoiselle Zouzou regrets. She has overslept," panted Placide.

And scarcely had she spoken when the young man Edouard made a penitent return.

" My angel, I have been to blame," he bleated. For twenty seconds nothing was in her mind but rapture at the coming reconciliation. Near to dancing with delight, she replied frigidly, "You have killed me." And, as he strove to embrace her, "No, no! Never will you understand me. It is wiser that we part."

"Ah, have mercy!"

"Do not persist. You pain us both for nothing. This time I am determined."

"I have not ceased to weep."

"I beg you be silent. I can endure no more."

"What misery! Each day I love you better—and each day I blunder worse. I am accursed. I could dash my head against the wall. Placide, pardon, pardon!"

"Am I not always pardoning? Ah, my poor friend, why cannot you improve? Our life would be so tranquil but for those nerves of yours. . . . What did you say? I am weak to listen! . . . Are you sure? Yes, yes, yes, I know, my darling boy! And I love you, in spite of all your tantrums—and of mine! I do, I do, I do. Hold me tight. And you shall *not* improve—I adore you as you are. *Ah!*" She broke from his arms in horror. "Again we are thirteen!"

"What?"

"The man's not here."

" Well ?   Fourteen, as at first."

" No—Zouzou is off.   There may be time to stop him—you must have passed him on the stairs."   She rushed to the telephone :   " Concierge, concierge !   Don't open the porte cochère. There's a gentleman that mustn't go.   The maid comes down."

So when the resentful Poupon had groped his way to the ground-floor at last, and crossed the courtyard, the outer door remained massively fast, and he stood shouting, " Cordon, cordon," to an invisible concierge without avail.   The rain was now descending with vigour, and there being no shelter from it by the porte cochère, Poupon's feet were getting wetter every minute. He was so much incensed, and the deluge on his umbrella was so boisterous that Mathilde had to call to him, from the portico, more than once before he heard her.

He bellowed back, " Tell the concierge to pull the cord ! "

" I have a message for monsieur."

" Give it to someone else this time !   You do not play the game with me again," cried Poupon, striding to her wrathfully.   " Where is your damnable concierge ? "

" But, monsieur, I assure monsieur——"

" Yes, I have not forgotten. ' It is an affair
of ceremony, I am invited to it.   How fortunate
I am in evening dress ! '   The ceremony here
doesn't impress me.   Let me out ! "

" Madame sends me to tell monsieur that, on
second thoughts, she cannot bear the idea of his
leaving.   She begs monsieur to make allowances
for her agitation just now, and to sup here as
intended."

" Hein ? " said Poupon, softening towards the
Siren Song.

" Madame is greatly concerned.   If I go back
without monsieur she will be furious with me.
Frankly, I tremble to do it," asseverated Mathilde,
thinking, " A fine fuss I have to make over a
fellow that gives two francs ! "

" Enfin," said Poupon, his robust resolve
melting into jelly, " I shall overlook the incident.
I go up again."

This time he made use of the hat-stand.   And
the smirk that he presented to Placide faded
painfully as he saw Edouard beyond her.

Edouard, however, was nearly as effusive as
she.   His presence was a clog, but apparently
not a danger.

" Ah, what beatitude ! " rhapsodised the lady.
" How forbearing of you, my friend ! "

" Hurra ! I am fortunate," gushed the host. " Monsieur, I rejoice at my opportunity to greet you."

" I have ill deserved your indulgence. But I was overwrought," lamented Placide, with plaintive eyes.

" I regret infinitely that my previous reception of you was, perhaps, abrupt. But as a man of the world, you realise that things happen," chimed in the gentleman.

Poupon recovered some cheerfulness, notwithstanding impeditive Edouard. " Madame, I am enchanted to regain a hospitality that—er—could not have been enhanced. Monsieur, the felicity is mine. Abrupt ? On my honour, I did not perceive it."

" How joyous a party now ! Everything arranges itself. I hope you have a good appetite ? You will find our friends very amusing. You must not be shy with them. They are like me—when I am happy I am only ten years old. How many children have you got ? If you are fond of company you will have a good time. I shall bring Aubrey to you by and by. My little innocent ! He does not dream what complications he has caused," Placide began.

But before she could say any more, guests

were arriving—all in the highest spirits, and the ladies in entrancing toilettes. The little salon was speedily crowded, and Poupon rejoiced to think that supper might be expected at any moment now, until, counting heads, he found that, inclusive of his own, there were not yet more than a dozen.

" We await Cricri and her husband," he heard Edouard tell someone. And the next minute, an hilarious blonde made a sprightly entrance, and was embracing and embraced.

" Where is Charles, love ? " asked the hostess, looking anxious.

" I am all on my little own, old dear," explained the new-comer. " I would have let you know the hubby wasn't turning up, but I only took the pool just now—he has eloped with Leonora."

" Ah," shrieked Placide, staggering under this final blow. " Again we are thirteen ! " She reeled to Poupon. " Be great, be great ! Be glorious and depart ! "

" What ? " howled Poupon, trembling with rage. " Ah no ! It is too thick ! You call me in—you turn me out. You call me in—you turn me out——"

" Upwards, upwards ! Your name will live always in my memory."

" Monsieur, we are overwhelmed," protested
Edouard. " But what is to be done ? Madame
has insuperable fear of the number 13, and you
know well we men must humour the fair sex.
Noblesse oblige, n'est-ce-pas ? "

" You call me in—you turn me out. You call
me in—you turn me out," fumed Poupon. " Is
that fair sex ? I do you favours—and you venture to speak of pulling my nose. Is that noblesse
oblige ? "

" Bravo, this is fine ! Who is he ? " chorused
the company, delighted at the entertainment.
Their laughter pealed. The blonde whose husband hadn't come was in such ecstasies of mirth
that she nearly choked.

" Who wants your supper anyway ? I shake
the dust of your sacré apartment from my feet.
But first I tell you frankly you are a couple
of——"

" Ah, take care, monsieur ! " interposed Edouard, with the dauntless valour of a man whose
opponent is no good. " Or I shall not only
' speak ' of pulling your nose."

" I spit at your supper," declared Poupon,
receding prudently. His climax was weak, but
the force of his kicks at all the candles on the
stairs, as he went down, put several of them out.

G

It was still pouring. He was in the streets when he might have been in bed; the mishap had cost him two precious francs. And he was so much disturbed that, when home was reached, the sandwich and the beer were tasteless. But when he tells the story, Poupon says, "What a romance! She could not bear to part with me. All through a shoelace! An adventure for a King!"

MATE

O N E morning a woman woke in the dawn, and presently her eyes filled and she wept without sound until her husband stirred. Then, because she loved him, she feigned to be sleeping still. The man slipped from the bed, and dressed quickly. He tucked a blanket closer round the baby in the cot—looked again at his wife, and left the house.

It was a little wooden house, partitioned into two; the smaller part was occupied by the Operator. The woman's husband banged at the Operator's door, and stood staring across the river, which foamed furiously. The country— all of it that concerned him—was white, peak and field. It was May, and the sun was melting the mountain snow to swell the rivers and flood the land. May was the month of menace : it was sometimes called the " month of death."

The man was the section foreman at Kaspar, the last flag station on the track. He was young, and big, and strong, and he looked a finer fellow still beside the little hunchback that came to the door.

" Any worse news from Allan's Point, Jim ? " he asked.

" No. Thought I heard you start two hours ago."

" You heard the men go. The missus took on so at the thought of being left alone all night that I had to stay with her a bit. I had no idea before that she funked the place so bad."

" So ? " said the hunchback. He was a man of few words, excepting when he swore.

The other moved slowly down the three wooden steps. " She's asleep now. And she's going to make the kid's new frock to-day— that'll keep her cheerful when she gets up. It's till then I'm thinking of—if she wakes again. She's that timid, got the bears and tramps on her mind ! She's safe enough, really, but—— Keep an eye on her, mate ! "

" Right ! "

Lower on the track, a passenger train had been wrecked. Bridges were in danger of being swept away, and already most of them had been damaged. It was to the bridge at Allan's Point, about seven miles distant, that the foreman was going. As he strode from sleeper to sleeper with the deftness of practice, his thoughts were wistful. His house lay back out of the course of the mountain water, but he was thinking of his wife. She was awake now perhaps? She was dressing the baby. She had had her breakfast, a poor enough meal, he was certain. She was busy in the kitchen; he knew just what was going on there, and how she looked—a neat little thing, moving lightly, with her eyes ever on the boy. Now it was time he went to sleep again—Letty would be singing to him. And the man on the track whistled the familiar tune.

At Kaspar, the hunchback whom he had left behind stood smoking idly. For several days, since there were no trains to be signalled, there had been little to do. But for the fact that he must remain by the apparatus he would have gone as well. Not that he would have been of much use, he thought bitterly! "Mate"? Nobody guessed it, but the word stabbed him as often as it fell. In truth he was no man's mate, with this back of his. It debarred him from the comradeship of men, and the love of women. He was quite aware that the woman next door had never taken to him, and she was the gentlest creature he had ever known. He lounged there, in the doorway, till the sun rose and showed the colour of the lake, and the awful beauties of the maddened river.

He was very cold, so he lit a fire and sat over it half the morning with his pipe. He, too, could conjecture pretty well what was going on in the foreman's kitchen, for the partition was thin, and the woman's image was as clear in his mind as if there were no partition at all. . . .

And Harry didn't know that she was wretched in this God-forgotten hole, he mused. The damned fool. Why, *he* had known it all along, ever since the first morning he had seen her, afraid to step out, and afraid to shut herself in. A sad little shrinking creature, with a beautiful smile for him when he passed, although she hadn't taken to him. She had never grown used to the wilderness—the frowning mountains, and the loneliness, and the prowl of bears. No wonder, coming from a little garden in England ! It was enough to damp a stouter heart than hers.

He knew she couldn't help her cowardice. She tried to hide it, but the bluff didn't deceive *him*. Hadn't he seen her times out of number come tearing back along the track, white and shaking from the sight of an animal's footprint, or the gaunt face of a tramp ? And hadn't he

seen her force herself to go out again to meet
her husband, her frightened eyes looking this way
and that until she caught sight of him in the
distance? She might laugh when they were
together, but the hunchback knew how she sobbed
when she was alone. He had heard her sobbing
in the other room so often before the baby
came. Not since; the baby had made a difference. Still, she was always scared, and always
shamming that she wasn't.

This morning he could hear her singing. He
listened for some time; then got up suddenly
and went to the wood-shed, and chopped enough
wood from the great round blocks to last for
two or three weeks. Once Letty looked in. He
did not stop his work. Would he lend her a
little, she asked: Harry had forgotten to chop
some for her before he went. The sweep of
the axe indicated that she might help herself.
She filled her apron, and thanked her taciturn
neighbour awkwardly. When she had gone,
he went to Harry's wood-shed and chopped
there for an hour.

Not until late in the evening did he see her
again. She came to the door.

" They're having a bad time at Allan's Point,"
she said, speaking as if she were out of breath.

" They're up to their waists in water, damming it all they can ! "

" Who brought word ? "

" A stranger on his way to Sulby. Harry sent love—I dragged the news out of the man."

Jim looked across the track, where a man's figure was fading in the gloom. The next moment the whole mountain-side was vivid under the first lightning flash of a coming storm.

He heard a smothered cry.

" It won't be much," he said quickly.

But he spoke only to the darkness. She was gone; her door was banged. He stood there for a minute, seeming still to see her quivering face under the old shawl. Then he lit his pipe and pondered.

The storm crashed, and the woman went to bed, to shut out sight and sound under the blankets. She did not hear his knock. He had gone to ask her if she was all right. As there was no answer, no light showing through the chinks, he returned to his room and filled the pipe again.

As if it had needed a storm to make things worse for her ! He cursed immoderately. Was she asleep ? Not likely. Trembling and crying, of course. And he could do nothing but smoke like a blasted smouldering log. He wished he had thought to tell her he meant to sit up all night. It might have comforted her to know that even a hunchback was awake close by.

By and by he went and pottered round her windows. He fancied that he heard the baby crying. Well, it was better for her to think of the baby than of her loneliness and the storm.

She could not pacify the child. She paced the room with him for nearly an hour, in abject terror, pretending enjoyment. The blinding flashes, through the crevices of the shutters, were a " pretty light," she told him, and the thunders that rocked the earth were " only the clouds having a funny game." Then, at last, when she could put him in the cot again, she crept back to her own pillow and hid her head.

At the hint of a footstep her heart missed a beat—and thudded in her ears as she tried to listen. Fearing that someone threatened the house, she prayed for nerve to look boldly out and prove that she was wrong. The hope that it might be her neighbour was too feeble to encourage her; he wasn't likely to be astir on such a night. That it was his method of taking care of her, that he was thinking of her at all, did not cross her mind. But the hint faded, and as the storm spent itself gradually the nervous woman lay painfully straight and taut, her gaze fastened on the candle she had lighted when the baby woke.

Silence. A prolonged, burdensome silence. It was intense. It seemed to her unnatural. She listened for a coming freight train, forgetting for some seconds that none could pass that night. She lay oppressed by the strange silence. And next, vague sounds stole into it, sounds that perhaps existed only in her fancy.

Startling her, as the candle guttered, there came a noise that was unmistakable. Someone was knocking at the outer door.

Her feet were on the ground before she hesitated. Then the knocking was repeated, and there leapt to her remembrance the coming of a tramp, and her skin turned clammy. He had appeared one evening, begging for food. She was alone, and gave liberally in her eagerness to be rid of him, but he had thrust his foot inside the door, and—— How she managed to shut it against him at last she never knew. To open it to a stranger in the dead of night would be madness.

The knocking became imperative. She huddled on some clothes. For an instant a new fear thrust the first one out. Perhaps it was a messenger—Harry was ill, an accident had happened!

She ran across the kitchen and a voice was calling.

" Jim! " She fell upon the bar and tore it down. " What is it? " She had to shout, for it was as if the clamour of an ocean had burst upon her. " What's wrong? "

" It's the house. The water's breaking our way. It's coming quick. If we can't turn it— will you help me? I wouldn't have woke you if I could ha' done it myself."

" I'll come," she said, shuddering. " Have you got a light? " She groped about the room. " I can't leave baby in the dark."

He came in and struck a match as she pushed the lamp towards him.

" You've not slept; you've had a bad time."

" How do you know? "

" That's easy to see."

She took the lamp up, her bare feet padding to the bedroom. As yet she did not understand that, for two, the task was almost hopeless. But the hunchback felt they were to die together, and in the morbid exultation that possessed him, death held no terror, and pity played small part. Before they sank, he meant to tell her that he loved her. It'd be no treachery then. And though she wouldn't care, it'd be sweet to say it. He would drown with his arms round her!

The woman came out again, wearing thick boots, and a small shawl. Behind the house, she stepped into water before he remembered to warn her of the trench he had begun. He swore as he pulled her back, but his words were half lost in the uproar.

"It's come already!" she said, dazed.

Then she turned on him fiercely. "Why didn't you call me sooner? We could have built up some sort of bank by now."

"I thought——" But what he thought wasn't uttered as he seized his spade.

A moment later her hand was on his own, and he knew she repented her reproach. Then she fought for their safety, with a vigour that amazed him. She had opened the bedroom shutters and pulled the cot from the wall, that she might have the child in sight. The source of her strange strength was proclaimed by every look she cast towards the window. Her strength was the sleeping child.

Its volume swelling, the torrent made their

panting labours puny. Bushes and young trees it tossed past them. Something gigantic, wrenched up by the roots, swept by.

All at once the woman shrieked. In looking towards the child, she saw what the man had seen some minutes sooner. The cot stood, an inch deep, in water.

They had failed to allow for the slope on which the house, without foundation, had been built—for rivulets below it. Now they knew that, unless they laboured faster, the water would soon be far higher than the cot.

" What can we do ? " she wailed.

He hung over the shovel, exhausted, open-mouthed.

" Go on, Jim, go on ! "

But he couldn't go on yet.

Suddenly she appealed to God.

" God, this man can do no more—he has worked his strength out. Only you can give it back to him. Oh ! God, can't you see for once ? " Her sobbing voice screamed above the riot of the flood. " Won't you give it back to him ? " She clutched at him convulsively. " Mate ! "

For the first time, the word had carried no sting. It had meant honour, incentive. Again they sweated, panting, side by side, and each load of the shovels felt weightier to their aching arms, and at every glance, the water in the room seemed higher. By and by they knew that it had risen several inches. Her face was frantic now, her tottering efforts futile. Even the empty shovel had grown too heavy to wield, and in her ears was a rushing different from the river's roar. The man gasped to her painfully, " Stop a bit." For answer, she looked again towards the flooded room.

The child turned in his cot. The blanket slipped, and a little hand, clutching an old rag doll, came out between the bars.

When she looked next, the doll was floating. And as long as she lived, the mother could see that coloured doll floating by her baby's bed that was soon to be submerged.

She tried to look less often, she tried to think of other things. She could not. What did the paint on the new chest of drawers matter any longer ? Or the things in the trunk ? Or her best hat in the box under the dressing-table ? Nothing mattered but the boy ! If Harry came back to find the house gone, and baby—— Supposing the men at Allan's Point had been drowned ? Supposing Harry never came back ?

The hunchback thought she was resting at last. She had let the spade drop, and was facing the window. But she could not see the window well now. She tried to wipe the sweat out of her eyes, but every second, the room and the child grew dimmer.

" Jim," she sobbed, " I can't see baby. The light's going out ! "

At daybreak, a shift of men at Allan's Point were free to draw breath in trucks on the line. The course of the water, hideous with the wrecks of houses, and screams of the doomed, would soon be turned now, it was reckoned, and for the men shambling to the trucks the work of saving the bridge was over. One of them muttered, " I'm going——" He had meant to say " home," but was afraid.

They warned him that it would be impossible to reach Kaspar yet, but he set out, saying that, where he couldn't walk, he would swim.

It was evening when he arrived, and the squat contour of his home was showing through the dusk. He wanted to shout thanksgiving, but his voice failed. He wanted to run very swiftly, but his legs trembled too much.

When he was near enough to call, he saw

pools under the house. So he did not call; he was suddenly afraid again. He cowered by the shuttered window, listening.

There was no sound, for a moment, but the drumming in his ears. Then he heard his wife singing the tune he had whistled on his way to Allan's Point, and he began to laugh hysterically.

A crooked figure came round the corner of the house.

"Hullo, Jim," said the man. "What are you at?"

"Keeping an eye on her," said Jim. "But I can chuck it now."

He went inside and slammed his door. At the husband's call, the other door was opened. And through the partition, the hunchback heard cries of joy.

THE VENGEANCE OF
MONSIEUR DUTRIPON

W H E N the fair landlady of the Chariot d'Or fled with the lion-tamer it was well for " Zambra the Dauntless " that her husband didn't know where they had gone. He was athirst to kill Zambra. During those early days when all Appeville-Sous-Bois was seething with the scandal, monsieur Dutripon hissed to his confidants that until he had shot Zambra he would never sleep again. He was not precisely heartbroken at the loss of his wife, for, though she was a fine woman, she was of a domineering disposition, and violent when opposed, but he had a dramatic temperament, and he felt that to shoot her lover was the thing to do.

The circus having come to grief, however, the troupe had been disbanded, and no one in Appeville had any idea where the guilty pair abode. Dutripon raved that he took steps to have them traced. " And then—you will see ! I follow, and I shoot him on sight." Whereat his father-in-law, old monsieur Bompard, the estate agent, embraced him fervently, quavering, " Good, good! The infamous scoundrel, to bring such disgrace upon me! I have been honoured in the town for forty-eight years—and now I am the father of a lion-tamer's mistress! It is agonising. Thou shalt avenge me, Victor."

A woman present, the pretty widow of the late postmaster, reminded Dutripon that he would have to suffer for his deed, but Dutripon swept the reminder to the winds, though he felt that his father-in-law's viewpoint was too personal. " I mock myself of the consequences," he clamoured. " The guillotine itself should not deter me."

" Excellent! " monsieur Bompard wheezed ecstatically. " To the devil with the consequences! Besides, he will be acquitted, I have no misgivings for him; the result of the trial disquiets me not at all."

The widow frowned upon this vicarious courage, but the old egotist was not to be repressed. " What a calamity for me that that circus came! " he snuffled. " Ah, mon Dieu, mon Dieu! They have spat on my grey hairs. For forty-eight years I have held my head high in Appeville, and now it is ignominy to me to tread its streets. Be sure the revolver is reliable, Victor! "

"Never shall I sleep again till he lies dead at my feet," thundered Dutripon, smiting his breast.

Every day he proclaimed his dread resolve to his intimates; and Appeville, normally a dull place, looked forward to his exploit with enthusiasm. It even made attempts to supply information, in the hope of expediting the affair. Only madame Lemoine, the pretty widow, seemed in the least perturbed by the thought of the penalty he might pay.

Nevertheless several weeks passed without result, and when spring had blossomed, the deserted husband found it practicable to give heed to other things when the day's work was done. He could again yield his attention to a newspaper, and as he perused *Le Journal* at his ease in the little salon behind the buffet, and lit, perhaps, a third cigar, there was some assuagement in the consciousness that he could sit and smoke there as late as he liked without incurring a blast of recrimination when he reached the bedroom. His wife was a firm believer in beauty sleep, and formerly, if he had lingered more than half an hour, he had been assailed by, " This is a fine time to come barging in ! Didn't I tell you to be quick ? "—and she would launch into a furious denunciation of his selfishness.

At first the room had appeared foreign to him

without her raging voice; instinctively he had listened for a sharp complaint, or a loud explosion; but by degrees the wondrous silence developed undoubted charm. Under its soothing influence he aspired less continuously to kill Zambra. Even he contemplated the act with less dramatic satisfaction; he began to think about it rather as a sacred but irksome duty. Relieved of his handsome termagant, Dutripon privately found life assuming a more agreeable air than it had worn for fifteen years. But as the town still jabbered about the matter, and looked to him to do something sanguinary, he had publicly, of course, to wring his hands and reiterate his threats of vengeance.

" I follow to the very limits of France," he proclaimed perpetually. " I empty my revolver into him ! "

When spring had ripened into summer without revealing the whereabouts of Zambra and the erring woman, Dutripon, though he was averse from recognising the fact, would have been entirely cheerful in his home life but for the frequent visits of his father-in-law. The intensity of the estate agent's attitude had not abated, and he would shuffle into the little salon, just when Dutripon had made himself comfortable, to solicit news, and pester for more active measures.

"Your procrastination is very bad for me; it is telling on my health," he whimpered in July. "At my age such delays are serious. Months and months go by, and nothing has been done. It is insupportable."

"I am of your opinion, père," said Dutripon. "It is maddening."

"I cannot bear it. You should bestir yourself. You sit here in an armchair. It is not moral."

"Not moral?" returned Dutripon with choler. "Where would you have me sit?"

"Mon Dieu, you should sit in a train! You should sit in a hundred trains. If I were of your age I could not rest while he walked the earth. No, I could not rest. My blood would revolt. You have not simply your own wrongs to attend to—you have mine. I have borne an honoured name in Appeville for forty-eight years, and now I conceal myself when a client enters my office. To that am I fallen—the father of your wife! The ravager of my honour—and of yours, and of my poor misguided child's—walks free, while you sit in an armchair. It is unspeakable."

"Never shall I sleep again till I see him dead at my feet," roared Dutripon once more.

"That I do not dispute, but I complain that you are too leisurely about it. Hurry up! At this rate you will never see him at all. I ask you, why not? He is a performer, he is a public spectacle—why should it require a miracle for you to view him? Other people can look at him for a franc."

"The world is wide," pleaded Dutripon; "how shall one divine to what parts he has travelled?"

"Are lions unnoticeable? He cannot put his lions in his baggage. Get a move on. Mon Dieu, in your place I would have shot him the next morning. Yes, I would have shot him the next morning, and brought Valentine back in the afternoon."

"*Comment donc?*" said Dutripon, stupefied. "You expect me to take her back?"

"Naturally it is my expectation," affirmed monsieur Bompard, nodding emphatically. "Do you ask me to believe you will condemn my poor girl to expiate her fault among lions? It would be barbarous; your heart would forbid. Also," he resumed, after wiping his eyes and nose emotionally, "you may have personal considerations that urge you to condone her error; I do not doubt that you are partly responsible for what has happened. She had a religious upbringing, my Valentine, her character was very pure—it is incontestable that she would never have taken such a course if you had not failed towards her in some respects."

" It's the limit," gasped Dutripon.

" I do not say your neglect was intentional, but without question, you are to blame. Alors, as a man of integrity you cannot hesitate. The pistol and the pardon impose themselves upon you, voyons ! "

As was his custom when he came, he remained till late, and ordered a lot of the best brandy without paying for it. And after this visit in particular Dutripon moaned at the sound of his shuffling footsteps in the hall.

Much more sympathetic was madame Lemoine when he happened to meet her in the market. With the frankness permitted by long acquaintance, she would own that she wasn't anxious for Zambra to be discovered. " On the contrary," she said one day, " I wish he would go to Cochin China and stop there. Mon pauvre ami, have you not suffered enough already ? Why should you sacrifice your liberty, and perhaps your life for an ideal ? "

" Because it is a lofty one," replied Dutripon gravely.

" How high-minded you are ! " she sighed. " And yet you are selfish too—I dare to say it. You have your friends to think about. Your punishment would fall heavily on them as well."

" On how many ? I make myself no illusions."

" On one at least," she murmured.

" That I believe," said Dutripon, touched. " You are a good sort. You also have deserved better luck than you got. Lemoine was all right in his way, but he was too old and sick to be the husband of a young woman like you."

" It was my mother's doing," she said pensively. " He was a martyr to rheumatism even then."

" He seemed to complain of a new ailment each time I saw him; I always thought you must find them confusing in the home. Well, I must return ! "

" And you will consider what I have said ? You will give up your wild intention ? "

" Ah, that never ! Never in this world."

" Men are amazing ! " she exclaimed. " You could not do more if she had been the apple of your eye. You pay her the greatest compliment in your power. One would think she had ruined your life by relieving you of her fiendish temper."

" Have I ever said she had a fiendish temper ? "

" You have never said she had two legs. There are things that do not need to be announced. We are speaking openly, and I confess I used to be very sorry for you. I used to say to myself,

'What a muddle Destiny makes of matters : a monsieur so charming and intellectual chained to a harridan ! ' Sometimes I have cried."

Dutripon expanded his chest, and was meditative for a moment. " Listen," he said gently. " I shall explain. I do not kill Zambra because— how shall I say it ?—because I exactly adored her, but because their association is a public insult to me which can only be balanced by his blood. I am out for myself, not Valentine. Speaking in confidence—I would not say it to anybody else—I do not violently lament her absence. What you say is true : Destiny is a muddler. Valentine was the wrong mate for me : that is a sure thing. But since I did throw myself away on her, and her caprice for a lion-tamer renders me ridiculous, my self-respect makes it imperative that I shoot him. And, without doubt, I shall do so. No matter how much expense it puts me to, to reach him, or how much I may privately deplore the necessity, I shall stretch him dead at my feet. Well, I must return ! Au revoir, dear friend."

" If they should be abroad ? Who knows ? In America perhaps. I pray the hotel may keep its end up while you are gone," she said solicitously. " Your little clerk is not capable of running it, you know."

"I know it well. But one must look on the bright side and hope I shall not have far to go. I see no reason to fear the swine is in America— I read that the immigration laws are very strict. It may even be that lion-tamers are excluded altogether. Certainly, if my errand should compel me to be absent long, the thought of the hotel would be a keen anxiety, but—que voulez-vous ? Perhaps, from time to time, if I may make the request, you would be so amiable as to look in there ? You could, at any rate, see to it that they kept the rooms clean."

"Bien sûr. I would do anything I could; I am honoured by the suggestion," she answered promptly. "And the hotel business has always fascinated me."

"So ? What do you know of it, you child ? "

"From experience, nothing," she smiled, "but for amusement I have sometimes imagined myself with an hotel. In my best imaginings it has been in Nice, or Monte Carlo, and I invented a feature that was a money-maker. I must consult you about it some day."

"Consult me now," said Dutripon gaily.

"Well, it appears that the smart hotels there have, beyond the dining-room, a room that is called the restaurant, where the food is the same, but the prices are double."

"Yes. People pay more in the restaurant because the company in it is more select."

"I venture to think that what they pay for is the satisfaction it gives them to walk, in their grand toilettes, with their noses in the air, past all the people who are dining more cheaply and looking envious."

"It is possible."

"Well, in *my* hotel there is yet another room, which is called the Restaurant de Luxe, and in which the prices are treble. In proceeding to it the super snobs can sneer, not only at the dining-room clients, but at the snobs in the first restaurant, too. It is such a success that I even think the prices should be increased."

"Upon my word, there may be something in it," chuckled Dutripon. "So the business interests you? All the better for me if I have to be away for long. By the by, if you would do me the favour to come in and take a cup of coffee one evening when you have an hour to spare, I could give you some idea how things are done. One evening when you are not occupied, hein? It would be very gracious of you. . . . Well, I must return!"

"I should love to be instructed; I shall take careful notes," she said devoutly. And this time she let him go.

Her visits were an exhilarating contrast to monsieur Bompard's, though Bompard resented them when he found her there. "She does not please me, that madame Lemoine," he sniffed. "I can keep an eye on the hotel for you myself, if necessary. You may tell her she is not required."

"No; it would distress me to put you to the trouble, père. The burden shall be hers," said his son-in-law with decision. And every day he was more exhilarated still.

It was on an evening at this stage that Poch, the photographer, bustled in, with the air of one bearing the best of news, to tell him that Zambra the Dauntless figured in an itinerant circus at Ker Breiz in Brittany.

Dutripon was conscious of swift depression. Of course, if an opportunity had occurred, it behoved him to get busy; but things had been very well as they were, and he surmised with annoyance that a place having the unknown name of Ker Breiz would involve a complicated trip.

"I trust you are not misinformed!" he exclaimed heroically.

"No fear of it; I have details," cried the photographer, beaming with merit. "The circus opened there yesterday—but for no more than three nights. So only to-morrow night remains

for you. No doubt you must start this evening.
Let us look at your railway guide!"

Dutripon began to entertain a strong dislike
for Poch. But he rushed for the railway guide,
as in honour bound.

They found that, to reach Ker Breiz, he had
first to go to Paris, and then proceed to Morlaix,
a journey of some nine hours. "Peste, how long
from Morlaix to Ker Breiz? I may arrive too
late!" he growled, with a hope that he strove
guiltily to stifle. However, after further study
of the guide, it appeared that, if he left Paris at
eight o'clock next morning, he would be able to
go to the circus in time to kill Zambra soon after
dinner.

When madame Lemoine entered he was alone,
oiling his revolver.

"What are you doing?" she faltered.

"I've learnt where they are. I'm off to Brittany," he said hurriedly.

"Ah, no, no! I entreat you!"

"It's vain to talk. I go at once. They
announce that he performs for three nights only.
They're right—he won't see a fourth."

"Don't go, don't go!" she sobbed. "You'll
kill me too."

Moved, as well as flattered by this avowal,
Dutripon stood silent for a second, trying to

think of a reply that would meet the case; but before he could hit on one, there were the shuffling footsteps, and all chance of a love scene was banished. The sight of her helpless tears and monsieur Bompard's jubilation both affected Dutripon very strongly, in different ways, as he strode to the taxi.

And, squeezed in a crowded second-class compartment, he found his thoughts straying to madame Lemoine oftener than was appropriate to his errand.

He slept ill for a few hours in Paris, at a little hotel which, he noted, had a good deal to learn from the Chariot d'Or; and it was not till the 8 a.m. train was duly steaming with him out of the Gare de Montparnasse that he was capable of concentrating upon his deadly purpose.

Dutripon was not an experienced traveller, and the force of his concentration didn't serve to prevent his finding it a very tedious matter, going to Morlaix. His restiveness under it, however, was as nothing compared with his vexation when, Morlaix being reached, he heard that he must resign himself to waiting leisurely for a train to St. Pol, and that, after that, he might expect to change twice again. The railway guide had misled him grossly.

He had stamped about an inhospitable station

for an hour and forty minutes when the final train of his requirements crawled into view at last, and when he eventually attained the platform of Ker Breiz the time was well past midnight.

Speeding to the exit, with his little valise in his hand, and his revolver in his pocket, Dutripon was chagrined, though not surprised, to find there were no vehicles outside. "How does one get to the town?" he demanded fiercely of the solitary porter; and then, as he stood gazing at the moonlit vacant prospect, he perceived the sign of an unpretentious hostelry across the road.

No sooner was he admitted to it than his professional judgment told him it was not one of the little hotels of good fare for which he knew Brittany to be famous, but since there was small likelihood of his being at liberty to return to it when his job was done, its deficiencies didn't matter. He threw the valise into a cheerless room, had a hasty snack and a drink, and inquired the way to the circus.

The landlord's mouth fell open, and he stared, round-eyed. "The circus?" he stammered. "At half-past twelve? It is over."

"I do not want to see the performance," roared Dutripon, provoked beyond measure. "I ask you quite simply the way to the circus. I have business there."

The man gave him slowly interminable directions, beginning, " You have only to follow——" and Dutripon's feet sprung echoes in a deserted byway, which yielded tardily the sight of a straggling main street, wrapt in slumber. Traversing it, and envying the residents their repose, he entered on a region where the flatness of the vista was relieved solely by clumps of broom— and where, after unrequited trudging, he realised that he must have taken the wrong course.

A groan broke from him. He thought of his cosy bed at the Chariot d'Or, and it seemed to him that many weary days had passed since he started on his journey. Retracing his steps as far as the last cottage he had passed, he rapped loudly and long at its door, and by and by a peasant thrust an angry face out of a window.

" I apologise for disturbing you. Can you direct me ? I am a stranger. I seek the circus," explained Dutripon, and this time he made haste to add, " I do not think of seeing the performance—it is a matter of business."

The clink of cash in his palm proved mollifying, but the tongue spoken by this simple Breton was in moments obscure to Dutripon's agitated mind. Fearful of again mistaking instructions, he offered ten francs to be conducted to the spot—

and the Breton could have made a better bargain, if he had known it. The offer was promptly accepted, and when the man had reappeared with some clothes on, Dutripon resumed his disheartening walk in company. He thought to himself, as they tramped along, " You will have an interesting tale to tell, my guide ! I am conferring publicity upon you."

At a quarter to two, on the confines of the sleeping circus, the peasant took leave of him, and he paused while the man clumped away. The big tent itself had been taken down, in readiness for the migration, but many other patched tents, of various forms and dimensions, were still grouped about the gaudy coach, and he wondered which of them to make for first.

Picking his way among pegs and halters and lorries, then skirting animals' cages, over which some rough covering had been flung, Dutripon remarked that many of the tents were scrawled with performers' names. In the vivid moonlight the scrawls were fairly legible and, encouraged by the assistance, he embarked on a rapid tour of them. The fifth name that he examined was " Zambra." " Ah," panted Dutripon. He fumbled with the flap of the tent, and stepped commandingly inside.

I

As he did so, a woman's bellicose voice shouted, "This is a fine time to come barging in! Didn't I tell you to be quick?"

At these familiar words, in accents that had terrorised him for years, Dutripon's stature shrank and, turning, he saw his wife, a figure of fury, sitting up in bed alone.

"You?" she exclaimed, agape.

"Miserable woman, where is your lover?" demanded Dutripon, beginning his indictment more diffidently than he had foreseen.

The question seemed to aggravate her grievance. "You may well ask!" she stormed. "But don't give yourself airs, for I am in no mood for them, I tell you straight! I let him go to a café for a drink at ten o'clock, and he isn't back yet. What time is it, what does your watch say?"

"I have not travelled all this distance to tell you the time," answered Dutripon hotly. "Have you no sense of decency?"

The vigour of her reply induced him to tell her the time, after all, and it was evidently the only matter that had any interest for her.

"Mon Dieu! he shall remember this night," she swore, choking with passion. "Two o'clock—and he went at ten, after his turn. It is the last café of his life! He shall have something to remember it by, when he comes—it shall cost him more than he spent there, the sot!"

Dutripon stood uncertain what to do. Primarily resolved to await the coming, immovable by the bedside, he strove to sustain his position by reproaching her for her infidelity, but she was, for a long while, far too noisy about her punitive intentions to hear what he was saying. When she did so, she diverged into a vehement summary of all the unfavourable opinions she had formed of him during fifteen years. He felt that a betrayed husband, being bullied, looked very undignified, waiting there indefinitely.

"I waste no breath on you," he sneered, withdrawing to wait outside, instead. "My affair is with *him*."

"After mine! Wait your turn, or you will come off worse than *he* does," she volleyed. "Ladies first!"

It was when he had maintained his monotonous vigil for twenty minutes, marvelling that any café was open so late in the unpeopled townlet he had seen, that suspicion swept Dutripon. Perhaps Zambra had noted his approach, and taken cover! Perhaps, even, he lay concealed beneath his own bed!

Dashing back into the tent, regardless of the frenzy of his reception, Dutripon extended himself on the matting and peered under the bed laboriously. But the view was disappointing. His wife's ribald abuse scorched his ears as he got up, and he bellowed, " I shall find him, all the same—he is hidden somewhere or other ! You will see—I search every tent in the show ! "

The suspicion hurled him to redoubled energy, and the indignation of the startled troupe was boundless. Cursed by the men, and screamed at by the women, he sprawled, gasping apologies, by the beds of equestrians, and acrobats, and trumpeters, and clowns. His breathless explanations could not pacify the company, and " Mlle. Dainty Darling " hit him on the head. But nothing could deter him now. Not a tent on the field escaped his helter-skelter rush, and he clambered on the lorries, and investigated the coach. . . . And when the dawn broke and his quest had failed, and the manager was going to horsewhip him, Dutripon drooped from the circus despairing, and dragged his poor legs back to the cheerless room.

He slept till late in the afternoon, and breakfasted languidly between the sheets. The knowledge that the circus must have removed many hours ago did not excite him. While the dramatic side of his nature still claimed that it was compulsory to shoot Zambra, the other protested piteously against any further exertion to that end. Smoking cigar after cigar, he lay brooding deeply over his dilemma. And then, as he thought again of the charms of madame Lemoine, he questioned whether his paramount duty might not be to preserve her peace of mind. She had declared that, if the law took an ungenerous view of his righteous act, she would suffer terribly. She had even said she could not survive his punishment. Nobly to forgo his vengeance for a woman's sake would also be dramatic! It would even be sublime! Arriving at this conclusion with infinite relief, Dutripon rang the bell, and ordered champagne with his dinner.

The buffet of the Chariot d'Or was thronged on the day of his return; and when he wailed that he had reached Ker Breiz only to learn that the shameless pair had sailed from Marseilles on a professional tour of the United States, Australasia, and South Africa, none but his father-in-law condemned him as a slacker for not pursuing them all over the world.

To the ear of madame Lemoine alone did Dutripon whisper that he had made a stupendous sacrifice merely to spare her pain. She blushed with pride. And after he had obtained a divorce, and his ex-spouse had forced Zambra to legalise their position, Dutripon and the pretty widow were married amid the congratulations of all Appeville, except monsieur Bompard, who never spoke to either of them again. She proved a perfect wife and, remembering how easily he might have been in prison, instead of in clover, Dutripon gave daily thanks that some mysterious café had saved him from slaying the lion-tamer on that dreadful night.

Long afterwards the two men chanced to meet, and Dutripon said, " You need not be ill at ease. You rendered me a great service, and I have nothing against you any more. But, take it from me, you were lucky I did not find you at Ker Breiz ! "

" Perhaps," murmured Zambra doubtfully. " Life with Valentine is no treat, though."

" That does not concern me now," said Dutripon. " But what I have never understood is how any café in that hole remained open for you to carouse in all night long."

" I was back by one o'clock," demurred the other.

" Impossible ! I found Valentine alone—and I searched for you everywhere."

" Not quite," said Zambra, embarrassed; " I had promised to be back by eleven, and I knew what hell I should get when I went in. I was so scared that—well, I could not pluck up courage to face her," he explained shyly, " so I slept with the lions instead."

POOR DEAR GEORGE

O N E afternoon in August, Mr. Hooper, of Eastjoy-on-Sea, prepared surreptitiously to leave the house. As he passed the parlour, which was on the ground floor, his wife cried " 'Oward ! "

Howard turned discomfited. " 'Allo, 'Azel ! "

" What are you at ? " said Hazel. " You can't go out ! What you thinking about, for goodness' sake ? "

" Only going to the beach for a bit of a paddle," murmured Howard.

" Bit of a paddle ? Didn't I tell you I was going to take mother on the pier for 'er 'eadache ? You must wait till we come back."

" Can't see what for," he sighed. But he hung up his cap, and followed her into the parlour.

" Oh, you can't ? P'raps you don't know we're 'oping for a paying guest—you 'aven't 'eard me mention it ? " She pointed to a copy of the local *Times*. " We 'aven't put an ad. in, I suppose ? "

" *You* 'ave. I can't say *I* 'ad anything to do with it. Don't want no boarder, myself."

" ' Paying guest ' I said—don't be so common !
Advertise for a paying guest, and then you start
to go paddling like a lord, instead of stopping
at 'ome to see 'oo comes ! If I 'adn't 'eard you,
I should 'ave 'ad to stop at 'ome myself. Piece
o' disgusting selfishness I call it."

" Depends 'ow you look at it. If a chap
that's been at work all the week can't go down
to the beach on early closing day——"

" You'll tell me next you grudge me taking
mother out for a breath of air when she's spending a month with us and——"

" Oh no, 'Azel," said Howard mildly, " I
should never——"

" 'Tain't manners to interrupt. Spending a
month with us and I want to make it pleasant
for 'er. Pleasant as I can, that's to say, with a
'usband that expects things all his own way and's
got the nerve to talk o' paddling when visitors
are coming down in their 'undreds, and any
minute may bring a ring at the bell and a lady
or gent only too thankful to find bed and board
at any terms at all, let alone two guineas and a
half, which is all I'm asking, and——"

" I——"

" *Will* you let me get a word in sideways ?
'Oo do you think was going to settle with 'ooever
come, if there was no one in the 'ouse but

Doreen ? " She called to the maid, who was a very grubby child, with a sniff, " Doreen ! I'm going out with me mother. If anybody comes about the ad. it's Mr. 'Ooper you're to tell."

" I see," said Doreen.

" And don't leave them standing on the step, because there's a card up next door. Let 'em in before they can change their mind."

" I see," said Doreen.

" And if they're under'and enough to ask you any questions, you're to say it's the best English meat always."

" I see," said Doreen.

The householder was at the point of solacing himself with a pipe, but an exclamation from his wife checked him.

" 'Oward ! Must I tell you again not to smoke about the place while mother's 'ere ? You know she can't bear the smell. Can't think 'ow you can be so selfish."

" I ain't selfish," demurred Howard, putting the pipe away. He added reflectively, " Be better for me if I was."

" Oh, you're very 'ardly done by ! Wish you'd known the young feller I was engaged to before I met you. Couldn't do enough for me, 'e couldn't."

" That's it, trot 'im out again," groaned her

husband. " Fact is, the young feller you was engaged to before we met is just what makes the trouble in this 'ouse. Always shoving 'im down my throat. Sick of 'im. No matter 'ow much I give in, it ain't as much as the gentleman called George something."

" 'E wasn't called George Something—'e was called George Perkins. 'Andsomest boy in Cricklewood. Give in ? 'E revelled in giving in. The more 'e give in the joyfuller 'e grew. A model for any 'usband, poor dear George ! "

" Mystery to me 'ow you let 'im slip. Couldn't expect to find another chap as 'eavenly as George what's his name ! "

" George *Perkins*, I said. Ah, I was 'asty when I threw 'im over. When I was a girl I 'adn't got my temper under control like I 'ave now. Not that I thought 'e'd take me at my word—I thought 'e'd 'ave been round the next day begging of me to make it up."

" Bit strange 'e didn't come, if 'e was so sweet on you, ain't it ? "

" No, it ain't strange at all. 'Cos I'd broke 'is 'eart, and 'e rushed off in despair. No one in Cricklewood ever 'eard of 'im again."

" Wish *I* was in Cricklewood. *I've* 'eard of 'im more than enough. 'Eard 'im jawed about as a pattern from the day I married you."

" Poor dear George.   'E was a delicate boy,"
she said reminiscently.   " When I broke it off
with 'im I expect it did 'im in; I often fancy 'im
wasting away to a shadder.   Well, I must go
and get my things on, or mother'll be ready first.
What did Doreen do with them shoes ? "

She went in search of them, and her husband's
hand strayed towards his pipe.   Then, remembering it was forbidden, he dropped with a sigh
on the starched antimacassars of the couch.   A
piano organ burst into riot opposite the window,
and Hazel reappeared wrathfully.

" 'Aven't I told you mother's 'ead's bad ?
Why don't you send 'im away ? "   She made
peremptory signs to the disturber till the clamour
ceased.   " What you doing, mucking up the sofa
like that ?   Come off it ! "

" Good Lord, ain't there *no* peace ? " wailed
Howard.   " Didn't the perfect George ever get
on a sofa ? "

" No, 'e didn't !   And if 'e *'ad* so far forgot
'imself for once, 'e was too much the gentleman
to complain when 'e was told of it.   Come on
off, d'ye hear ? "

Her voice was high.   And her mother, who
entered now, with her bonnet on, inquired passionately, " Is it done a-purpose ?   Never 'eard
such a 'ullabaloo in my life !   As sure as I lay

my 'ead on the piller the 'ouse is a 'ell." She arraigned her son-in-law. "What you been hexasperatin' 'er about? Seems a strange thing you can't get on with 'er, I must say—a good wife like 'er. What you got to complain of, I'd like to know?"

"George Gherkins," replied Howard.

"*Perkins*, I tell you," screamed Hazel.

"Ah! '*E* knew 'ow to value 'er," said Mrs. Price. "Fair did for 'im when she chucked 'im up. Dessay 'e's gone to 'is grave all along o' losing 'er. Biggest mistake *you* ever made, my gal."

"I don't see as you've any call to say that," said Howard plaintively. "I make 'Azel a good 'usband."

"As 'usbands go," conceded Mrs. Price. "But you come very short of treating 'er as tender as she deserves. Pity you didn't know 'im! 'E'd 'ave learnt you better. You got to remember she never knew what it was to 'ear a 'arsh word till she married." Noting that her daughter wasn't ready to go out yet, she broke off angrily, "Now then, girl, 'urry up, drat it! Never in time, are you? Always be'ind, like a donkey's tail."

"Shan't be two minutes," said Hazel, scampering.

" I was just saying——" began Howard, with a nervous clearing of the throat.

" Nothing against 'Azel now, or you'd best not say it twice ! You found a treasure."

" It's a little 'abit you've both got. That there George. I was saying we should be 'appier if 'e wasn't 'eld up to me as a sort of 'oly text all the time. Bit sickening. Can't open my mouth but it's 'ow different 'er first fancy was. Gives me the pip. I mean to say, I'm not one of your masterful kind—I can put up with more than my share for the sake of a quiet life—but it do seem to me, sometimes, regular 'opeless. Seems to me I couldn't eat as much 'umble pie as she says that chap relished, not if I was to stuff it till I bust."

" 'Oward 'Ooper," said Mrs. Price, impressively, " I am surprised at your brazen cheek. 'Cos poor dear George 'ad a better 'eart than what you 'ave, you got the face to blame 'er and me ! Blame yourself, 'Oward. Try to act to 'er more like 'e did."

She set forth soon afterwards, her daughter's toilette having been hasty, and Howard sought recreation in trying to catch flies on the window-panes. When this palled, he treated himself to a daydream, in which he spoke with calm authority and sensational effect. And just as he concluded, " What's more, we take no boarder," Doreen

put her head in at the door and said, " Gent
about the room."

" Oh ? " said Howard, bumping to realities.
" Oh, well, I got to see 'im. In 'ere."

Doreen turned her head the other way, and
said " Sst ! "

The plump young cockney who came in beaming, with his luggage, was dressed with care.
Nothing more nautical could have been found on
any Parade in England. His shirt was thrown
open to display so much of his manly chest that
it afforded generous glimpses of his abdomen.
He said :

" Phew ! 'Afternoon. 'Appened to see your
ad. Thought I'd look in and ask the figure."

" Won't you sit down ? "

" Don't mind if I do. Bit of a pull up 'ere,
with your bag to kerry. Tidy long way from
the sea, ain't it ? "

" Oh no," said Howard suavely, " we call it
no way at all."

" *I* call it a blooming mile and a 'alf. Don't
mind telling you, if I'd known what I was in
for, I'd never 'ave started on this game of 'ide-
and-seek. Like to 'ave the sea close and 'andy
when I get my fortnight. A real boarding-'ouse
near the front's my mark. I grant you the com-

pany's often a bit mixed, but a gentleman can always keep people at a distance, if they ain't his class." He looked around. " Still, now I'm 'ere—— 'Ow 'orrible's the bedroom ? Tell me as man to man. 'Tain't worth your while or mine to take on the stairs if you know it's one of them rooms me and my bag couldn't both get into at the same time."

" It's a bright airy room."

" Break the terms to me gentle."

" Two guineas and a half."

" ' Inclusive,' mind yer ! Can't stick extras— they give me the shudders. 'Ow about meals ? For breakfast I'm partial to a bloater with a nice 'ard roe. Dinner—pretty near anything, so long as it's 'olesome, and the lady asks me if I'd like some more."

" There's no stint. As for 'olesomeness, my wife's mother's 'ere. She can't touch nothing but the best—when she's on a visit."

" Nuff said. I'll chance it. Don't want to pick myself out of this chair before I'm drove to it. Tell you the truth, I've 'ad my work cut out to find a room in the place at all. Going strong 'ere this summer, aren't you ? Right-o. It's a go, Mr.—er——"

" 'Ooper. Mr. and Mrs. 'Oward 'Ooper."

" 'Ope you'll find me a little ray of sunshine about the 'ouse, Mr. 'Ooper. Mine's Perkins—Mr. George Perkins."

" Eh ? . . . I say, I suppose you don't 'appen to be the George Perkins that used to live at Cricklewood ? "

" 'Ello ! That's me."

" My word ! " said Howard with intensity. " 'im ! "

" You've 'eard of me ? " asked the young man, gratified.

" 'Eard of you ? " panted Howard. " I'm fair fed up with you."

" 'Ere, steady on ! What you mean ? "

" You been my curse."

" Me ! Been your curse ? Never clapped eyes on you in my life before, s'elp me bob ! "

" Only wish I was big enough to set about you, that's all. You ain't ' wasted away ' too pathetic, 'ave you ? Shouldn't 'ave mistook you for a ' shadder ' myself."

" Set about me ? Shadder ? I say, you know, this is some bally misunderstanding."

" I 'ate you. See ? I 'ate you."

" 'Ate then, and enjoy yourself," exclaimed Perkins, jumping up. " But *whaffor* ? "

" You're the man that ruined my 'ome."

" 'Elp ! It's a lunatic asylum. I'm off. 'Oo d'ye think you are, Barmy ? "

" I'm the gentleman what married Miss 'Azel Price."

" Well, I be jiggered ! " He stood transfixed. " Mean to say she lives 'ere ? I 'eard she'd 'ooked some silly foo—I mean, I 'eard she'd married someone, but—*well* ! Fancy me 'aving walked bang into 'er 'ouse. Er—get on all right ? "

" Should do, if it wasn't for *you*."

" Me ? . . . Blimey ! You aren't going to tell me she's nuts on me still ? "

" Wouldn't go so far as to say ' nuts.' But from all I 'ear you spoilt 'er something shameful when she was engaged to you—made 'er a fair terror for the chap that married 'er. Can't smoke me own pipe cos of *you*."

" Don't say that, 'Ooper," said George humbly.

" Can't put me feet on my own sofa cos of *you*."

" Don't speak too 'arsh, 'Ooper—I got a 'eart, I 'ave," begged George.

" Wicked, the way you give in to 'er ! Do my best to make 'er 'appy. Think she thanks me for it ? No. Tells me what a idol poor dear George made of 'er."

K

" 'Ear me! I was more sinned against than sinning. Give in to 'er? Yes. 'Cos why? 'Cos I thundering well 'ad to! She sat on me fine. I ain't speaking in the spoony meaning of the word; no objection to 'er sitting on my knee, of course——"

"Not so much o' your knee! I don't want to 'ear nothing about that."

"Right-o! 'Ad to say black was white from the night I popped the question. Daresn't even say it was grey. 'Adn't got the nerve to put me foot down in those days. Made a fair martyr of me they did, she and 'er never-mind-what mother! 'Ere! I don't mind telling you that when your missus give me the chuck, it jollied me up so that life looked like one long Bank 'oliday."

"Always understood you faded away with sorrer."

"No, old sport. I went strong and relished me victuals. Only fear I'd got was that she might change 'er mind. So I packed me traps and 'opped it from Cricklewood before she 'ad time to say she'd forgive me. You got no call to 'ate me, 'Ooper. *I* got a feller-feelin' for *you*— I know what you're up against; I 'ad some myself."

"I wouldn't 'alf like you to tell 'er so," said Howard fervently; "I reckon I wouldn't 'ave 'poor dear George' held up to me no more!"

"Like me to tell 'er so?" responded George with enthusiasm. "Friendy, it'd do me a treat! When I think of what I was mug enough to put up with from 'er and the old 'ag, it makes me blood boil. Leave it to me. I tell you I'm sorry for you—I got a 'eart, I 'ave. I'll do you a turn, and get a bit o' my own back at the same time. Where is she?"

"Out."

"Well, I could do with a wash. Don't give it away that it's me if she comes in—just say a gentleman's took the room. Whereabouts is it?"

"Top floor front."

"You buck up, 'Ooper, old pal," said George; withdrawing buoyantly. "I'm going to do you a bit o' good. You'll be 'appy I blew in."

Less than five minutes later the ladies returned, Mrs. Price explaining that "the 'eat 'ad been too much for 'er 'ead"; and Hazel's satisfaction at the news awaiting her was damped when she heard the word "inclusive."

"What about 'is shoes, and 'is Saturday night bath?" she complained. "Not a penny extra

for 'em ?   You might be a child, 'pon my word !
I can't so much as take my 'and off you."

"Might be sure 'e'd mess it up somehow,"
commented Mrs. Price.   "Seem to 'ave no feelin'
for your wife—let 'er work 'erself to skin and
bone ! "

"*I* never asked 'er to take no boarder at all.
No wish o' mine, I'm sure."

"'Eartless, I call it !   Oh, my 'ead, my 'ead ! "
She retired to make a cup of strong tea, and her
daughter went on :

"Well, 'e can clean 'em 'imself—and make do
with the sea.   'E won't get no bath in the 'ouse.
I 'ope 'e's respectable ? "

"Seems a pleasant-spoken chap enough,"
answered Howard.   "'Ark, 'e's coming down."

"I'll open 'is eyes about them shoes and baths
right off," said Hazel firmly.

George's fat face was bent over the pages of
Saucy Bits as he entered, and she said, " Ahem !
Good-afternoon," without attracting attention.

"'Ard of 'earing ? " she inquired of her husband.   "Ahem !   There's a little thing I want
to speak about——"

"Beg pardon ? " said the boarder, looking up.

"George ! " she gasped, jerking electrically.
"Mean to say, 'Mr. Perkins ' ! "

" What, 'Azel ? " cried the boarder, overcome
with astonishment and pleasure.   " It ain't never
'Azel Price ? "   He stared from her to Howard
bewildered.   " You aren't going to tell me——? "

" 'E's my 'usband."

" Well, I never did ! "

" You *'ave* changed from what you was ! " she
faltered resentfully.   " *You've* been pretty 'ale and
'earty since I saw you last."

" Old friends, me and 'er," announced George,
slapping his host on the back.   " Good lad !
Me bes' respex to the 'appy pair."

" This," said Howard, in deep perplexity,
" ain't never the Mr. Perkins what faded to a
shadder ? "

" Never mind about that," said Hazel sharply.
" Now you'll see the way to beyave to me."

" And 'ow you been keeping ? " George asked
her, filling his pipe.   " Only fancy me tumbling
into clover like this !   Be a jolly little party, and
no mistake.   'Adn't you got a mother or something ?   'Ow's *she ?*   Well, I declare, it's prime !
Meant to go on the front and give the gals a
treat, but we'll 'ave a cosy time at 'ome instead."

"Mother's staying with us," she said.   " You've
forgotten something."

" What's that ? "

" She can't bear the smell o' tobaccer."

" Oh, ah—no more she couldn't, I remember," said George, striking a match and puffing peacefully.

" So my 'usband don't smoke in the 'ouse," she added, agitated.

" Go on ! " laughed George. " Don't mean to tell me you take notice o' fads like that, 'Ooper ? What was I going to say ? Oh yes—about the gals. What sort o' lot you got down 'ere this year ? Suppose there's no objection to me bringing one in, if I pick up with something tasty ? "

" Well, upon my word ! " flared Hazel. " What you take the 'ouse for ? "

" A ' 'ome from 'ome,' you said in the ad. Little thought I was going to settle with an old friend when I saw it ! Ain't the world small ? Came precious near to being a lump more than friends too ! Didn't we, 'Azel ? Mustn't get the needle, 'Ooper, but she'd 'ave been Mrs. Perkins to-day if——"

" If I 'adn't 'ad the sense not to," she snapped.

" That's it," assented George genially. " Absolutely unsuited to each other, 'Ooper. Take it from *me*. But, bless you, *I* 'adn't the 'ead to get out of it. Reg'lar stew I was in, mind you !

Knew I'd put me foot in it *wallop*—and there I was without the sense to countermand the order! It was *'er* that saved my bacon. Good sort! Cheer-o, 'Azel!"

" *Well!* " she exclaimed, glaring. " Your manners ain't improved, I *must* say ! "

" What you mean? " he asked, mystified. " Notice I go stronger with the ladies every summer. Nothing the matter with me perlite-ness, 'Ooper, I 'ope and trust? "

" Bit of 'er fun, that's all," said Howard assuringly.

" You shut up," said Hazel.

" Crumbs! 'Ow them tender words kerry me back! " remarked George. " Shall begin to fancy we're engaged again before me fortnight's up." He stretched himself on the sofa. " Bit lumpy, ain't it? "

" Tell you what it is," she said tartly—" not sure I want you 'ere at all! And please don't put your dirty shoes on the sofa."

" 'Ow the past do revive! Go on, Fuss-box. What time's tea? "

" Tea-supper's at seven."

" Seven? Seven be blowed! Touch the bell."

" 'Oo you giving orders to? Making your-self pretty much at 'ome, ain't you? "

"Well, I suppose I got a *say* on the subject?" inquired George, with mild expostulation. "I ain't courting now, you know—I'm a paying guest. Not took no liberty, 'Ooper, I 'ope?"

"You got to ask *me* them things," said Hazel, "not *'im*."

"Oh, that's 'ow it is? I see!" He rang the bell vigorously. "Lucky thing for you you didn't take *me* on, old girl."

"*Very* lucky, *I* think," retorted the lady, red in the face.

"Tea immediately, if not sooner!" commanded the paying guest, when Doreen appeared. "Ermyntrude, you've got a smudge on your nose. Don't let it occur again. Like to see a gal look clean and neat about the 'ouse," he mentioned to his hostess. "You want to watch it while I'm 'ere."

"That's done it!" she said thickly. "You'll 'ave your tea, and then you'll go!" Another organ hurled forth tumult, and she cried, "What did I tell you before, 'Oward? Send 'im away."

"Oh, that don't 'urt," said George: "I like a tune."

"'Er mother ain't well."

"What, dear old mother? Do 'er good." Reaching the window first, he saluted the Italian

with affectionate antics. " Bravo ! 'Ip, 'ip, 'ooo-
rayo ! Damma fino ! Now, don't come bob-
bing in the way, you two—I tell you I like it.
Raises me spirits." He threw money. " 'Ave
sixpence to buy a motor-car ! Pleased to meet
you, signor ! My love to Mussolini when you
write. 'Allo, 'ere's the tea-things, if there ain't
no tea ! We'll 'ave it over there, Peg o' my
'Eart—on the bamboo table. Snugger like."

" No, we won't—'tain't safe," rapped Hazel.
" That tea-service was a wedding present from
mother."

" This way, madam, for the Bamboo Department," directed George, with a wave of the hand.

" 'Ear me, Doreen ? "

" Through the Ironmongery, and past the 'ole
in the carpet, madam," insisted George. " Allow
me, madam." He swept a few articles from the
table negligently. " Shouldn't keep a lot o'
rubbish on it," he told Hazel; " it'll be a
'andy little table for me pipes."

" 'Ere, go and fetch 'is things down," she
shouted to the girl; " I'm putting 'im out."

" I see," said Doreen.

" What a one you are to chaff ! " chuckled
George. He carolled gaily to the organ's rag-
time. " 'Eard that song down 'ere ? Shouldn't

wonder if I went on the 'Alls myself some day. Not so much singing, mind you, as a bit o' juggling. Learnt of an evening, after business. Only nerve. Keep your 'ead, and the thing comes down and meets your 'and!"

Before she apprehended his purpose he had tossed a plate high in the air. "Look!" he said proudly. And the plate fell in fragments on the floor.

"Are you up the pole?" she screamed, livid with rage.

"Sorry! Can't think 'ow it 'appened. Expect the plate must 'ave been cracked. I can work three of 'em all right. Got a gift for it. Makes me pop'lar in company. Keep your 'ead, and the thing comes down and meets your 'and! Look!"

Swifter than thought, he pitched up three more plates—and they were shattered in various parts of the room.

"You—you—my Gawd! If my 'usband was a bigger chap 'e should break every bone in your body," she howled. Snatching his belongings from Doreen, she flung them at his feet. "Get out!"

"Whatever *is* a-going on in 'ere, for 'Eaven's sake?" screeched Mrs. Price, reappearing in a state of frenzy. "What, George Perkins? Where did 'e spring from?"

" 'Ell. It's 'im that's making all the row."

" My 'ead's fit to split with it."

" Got a 'ead, 'ave you?" mourned George. He approached her persuasively. "Why don't you give the 'abit up and take the Pledge?"

" What? 'Ow dare you? Oh, 'e's insulted me. I been insulted in my daughter's 'ouse. Give the 'abit up—and me next door to Prohibition? What you mean by it? Did you 'ear what 'e said to me, 'Azel?"

" 'E wants a good 'iding, that's what '*e* wants."

" Been saying it was a lucky thing for 'im 'e didn't marry 'er," whispered Howard. " Sauced her terrible, 'e did."

" Never been so insulted since I was born, never! 'Oo smashed them plates I give you?"

" 'Im, the 'og," said her daughter.

" I see by the paper, the other day," observed George, in the tones of one introducing a new and pleasing topic, " that there wouldn't be no poverty in the world if it wasn't for the drink."

" I won't put up with it, I won't!" shrieked Mrs. Price. " Turn 'im out."

" Only speaking for your own good," said George wheedlingly. " Why not try cocoa?"

He continued, drawing her to his knee, " What I always say about cocoa——"

" Stop it ! " she stormed, struggling.

" The advantages o' cocoa——"

" Let go of me—let go ! I'll 'ave the law on you."

" Where you'd be so much better off with cocoa——"

" Let me go, I tell you ! "

" Oh, well, if you won't chat it over, you won't. But you see for yourself what the 'abit leads to—makes you violent. Now, cocoa——"

" Get out o' my 'ouse. This minute ! D'ye 'ear ? Or I'll fetch the perlice to you," yelled Hazel.

" You bid me leave your 'ouse ? " spouted George. " Ever see ' David Garrick ' ? Bit of all right. Can't think what you're so touchy for, you and 'er ! If you was 'alf a man, 'Ooper, you'd see to it they treated me warmer."

" You leave my 'usband alone—'e's a better man than what *you* are, by a long sight ! "

" They need a bit of firmness, my lad. You may think it's no business o' mine, but I don't look on you as a stranger. *Your* wife might ha' been *my* wife—it's a sort o' relationship, ain't it ? I tell you straight, you 'andle 'er too mild."

" 'E don't want your opinion ! " " Keep your advice till it's asked for ! " the ladies interposed together.

" Even when she was young——"

" *Was* young ? " blazed Hazel.

" —she was 'ot-tempered," proceeded George, judicially; " now she's getting on in years, she's a regular 'igh explosive. Only wonder is, she ain't worse still. Look at that Awful Warning ! " He indicated her parent. " What can you expect of ole Mother Price's daughter ? It's hereddy-derryterry. 'Allo, old 'un, got the 'orrors come on now ? What did I tell you ? If you'd only take up cocoa——"

" I can't bear no more, I can't stand it ! 'Ere's a 'oliday for me ! " quavered Mrs. Price.

" Mother ! Come to your room ! "

" Now's your chance," said George, in an undertone to Howard. " I ain't stopping—say you're going to throw me out of the winder when they've gone; I can 'op it easy. Say you'll break me 'ead. Take your coat off."

" I'm going to throw you out of the winder when the ladies 'ave gone," proclaimed Howard with resolution.

" You ? Try it, that's all." He advanced menacingly—and winked.

"I'm going to break your 'ead," maintained Howard, undaunted.

"'Oward! What you doing, lovey? You'll get 'urt," cried Hazel, clinging to him in terror.

"You got pluck," admitted George. "You're a brave man, I'll say that for you. But if you lay your 'and on me she'll be a widder."

"I can't look on, I can't," wailed Mrs. Price, stumbling from the room. "Oh lor, oh lor! Send for the perlice!"

"You 'arm my 'usband, and I'll tear your eyes out!" Hazel volleyed. "Doreen! Where are you, Doreen? Fetch a pleeceman!" She rushed into the kitchen, calling "'Elp!"

"That's the ticket," said George. "Turn the key on 'em. Now shout at me fierce."

"You 'ound! You're a 'ound," bellowed Howard. "That's what you are. I say you're a 'ound!"

"Bit o' variety. Low-lived dog."

"You're a low-lived dog," bellowed Howard, straining his voice.

"'Ere comes the clash o' combat, 'Ooper," said George, picking up the fire-irons and producing a dreadful din.

"'Oward! Open the door!" shrieked Hazel, banging at it.

"Stop it—or I'll scream the 'ouse down?" shrilled Mrs. Price.

"I won't go—I won't, I won't!" roared George. . . . "'Ow's that, 'Ooper? Going strong, ain't we? . . . I'll fight yer—with my last—breath," he roared again, stamping desperately. . . . "Told you I'd do yer a bit o' good before I went! You'll be a bally 'ero in a minute. Mind you keep it up afterwards!"

"You bet!" said Howard. "You been a pal, ole chap—you been a real pal."

"*I* got to thank *you* for a 'appy afternoon," said George, putting his bag over the window sill, and following blithely. "Wouldn't 'ave missed it for a 'undred quid. Cheer-o!"

"Gone. Chucked 'im through the winder," replied Howard, to affrighted questions, when he opened the door. "And, be it understood," he decreed, sprawling on the sofa with his pipe, "we never 'ear no more of ' poor dear George '!"

"No, 'Oward," said the awestruck ladies.

W H E N she was a little child it was said in Lucy's presence that she had a "very forgiving nature." And as this beautiful quality of her nature excited many glances and whispers that were gratifying to Lucy, she resolved to cultivate it as much as she could. In the nursery she forgave other children, who used to reply, "What for?" In the schoolroom her forgiveness was extended to a governess who corrected her. In course of time she forgave her husband. It was a disconcerting truth, and it took her a long while to realise it, but Lucy's beautiful quality was the cause of her worst troubles.

Of course she married much too young, and so did he. For another thing, he wasn't in a position to marry. But he was supposed to have prospects with the firm, and there was the three hundred a year of his own—and her mother, who was the widow of a poor parson, and had a large family, and an infinitesimal income, beamed a blessing. Lucy married Jack Willoughby, and went to live in a semi-detached suburban villa, when they contrived to find one. They called it "The Dovecote."

It was a suggestion of the bride's. They were sitting in the cheap drawing-room, seeking a name for their Eden. "What about 'The Dovecote'?" she had said, with an air of inspiration. And he had kissed her approvingly.

Some weeks later the name on the little gate began to embarrass him. Fond as he was of her, he told himself he looked a "soppy fool," watering the geraniums of a house called The Dovecote, and imagined amusement in the eyes of the neighbours. It was exaggerating their intelligence, but the notion rasped him, and one morning there was a quarrel at the breakfast-table.

It was their first quarrel. Lucy came out of it limp and disillusioned, and Willoughby shut the offending gate with a bang.

"What on earth had he said to make her cry like that?" he asked himself, striding to the station. She had behaved like a girl in some damned old-fashioned novel. What rot she had talked! What sticky Victorian sentiment she had been brought up on!

And Lucy was wondering what on earth she had said to make him laugh so brutally. What

L

had she done to make him angry? She had
only cried. Naturally, she had cried on seeing he
didn't love her any more, that he was ashamed
even of their dear little home! Oh, never would
she be able to forget the nasty clever things he
had said! She hadn't understood them all, but
they had cut her to the quick.

He came back in the evening repentant. He
kissed her tenderly, and mentioned that he had
booked seats at a theatre for the next night. A
more sensible girl would have been content with
the tacit admission of his fault, and have made no
reference to the quarrel. But Lucy's beautiful
quality displayed itself. Presently she placed her
hand on his gently, and murmured, with a holy
expression in her eyes, " Jack, I forgive you."

Jack stared; and somehow the evening was
less cheerful afterwards.

But that did not save her from forgiving him
over and over again. When Jack Willoughby
brooded—and during the following year he
brooded much oftener than a young man ought
to do—he said, " It's her infernal 'forgiveness'
that's dividing us ! "

He bought an office desk, second hand, and
converted an empty attic into a study, explaining
that there was a lot of work for the firm that he

had to do at home now. Lucy sat in the drawing-room, sewing, and crying, and Willoughby sat, with his feet on the superfluous desk, wishing he hadn't married.

The " scandal," as her people called it, though the young couple were far too obscure for their affairs to cause much gossip, occurred some six months after the desk had been installed. Her eyes were red, but her voice was fairly steady as she announced her intention to him. He was shaving, and wished she had chosen another moment.

" The fact is, we ought never to have married," she said. " We're utterly unsuited to each other."

" Well, what do you want me to do about it ? " he asked.

" I want you to arrange for a legal separation."

She had often threatened hysterically to return to her mother, but this time he saw she meant it. He couldn't pretend to feel it was bad news.

" All right," he said. " I've done my best— that's all I can say."

She laughed painfully. " Your best ? I've forgiven you till I'm tired of forgiving you, Jack. You've never understood me; you never *would* understand me, even if we went on with it for years. What's the use ? We were never meant for each other. I'm acting as much for your sake as my own."

He made his finger bleed, wiping the safety blade, and now he wouldn't be able to fasten his collar ! But he was feeling so much relieved by her decision that he didn't say " damn."

" Quite," he said, more cheerfully than he knew.

" I'm going *home*," she said, with a sob. " I'm going now."

For some weeks her mother and five sisters made an enormous fuss of Lucy. They continued to treat her as a martyr, even when they began to understand that she had really come back for good. Special dishes were prepared to tempt her appetite, and as she lolled in the best armchair, monopolising most of the cushions, her slow, sweet, sad smile was enough to bring tears to their eyes.

Willoughby had waived his dividends to her munificently, plus the furniture—he was understood to be indecorously cheerful in lodgings on his meagre salary; and after protesting that she would accept nothing, she warehoused the furniture, and drew the three hundred a year. Perhaps it was because the income made her feel independent that, despite their affection, her family found her rather trying as the months wore by.

Anyhow, it was recognised by degrees that she expected a good deal in return for what she contributed to the housekeeping expenses. And the five unmarried sisters, four of whom went to town and worked for a living, confessed among themselves that the little presents that they received from her didn't compensate for all the attentions she wanted when they came home tired. Moreover, they resented her " forgiving " them when she had been wrong. " You're a great deal too ready to ' forgive,' " said the youngest, who was the modern one of the family, and rather pert; " I shouldn't wonder if Jack said so too ! "

Lucy knew that Jack had said so more than once, and momentarily she had misgivings.

The vexation simmered for the best part of a year, but at last it boiled over. To keep her with them demanded too much time, and too much patience. " She will have to be told," said the five unmarried sisters severally, and collectively— and sneaked off to bed, leaving the unhappy mother to tell her.

After many false starts, the lady reached the point of hinting to Lucy that, though she was intensely loved and profoundly pitied, they all felt it would be much more cheerful for her in a "nice boarding-house at the seaside, where she'd have other people to talk to." Or, better still, didn't she think that Jack might be willing to retrace the dreadful step they had both taken? It was a terrible position, for a woman to live separated from her husband. And there were many worse than Jack.

Lucy rose from the armchair, holding her halo tight.

"I quite understand," she said. "It isn't your fault, mother. I don't blame *anybody*."

Her mother bleated something too incoherent to be construed as a plea to her to remain, and a fortnight later Lucy drove away, with the trunks that had been encumbering the scanty landing. Her sisters said they "envied her, going to a jolly boarding-house at Brighton," and Lucy put all the forgiveness possible into the sweet, sad smile.

"If I thought that Jack would be willing!" she said to herself. It was for Jack to inquire her own views—Jack, who was the guilty party. Not a single error on her side could she recall. . . . Perhaps, if he ever did say how sorry he was, if he should ever write to her, humbly begging her to go back, she *might* consent to give him another trial! He must have realised the truth by this time; he would probably be more subdued, and less egotistical.

She remained at Brighton for nearly a year, going to the cinemas occasionally with women who, when she was out of the room, " wondered where her husband was," and taking long, solitary walks. Then, because one of the women told her what another woman had said, she left the house in disgust, and removed to a similar one in Worthing.

The penitent pages from Jack that she was waiting for hadn't come.

When she had been drifting among boarding-houses for two years longer, and never seeing anything for her in the letter-racks but letters from her family and the weekly bills, she began to feel old. As this was preposterous at her age, she told herself that what she needed was a thorough change, and, rather alarmed by the adventure, for she had never left England, she accompanied a woman who was returning to Wiesbaden. At Wiesbaden, the splendour of the larger theatre was a revelation to her, and the charm of the German servants and shopkeepers was an even greater one, but she felt no younger for them when the novelty wore off. An English family in the house, with whom she grew friendly, were going to Geneva before the summer began, and she went next to Geneva. She lived in continental pensions-de-famille, to her mother's consternation, till she was twenty-six—and then something deeper than her foibles drove her back to London.

She had for long prayed, on her knees, for the letter from Jack, when, craving a home again, she questioned whether she could find a flat within her means. The advertisements that she studied frightened her, and the high rents that were asked looked no lower because the people put " Only," but she didn't mind how tiny the flat might be, nor how far from town it was, and she took many trams and trains to agents far afield.

And then, one day, after she had been applying to agents for weeks without result, she saw an advertisement that held her magnetised. " Unfurnished : The Dovecote." . . . What a strange coincidence ! . . . Was it prophetic ?

She was not quite sure that she would care to live in the house, and she did not see how she was to afford it. But she knew definitely that she wanted to look at it.

She walked, by a young clerk's side, next morning down the street where she had walked so often, and she wished he were not there. The street seemed shabbier to her than it used to be, and the children that she saw looked commoner. The Dovecote itself had changed, excepting for the little gate. The path was weed-grown, and in place of the smart front door that she had always been proud of when the girl had polished the brass well, there were two mean doors now. The hall was darkened and divided by a partition, and the dining-room had disappeared. It belonged to the other side of the partition. Emptiness altered the few rooms that remained. Only the wallpaper in the drawing-room, and the " study," which had always been bare, were vivid with reminder.

She took the " maisonette," as it was called. And she went to the depository, and viewed the saddened furniture that was disclosed to her, and determined how much of it the shrunken Dovecote would contain. Moths had been feasting on the drapery of the best bed. She recalled, with a sigh, that, in the inventory, the depository people said they were not responsible for moths, fire, or the acts of God.

With a duster on her head, and another in her hand she superintended arrangements daily— and at last, the recovered half of the house was as it used to be, except that there was a dinner-table in a corner of the drawing-room. She had even restored the desk to the alleged study. Then. one evening, the poor girl sat down at it, and composed an amazing message :

" JACK, come back to Lucy at The Dovecote. Forgiven."

And she did not feel undignified; she did not tell herself any longer that it was for Jack to take the first step. There was self-approval in her gaze. She felt very noble when she read her message in a newspaper.

But nothing happened.

One day, when her mother came to see her— two of her sisters were happily married now, and did not come very often—the old lady said nervously :

" My poor Lucy, we've been seeing your advertisement. I thought you knew—— Oh, I don't mean *that !* " she cried, as Lucy's eyes widened with terror. " Oh, no, I don't mean *that !* I mean he's not likely to see it; I thought you knew he was abroad. I'm sure I wrote you, when we heard. I know I wrote, because I remember thinking it didn't seem right, as you had all the money, that——"

" What *are* you saying, mother ? "

" Well, dear, it seems he went to America two

or three years ago. We heard, in a roundabout way, that he was in New York, and dreadfully hard up. He said he was sorry he had gone there, and that he'd have done better to stay in London, but that he hadn't the money to go back."

Lucy withdrew her advertisement from the newspaper, and waited again, with solemn faith in a personal Deity who realised her perfections, for her husband's erring feet to be led to her. Periodically she paid visits to her mother, and never failed to ask, with as casual an air as she could affect, " Oh, and—er—any more news from anybody ? "

At last she was told that there *was* news of a sort. One of the married sisters thought she had seen Jack in Holborn. She was on a bus, and it had passed very quickly, but she was almost certain—and she had nearly cried.

" What did she nearly cry about ? "

" The way he looked, my dear ! So shabby and poor. Considering he has a right to share your income——"

" Why didn't she get off and speak to him then, if she thought it was Jack ? " said Lucy hotly. " Couldn't she stop the bus ? I don't suppose it was Jack at all. Lily always did fancy the most ridiculous things."

Nevertheless, it reappeared in the papers, that troubled and tactless message, and in course of time it reached him. He read it in a coffee-shop where he was dining on a bloater. The meal was inadequate, and the table was dirty, and he sat, ill-clothed, among the unwashed, but as he pondered the message with gloomy eyes, he reflected that, on the whole, he had less of a hump here than he used to have at The Dovecote.

As a matter of fact, he was not feeling as down-and-out as he looked. He had got back to London; and though there were only a few shillings in his pocket, he would win through yet, he thought. He needed money to go on with, and most urgently he needed shirts and a decent suit, but he knew a man who would be pretty sure to lend him a bit, and then he would make good. Lucy? Poor, well-meaning, impossible girl! Not even for three hundred a year, comparative affluence, would he put up with her again. He hoped her message didn't mean she was unhappy; he would have liked to shake hands with her, to show there was no ill-feeling; but to go back to her—— Not much!

For nearly a month after he saw her message, Lucy listened for a timid ring at the bell. Her welcome was prepared, she knew just what she

was going to say first. Jack shouldn't feel that
she was inconsiderate. She would not refer to
his failings, or let him dwell too much on his
repentance. And she wouldn't even repeat that
she forgave him, since the word had always irri-
tated him, for some reason or other. Everything
she said should be bright and encouraging—and
then she would kiss him very, very gently. And
if he should bow his head in her lap and weep, it
would be beautiful !

Her reverie was shattered, one evening, by an
imperative peal, and as much noise as could be
made with the little knocker. The woman who
came in by the day had gone, and Lucy went,
wondering, to the door herself.

" Hallo, Lucy," said her husband.

It was as unemotional as if he had been away
for a week-end. She stared at him dumbly, the
things she had meant to say forgotten.

" Aren't you going to let me in ? What the
devil have they been doing to the door ? "

" You startled me," she said. " What did you
knock and ring like that for ? "

" I'm sorry. The hall's got narrower, too,
hasn't it ? "

Incredulously she stared at him when they
were in the room. It wasn't only that he was

older, or that he hadn't shaved for days, or even that he seemed unnaturally, bewilderingly impenitent—his very voice was unfamiliar to her.

" You *are* Jack ? " she faltered.

" Oh, I'm Jack right enough," he said, with a short horrid laugh.

" There's nothing to laugh at. If I had seen you in the street I shouldn't have known you. You've changed very much, and—and you don't seem very sorry or anything, I must say."

Willoughby, who was feeling desperately ill, sat suddenly on the nearest chair. " That's all right," he said thickly, " don't worry about that ! I'm just about as humble as they make them, or I shouldn't be here." He paused, and she saw he was trying to find words. She waited eagerly.

" I want a few pounds to live on till I find a job," he blurted. " I wanted to manage without bothering you, but I couldn't. I'm not trying to go back on our arrangement—the interest on that money's all yours; I'm only asking for a loan. Got to get it somehow. You can see for yourself."

She mustn't be too critical ! He had always expressed himself clumsily. And the first few minutes must be terribly difficult for him.

"Of course you must have money," she said sweetly. "But there's time enough to talk about that; it isn't what we need talk about first, is it? So you've seen my message, and come! And what I said was true; I do forgive you, Jack."

She rose and went over to him, and laid her hand on his sleeve.

"I know just how you feel," she murmured, warming to the situation. "I know all that's in your heart—all that you want to say—much better than you can tell me. You've been punished frightfully, and now *He* has led you to me for consolation and help. There is no rancour in me, dear—only forgiveness and pity."

Before he could speak she had kissed him on the forehead.

"Come and look," she said; "I want to show you something. Your study is just as you left it—the desk's in the same place."

He did not answer; he felt incapable of talking as he had meant to do—too ill, or cowardly. It wasn't a thing to be parried, her forgiveness—it was something gigantic, with tentacles. And he couldn't refuse it without being a brute! . . . If he got up, he might find himself in her arms. He realised muzzily that he was an idiot to have come.

" You haven't got any whisky in the house, I suppose ? " he said; " I'm dead beat."

" There's some claret."

" That'll do," he said. " Anything."

He was swaying by the street door as she ran back to the room with a decanter and a glass.

" Where are you going ? " she exclaimed.

" I'm a fraud," he panted; " I'm not Jack Willoughby. Don't be afraid. I'll push off."

The glass slipped to the floor, and the awful pallor of her face was piteous. But the truth would hurt her more still.

" You're not Jack ? " she stammered.

" I thought I could get money out of you. Don't you see ? Don't be afraid. I'm off."

" You're not Jack ? "

" Let me go," he muttered.

The muzzy feeling in his head was worse, and the gate looked further away than it was. " Funny, something wrong with my eyes, too, now. Never mind, I shall make good ! " The confusion increased. He was seized by panic lest he should never reach the gate. Her voice was calling to him to stop, and he strove dizzily to go fast. " Sprint, you fool ! " he thought—and fell, like a child learning to walk.

She beat at the door of the next maisonette.

" My husband has fainted," she gasped. " Will you help me get him inside ? "

Willoughby lay ill at The Dovecote for a long time—much too ill for painful conversations—and when Lucy was not in the room, pretending to be bright, she was prostrate under the remembrance that he had lied because he didn't want to remain with her. He had preferred the worst straits to remaining with her. The humiliation was so deep that it might easily have resulted in her hating him, but happily it did not. It resulted in her doing the only other possible thing—she thought hard. Extraordinary as it appeared, Jack himself must have found a good deal to complain of in their brief life together. It was astounding, but it was evidently a fact. Lucy looked back assiduously. She looked back with confidence, with qualms, and at long last, with discomfiture. Lucy looked back with more enlightenment than most people have the good fortune to do until it is too late for enlightenment to be any use.

And when Willoughby was well enough to realise that the lie hadn't taken her in, and that she had nursed him devotedly and cheerfully in spite of the abominable humiliation he had put

M

upon her, there was light for Willoughby too.   It was a light that did not flatter him.   It displayed that his wife had far finer qualities than he had given her credit for, and that, if he had been as wise as he imagined, he would have seen them sooner.   It showed him a very sad and lonely little girl on those many evenings when he had sat upstairs in the " study," lamenting his marriage, and revealed that he would have been more kindly and sensibly employed bearing her company and trying to make the marriage a success.   But when he began to tell her so, she said, " I've forg—forgotten that," and he saw she wanted to avoid allusions to the past.

She alluded to it once herself, though.   He was saying that it was his fault they had crashed, and that he must have been an awful ass not to get on with her.   He said that, if she would risk another honeymoon before he started hustling for a job, he'd value her better this time—by God he would !   They were on the path, standing by the little gate of unhappy memories.   And a wonderful thing happened.   Lucy raised her face and said what no one had ever heard her say before.   She said :

" Forgive me ! "

T H E patient rose from the dentist's chair with reluctance.

"I regret infinitely that you can find nothing to do," he said.

"There is no cavity, monsieur—the tooth is sound."

"Is it not possible there may be an abscess at the root? If you were to bang it about some more, is there no chance that you might suggest pulling it out?" pleaded the young man.

"If there were an abscess, monsieur, you could not have borne half the tapping I have given it already. The sensitiveness is due to nothing but slight erosion. It is so very slight that I am surprised you feel it."

"Erosion? What is that—mayn't I return to the chair for it?" he asked eagerly. "I beg you not to hesitate to hurt me; I will submit to the severest treatment cheerfully. I have often reflected that a fretful patient must be tiresome— pray do not be deterred from inflicting agonies by the thought that you would find me a nuisance.

You don't know with what joy I have looked forward to this visit; I have been counting the days to it. If it were to last no more than five minutes, I should be grievously disappointed."

"Monsieur," replied the dentist, her tones strictly professional, though a faint blush tinged the beauty of her girlish face, "the only thing I could do for erosion would turn the tooth black, and as it is an incisor, the result would not be agreeable to you. Dab with a little milk of magnesia in the morning, and again at night. And avoid ice pudding."

"Its price compels me to. Do not take me for a spendthrift because I have a clean collar on. What abstruse knowledge you possess, mademoiselle! How little I divined when I saw you first that I was to have the benefit of your opinion. It was in the Garden of the Luxembourg last Sunday, and I wondered who you were."

"It is well not to drink anything hot for some time afterwards," she added gravely. "Dab after you have taken your morning coffee."

"How considerate of you to mention it! Dentistry is a career with which I didn't associate you. My impression on Sunday was that you were a poetess. You are fond of poetry, aren't you, mademoiselle?"

"Very fond, monsieur. If you follow my directions the sensitiveness will pass."

"And on Monday I rather fancied you were a singer. And then on Wednesday—I looked for you in vain on Tuesday—you had taken off your gloves, and your hands led me to think you might be a pianist. I cannot say what an astonishment it was to me to imagine the forceps in them! When you left the Luxembourg on Wednesday, I chanced to leave it also—I chanced to be behind you when you entered here. Startled, I read 'Mademoiselle Jibinsky, *Dentiste*,' on the brass plate. Yet even when I wrote requesting an appointment, even when I rang the bell this afternoon, I was still in doubt whether *you* were mademoiselle Jibinsky. You might have been a lodger on the next floor; you might have been a lady calling to have a tooth filled—I had no means of knowing. Even in the other room just now, while I sat striving to assuage impatience with an ancient copy of *Je Sais Tout*, the uncertainty continued. It was not till I saw you standing by those glittering instruments, so graceful, so dignified, in that white overall, that I ceased to tremble lest my appointment should turn out to be with some dejecting stranger."

"And always use a dry toothbrush," the girl

went on, as sedately as if she had not noticed him in the Garden of the Luxembourg, hadn't been aware he followed her, and wasn't thinking him rather nice. " By that I don't mean that you should try to clean your teeth without any water, as some of my patients have supposed—with distressing results—but that you should let the brush get thoroughly dry before you use it next. The best plan is to use two alternately."

In this fashion began an acquaintance that was to have strange consequences. We dare to say that not one among our readers has ever experienced consequences so strange from a visit to a dentist's. We dare to say that never has a professional appointment led any other dentist to diverge so heinously from the professional path.

The name of the enamoured patient was Edmond Bernier. Having served an apprenticeship of some years in the provinces, he was now a member of the Théâtre Duphot, where he was cast for painfully subordinate rôles, and understudied a self-satisfied leading man called André Cucq. The plays being commissioned by the actress-manageress, the leading man's parts were, naturally, nothing wonderful, but by comparison with Bernier's they were transcendent, and the poor boy, who was desperately anxious to

get on, aspired ardently to shine in them.
Cucq was pleasurably conscious of it. Ladies
in the audience who melted to the affected
hero's eyes, and attitudes, and noble sentiments
behind the footlights little guessed the malicious
tricks he could perpetrate behind the scenes. It
tickled his objectionable sense of humour to prepare disappointments for his understudy. More
than once he had arrived so late that the stage
manager cursed in a fever of apprehension, and
Bernier had been thrilled by a hurried message
that it " looked as if he might have to go on for
the part." On these occasions, when there had
come another message that he wasn't needed for
it, after all, his own humble lines seemed, of
course, more abject to him still, and Cucq, who
well knew how he felt, was mightily amused.

The Garden of the Luxembourg being a very
nice place for confidences, and mademoiselle
Jibinsky being in the habit of resorting there for
exercise and fresh air, it was not long before she
was familiar with the story of monsieur Bernier's
woes, ambitions and lack of prospects. And
meanwhile Bernier learnt that the young lady's
father, too, had been a dentist, and that a few of
the patients to whom she had sometimes attended
in his lifetime were the prop and stay of her scanty

practice. She might have stated that one of them was André Cucq, but she was, at this epoch, far too punctilious to introduce the teeth of one patient to another. Moreover, when a girl sits beside a man she has begun to like, she doesn't want to waste time talking about teeth.

Now, Cucq had not played his little trick on his understudy for many months, and he was contemplating a hoax on a more elaborate scale than any he had attempted hitherto. He said to his toady, an actor in the company, of the name of Mivart:

" If there is anybody who gets on my nerves it is that chap Bernier! He is the typical amateur. I am tempted to have a game with him."

Mivart, who had himself hoped to understudy Cucq, and who was accordingly jealous of Bernier, responded:

" Oh, do! I don't like him either."

" It would be humorous to see him gulled to the extent of dressing and making-up for my part one night. What fun, if he weren't undeceived till the very moment that he was about to step on to the stage. The shock to him! Figure yourself, his consternation, if he had no idea I was in the theatre till he stood waiting for the cue. He would be petrified when he saw me."

Mivart shouted with mirth. " It would be superb ! But how ? It would be difficult to carry it so far, hein ? "

" No, it only needs stage management. *You* could do it. You could go to his lodging in a high state of excitement—you have ' just called on me and found me down with the flu. A doctor there.' Say I have sent you running round to let him hear it is out of the question for me to play. He can make you no reproaches after-wards—it won't be *your* fault that I pluckily changed my mind. I can see a capital little scene for you. You might affect some envy. ' What an ordeal for you ! But one may be sure they'll make allowance for your inexperience '—that sort of thing."

Wherefore it happened that one afternoon, when Bernier was occupied in thinking deeply of Olga Jibinsky, and how much better it would be if she were called Olga Bernier instead, there came a peremptory rapping at his door, and Mivart burst in, puffing with perturbation. To do Mivart justice, his performance in the attic was better than any he had given on the boards. " Word of honour, I sympathise," he declared— " there isn't even time to call a rehearsal for you. I should be nervous of your job, myself. Still don't worry, mon petit; it is near the end of the run, and you can't do much harm to the piece—it will soon be coming off, anyhow."

Bernier's brain was spinning too fast for the gibe to wound. Moreover, he had long been letter-perfect in the part, and was thoroughly familiar with the " business." It was not even necessary that he should consider his clothes and pack a portmanteau, for it was always in readiness at the theatre—complete, to a dress tie. Within half an hour he was speeding to the boulevard du Mont-parnasse, to communicate the sensational tidings to mademoiselle Jibinsky.

" I thought it must be a millionaire, with a big case, pealing the bell like that," she said, as he went in.

" Do you know the date ? " he asked her.

" Have you hurried here to inquire ? "

" I inquire because it is a date to be graven on the tablets of your mind. To-night I appear in Paris as a leading man. Don't swoon. It has occurred at last ! It may lead to good things, who knows ? If I acquit myself tolerably, everybody will be astounded. The admission isn't gratifying to my vanity, but it is encouraging to my hopes. To astound one's circle is to take a stride forward. Seriously, they can hardly fail to give me better rôles in future if they are pleased with me this evening."

"How I congratulate you!" she cried. "Tell me more, tell me all. What has happened? Cucq is sick? Not dangerously?"

"No, not dangerously, I trust. There is no reason to think so. He has flu. People have been known to recover from it. Even his sycophant Mivart does not pretend to quake for Cucq's life. But he must keep his bed for a day or two. So to-night, mademoiselle, at a quarter to nine—though you will not be present, because the knowledge that you were there would paralyse me—you will think of me a little, and wish me well, hein? I wonder if you would give me something for luck?"

"For luck? Why yes. What shall I give you?"

"If you will be kind enough, give me that bunch of violets that I see—and the rest of the afternoon."

"But if there should be a patient?"

"What far-fetched ideas you have! Anyhow, be reckless. I want to stay and talk to you. My heart is so full this afternoon."

"To be a true friend, I think I should send you home to study."

"Mais non, mais non. I know the lines as

well as I know the way here. I want to stop.
No, I want to take you to the Dôme for coffee;
I want to take you to the Rotonde for a ' pichet
blanc '—I don't know what I want. Yes, let's
go to a café—I want you to drink a glass of something and toast my opportunity ! I entreat you.
Put on your hat."

How Cucq and Mivart would have held their
sides !

And, after the return from the café, how they
would have roared at the castle in the air that was
erected in the firelight ! Beginning with the
audacious notion of his salary being doubled soon,
the dupe gave fancy full rein. The figures rose
with every phrase, and in a quarter of an hour he
was offered " lead " at half the theatres on the
Grand Boulevard. In circumstances so opulent,
what more natural than that he should confess his
love ? And since the sentiment was not all on his
side, what more natural than that his hostess should
listen ? Before it was compulsory for him to go,
the rent of the castle was discussed, and they had
even decided on some of the furniture. They
were actually affianced. And all on the strength
of a hoax.

With what emotion he parted from her ! And
with what joyful anticipation she stole, unknown

to him, into the fauteuils de balcon to witness his
triumph! When the curtain rose there was, in all
the house, no gaze so rapt as hers, though she had
seen the piece twice already. As the moment
approached for the hero's entrance, she shook in
her chair; when the moment dawned, she held
her breath. And then, of course, André Cucq
strolled on to the stage as usual—and she thought
she was going to faint. Indeed, as her tense
figure suddenly relaxed and her chin dipped to
her chest, an ardent playgoer in the next seat
thought so too, and was furious at the threatened
interruption. In every second of those long,
long acts she yearned for vengeance on the postur-
ing hero—her instinct divined the truth. And
more piteous than her own despondence was
the thought of the misery that must be bowing
Bernier in the dressing-room. It is a strong statement, but rarely has a man inspired deeper execra-
tion in a woman than the hilarious Cucq inspired
that night in Olga Jibinsky.

How exquisite was her sympathy at the stage
door! Never in Bernier's most dazzling day-
dreams had it been excelled. Within five minutes,
and a taxi, he was vowing, " word of honour, to
have you make so much of me, I would go
through it all again, frightful as it was."

"The cad!" she cried. "The odious contemptible cad. What did he say, chéri?"

"He said carelessly, 'Here I am, after all, though, no doubt, it is rash.' And as for *me*, what could *I* say? He saw very well I knew I had been tricked, but to upbraid him would only have been to increase his satisfaction."

"If I could revenge you!" she gasped. And with never an inkling that an opportunity was to emanate from the fact, she reflected anew that Cucq was on her exiguous list of patients.

Observe how intricate is the web of Destiny. More than seven years earlier, a stranger in Paris, suffering from pyorrhœa, had been recommended to a worthy monsieur Jibinsky, since defunct, who extracted an assortment of his upper teeth, and made him an excellent plate in their stead. The stranger was no other than André Cucq. And since mademoiselle Jibinsky had been her father's assistant, and knew all about the matter, Cucq had subsequently sought her services, and resigned himself to exhibiting his mouth to her, on occasions when any of his remaining teeth needed to be filled. He was morbidly anxious that no one should hear that he wore artificial teeth, and he preferred the secret to remain in the Jibinsky family. How could he foresee that he would one day have an understudy with whom mademoiselle

Jibinsky was to fall in love ? How could he fore-see that he was destined to arouse in the heart of his fair dentist a remorseless hate ?

Trouble was already at his heels. Some few weeks after his discreditable influenza prank, a new drama was put into rehearsal at the Duphot, and to his surprise, the hero of it proved to be less insignificant than was customary there. Though, of course, negligible by comparison with the heroine, he had for once more to do than loiter around in scenes in which the actress-manageress was voluble and acclaimed. Cucq was not a little elated. And as to Bernier, all his previous aspirations were as naught beside his devouring hope that at some distant date he might be privileged to manifest his abilities in the royal vesture of King Casparillo. Privately he rejoiced in rehearsing the part—and, sad to say, his own meagre part of the monarch's valet left him plenty of time to do so.

" How atrocious it is, that fellow as a King, and you as a valet ! " bemoaned Olga Jibinsky. " Has the valet many lines ? "

" Alas ! " sighed Bernier, "he speaks frequently, but what he says is chiefly, ' Yes, sire.' "

The production was finally announced for January 7th. And on the morning of January 7th, André Cucq, lunching in his little flat in the rue Cambon, and musing on the superb apparel he was to don that evening, and how prodigiously ladies in front would admire him in it, turned, on a sudden, damp with misgiving. He ceased to masticate, and for perhaps ten seconds remained rigid, without nerve to determine his dread. When he at last put out his tongue and extricated the disturbing substance he had felt on it, his blood ran cold. The substance was an artificial tooth. Tottering to the mirror, he forced his blanched face into a sickly smile before it, praying that the tooth might prove to be a back one. On the contrary: it was one of the centrals.

"Mon Dieu!—mon Dieu!" yelled Cucq, throwing up his arms. "Now, how am I to go on the thtage a thight like thith?" Whereat he discovered further that the gap endowed him with a slight lisp.

With his next comments we refuse to pollute our pages. Wet with perspiration, he questioned whether it was possible for the disaster to be remedied by the evening. Then, snatching his hat, he pelted down the stairs, signed frantically to a chauffeur, and burst into the surgery of his dentist like a man demented.

"Mademoiselle, mademoiselle, regard the catastrophe!" he panted, always with the lisp that wrung his heart as he heard it. "Repair it by this evening, I entreat you. I cannot appear without it. And to-night's the night—I must have it! I must have it at any cost. Mademoiselle, say it can be done."

For a space she made no reply. Her eyes were hard, disdainful. The proximity of this creature who had sported with the hopes of her betrothed, who found diversion in creating torments for the man she loved, was revolting to her. So far from hastening to allay the suspense that she beheld, she inclined to prolong it, to feign uncertainty if the work could be accomplished in the time. But conscientiousness prevailed.

"It can be done," she owned.

"Ah, heaven be praised! What a relief! What I have suffered! How soon can it be ready? The sooner the better."

"I am much occupied," she returned haughtily. "However, if you leave the plate now, you might call for it at seven o'clock."

"Seven o'clock?" he expostulated. "To-night I must be in the theatre early to dress. Seven o'clock would be cutting it very fine. Say, six. You can manage it for me by six, mademoiselle, n'est-ce-pas?"

"I fear that seven is quite the best I can do,"

N

said she. And when he had pulled the plate out, and an expanse of vacant gum made him look very unheroic indeed, she could not resist adding, " Meantime, remain indoors—do not expose your mouth to the air while you have no teeth worth mentioning."

As the door closed, she sank to a chair. The plate, prominent in a glass beside the basin, seemed a live and formidable presence. Ah, stroke of fate that it should devolve on *her* to rescue him ! Thrice-bitter fate that mocked her with a chance she might not seize to lift her lover to renown ! Not for one moment did she doubt that were Cucq incapable of playing that night, his understudy would be glorious on the morrow. She pictured the headlines : " Sensational Success "—" Unknown Actor Leaps to Fame." And a temptation, terrible in its tenacity, clamoured to her that the consummation was within her reach. The means lay before her, in a glass of water. She might restore the plate too late—she might assert that it had met with an accident in the vulcaniser. Retribution well deserved ! But conscience recoiled—her unquenchable probity abhorred a lie.

" Ah, my Edmond, my Edmond ! " wept the girl. Her mind was torn in twain. None but a dentist who has passionately loved can realise the intensity of this struggle between devotion and professional rectitude.

No sound was in the room but the clock's admonitory tick. The clock ticked on, but the plate lay still untouched. All her sensibilities shrank from approaching it. And now, to her distracted gaze, the teeth in the tumbler glistened, as in an evil grin, deriding her despair. . . . Suddenly she sprang to her feet, intrepid and implacable. Her long-pent hatred of her lover's torturer had discerned a prouder course than subterfuge. She would front him valorously when he came—she would deal this miscreant pang for pang !

Monsieur Cucq was agitated during the afternoon by a telephone call. His dentist inquired solicitously the precise time at which King Casparillo was to make his first entrance, and she suggested that it might be well for monsieur Cucq to dress for the part before he came to her. This could only be construed to mean that seven o'clock might not see the work completed, and his reply was vehement and prolonged. However, he adopted the suggestion. He sent excited instructions to his dresser to come to the flat at once with the uniform that was to be worn in

Act I, and there, in the bedroom, he was duly attired—keeping his lips tightened to conceal his misfortune. "I have a sore throat," he lisped. "Ask me no questions—I fear for my voice to-night." The grandeur of his appearance, in azure and gold, with an array of decorations on his padded chest, gratified him so much, that involuntarily he smiled, but happily the dresser wasn't looking.

"I shall be at the show, to make up, at eight o'clock sharp. Mind everything is put out," commanded Cucq, pluming himself before the mirror. "Now get me a taxi." And he regretted that the cold weather compelled him to hide his magnificence under a long overcoat.

His greeting to his dentist was censorious. "Your message deranged me very much, mademoiselle. The plate is ready?"

"I need detain you no more than a few minutes, monsieur," said she, ringing the bell.

"Ah! Upon my word, you made me question whether the curtain would rise to-night."

"But why? There is always your understudy, n'est-ce-pas?" she inquired.

"My understudy?" scoffed Cucq. "It would be a fine production with my understudy in the part! Phew! it is hot here," he added, remov-

ing the overcoat to exhibit his gorgeousness.
" You see I did as you said, but it has put me to
terrible inconvenience."

" It is a handsome costume," observed mademoiselle Jibinsky, regarding it critically. " Is it
designed to fit your understudy without altera-
tions ? "

" How should I know ? " said Cucq, with an
impatient shrug. " I am pressed for time,
mademoiselle. If you will kindly hasten ! "

" Excuse me one moment, monsieur. Be
seated," she returned. And to a servant who had
entered she said, " Light the gas in the next room,
Hortense, and then put on your shawl. I shall
send you on an errand directly, in a taxi."

Cucq tapped irritably on his knee. " I have
still to make up, mademoiselle. May I beg that
you postpone your domestic arrangements till
you have attended to me ? By eight o'clock I
must be in the theatre."

" No doubt it is a slow process for a player to
dress and make up," said the lady. And she continued, " I wonder how long your understudy
would need ? "

At these strange and constant references to his
understudy, an indefinable apprehension began
to steal through Cucq. He eyed her searchingly.

" My understudy—my understudy ? I do not understand," he faltered. " You speak always of my understudy."

" He is always in my mind, monsieur. We are betrothed."

" Betrothed ? " echoed Cucq, with growing uneasiness.

" It is in my mind, too, that there was a night when it diverted you to prepare for him the humiliation of dressing for a part he was never to perform. . . . Did you say it was ' thoughtless ' of me to bring you here in the costume of King Casparillo, monsieur ? "

His sensation was akin to a swirl of seasickness. She had cast the mask aside, and her tones were dread with menace. He sat livid, unable to articulate. Then, leaping from the chair with a burst of fury, marred only by the lisp, he roared, " Give me my teeth ! I demand them instantly. Don't dare to delay another second. I refuse to wait. I refuse to wait, I tell you. Give me my teeth, you devil, or I'll wring your neck ! "

A contemptuous smile curved her perfect lips.

" Please don't rant. It will serve you better to listen. Your plate will be forwarded to you a week hence, when the success that I'm confident

monsieur Bernier will achieve this evening has
been fully confirmed. For the rest, you are free
to go as soon as you have 'phoned to the theatre
that you are unable to appear. Violence is futile.
The tables have been turned—and to-night the
valet will be King. But, if you are discreet, I will
show you more leniency than you deserve."

" Give me my teeth," screamed Cucq. " Do
you figure to yourself that you are talking to a
child ? Give me my teeth, or you shall suffer for
it all your life—you and your accomplice in this
conspiracy. I will have him discharged from the
theatre; I'll see to it that he gets no other engagement to the end of his days."

" Monsieur Bernier knows nothing of what I
do ! " she cried out.

" I don't believe it—and even if it be true, no
one else will believe it, either. Hysterical fool,
to dream that you could victimise me, that you
had power to dictate ! My teeth, quick, girl !—
and I may yet overlook your ravings. Exasperate
me any further, and it is not only your lover that
will be punished. I'll have you expelled from
your profession. I'll prosecute you—you commit a crime."

"Yes," she answered, " professionally I commit
a crime; but ethically I find myself faultless.

have communed with my conscience much to-day.
I obey higher laws than the Dental Association's.
And I have communed with my judgment, too,
monsieur, and your threats leave me undisturbed
—for publicity would be disastrous to you. You
will announce at once that you are too sick to play.
Be grateful for the clemency that permits you
to disguise the truth.   Submit, or I proclaim it
myself!   I expose you to the banter of your col-
leagues, to lampoons in the Press, to the derision
of silly women who find you attractive now.   I
make you the laughing-stock of Paris—the young
romantic actor who could not appear because he
had lost his false teeth.   A fig for your bluster!
It is *your* career that is in *my* hands!"

"Girl, give me my teeth," wailed Cucq.
And in all the effulgence of his sovereign splendour he went down on his knees.

Inexorable, she pointed to the telephone.

He staggered to it at last. "Thentral: thikthy-
theven, theventy-thikth," quavered Cucq, so hard
to understand in his distraction that the woman at
the exchange was rude to him.

Olga Jibinsky took the receiver from his nerve-
less hand.   Her tones were even, though her heart
throbbed fast.   Silence—and next, the fateful
words.

" I speak for monsieur Cucq. Monsieur Cucq cannot appear to-night. He has lost his——"

" No, no ! " shrilled Cucq beseechingly.

" Voice," she conceded. " Monsieur Cucq hoped to appear; he even dressed for the part. Monsieur Bernier must be informed immediately. Monsieur Cucq is about to remove the costume, and send it to the theatre for him." She rose. " You will find a light in the next room, monsieur, and my maid waits to take the costume in a taxi."

" But—hell ! What clothes am I to go home in, fiend ? " wept Cucq.

"I presume you have underwear on," she replied imperiously. " And the overcoat will cover it up."

After a sleepless night, monsieur Cucq lay surrounded by the morning papers, which shattered him completely by the news that his understudy had made a brilliant hit. The hit was so marked that soon after Cucq's teeth had been restored to him, young Bernier was offered leading business at the Palais-Dramatique; and the terms being handsome, he espoused Olga in the spring—to the unwavering felicity of both.

ONE summer's day, mademoiselle Vernet travelled from Rouen to Paris, and went to see the chief of the detective force.

As she went by appointment she did not have to wait long.

" I am delighted to make your acquaintance, mademoiselle," said Laperche, rising, and looking at her with interest.

" It was exceedingly good of you to let me come," said the girl. " I wrote with a great deal of misgiving, though my mother often spoke about you to me."

" Did she ? I had the honour of being a friend of your mother's ages ago. I rarely saw her after her marriage."

" We lived in England so many years, monsieur—we went there when I was quite a child."

" What can I do for you ? "

" Monsieur, my father left us very poorly provided for, and my mother and I had to earn our living. Since I lost her I have been teaching English in Rouen—I am really more at home in English than in French."

" You speak French perfectly," said Laperche, with a bow.

" Well, the work is badly paid; it leads to nothing, and I hate it besides. There is one calling that has always attracted me, and I think that I have aptitude for it. Others have thought so too. Of course, I know that I need training, but, with experience, I should make a good detective. Will you be generous enough to give me a trial ? "

" Ah, mademoiselle," exclaimed Laperche, shrugging his shoulders almost to his ears, " you don't know what you propose ! You hate your present work ? I assure you, you would hate the work of a detective much more. I would with infinite pleasure do anything I could for you, but I cannot do what you ask."

" You employ women ? " she persisted.

" Yes."

" Ladies ? "

" Some of them."

" Then why not me ? I have not come to you on impulse—it isn't any sudden whim. I have been enthusiastic about it all my life, and I'm not afraid of the risks. And I am ready to begin at the foot of the ladder. Why not me ? "

" Because, as I say, I should be doing you an

ill turn. You picture the romantic side of the profession; you see yourself frustrating villainy and aiding virtue in distress—for ever glowing with the consciousness of a helpful action. But, mademoiselle, a detective must do many things that are not romantic—things that would be odious to you, repugnant. I speak from my heart. Your age is only . . . about twenty-six, and you are beautiful—there is a happier career before you than any *I* can offer. And at the very worst, you would do better to resign yourself for life to the calling you detest than to adopt the work you want."

Most girls would have felt there was no more for them to say. This pale, slight, delicate-looking girl stood her ground. She even spoke without any sign of discomposure.

" Monsieur, may I hint that you cannot know all the mournfulness of a position you have never tried ? You refuse. I was half prepared for it. I should have been quite prepared but for something you once said. I think you told my mother once that, if at any time, no matter how far distant, you could render her a service, you would do it. Though speeches like that are soon forgotten as a rule, I hoped you might remember and serve her child."

"I do remember, mademoiselle," said Laperche with dignity. "I told your mother that in the Garden of the Luxembourg, twenty-eight years ago, on a seat facing the Médicis Fountain. I had not known her until she was already devoted to the gentleman who became your father, but she was very dear to me and, poor as I was, I wanted her for my wife. Your mother remains a vivid memory to me, though I am a family man and an old man now. I will not help the daughter of the girl I loved to enter a profession in which I would not place a daughter of my own."

"I beg your pardon, monsieur," said mademoiselle Vernet softly, and there was a moment's silence. She went on: "You refuse in kindness to me, I understand. And it may be true that I was more attracted by the romantic side of the thing than I saw; after what you have said I realise clearly enough that it must have its uncongenial, sordid side as well. If I were independent, no doubt I should thank you for your frank advice and take it. But again, monsieur, I have my living to earn. I should be a fool to neglect a career for which I am convinced I have ability simply because it isn't a bed of roses. Also, however heavy its drawbacks proved, it would be more to my taste than the drudgery that I'm putting up with now. As I do have to work, you will forgive me for deciding to do the work that is most congenial."

"Since I cannot offer you employment, there will be nothing for me to forgive," said Laperche dryly.

"Monsieur, I am in earnest. If *you* won't help me, I shall have to see what others will do—there are private inquiry agents; and there's London."

"Any valuable introductions there?"

"No."

"Friends to turn to when your money gives out?"

She shook her head.

"You might have reason to repent your adventure as long as you lived. Listen," he said, distressed. "It is most improbable that anyone would take you on; if you were not good-looking I should say it was certain no one would take you on—but I admit that your appearance might possibly recommend you to some snide quarter for a certain sort of affair. What do you suppose would come of that? Not permanent work, believe me! And you would find the job degrading; you might find you had exposed yourself to other dangers than those you are thinking of."

"I am used to taking care of myself; I am not a child."

"I can't dissuade you?"

"Monsieur, I appreciate what you say; I know you mean it all most kindly, but——"

"But you are resolved to do an unwise thing."

There was a pause again, a long pause this time. Laperche leant back in the chair with his heavy brows knit, his gaze brooding on her.

"I wonder if you really *are* any good," he said abruptly. "Look here, I have given you good advice, and you won't take it. If you were anybody else on earth that would end the matter for me, but, as it is, you make me vacillate. Of the two evils, I would rather give you work myself than see you come to grief in bad hands. ... Well, I will consider. But I promise nothing. You shall hear from me. I must send you away now." He got up. "You are a foolish girl, and I ought to be very angry with you. Be off. If you come to your senses before I write, I shall be happy to hear it."

Mademoiselle Vernet went back to Rouen feeling rather sanguine. In saying that she had qualifications for such employment she was not mistaken, but, odd as it sounds, she did not recognise the outstanding one. Her faculty for deduction, if above the average girl's, would not have moved Laperche to enthusiasm. What was remarkable was a gift she had for appealing to the most diverse characters so strongly that they grew confidential with her on brief acquaintance. When she was two-and-twenty a man of the world had asked her, " How on earth have you learnt so much about life ? " And she said, " I always make friends with people, even people I don't like much, till I've heard everything worth while that they can tell me." " Isn't that rather insincere ? " said he. " I don't know," she murmured. " I've never thought about it like that. It doesn't do them any harm." And she had captured his own interest so firmly that all the man said was, " Well, I don't care if you *are* insincere to other people—but be sincere to *me !* " The fact has nothing to do with this story, but she proved sensationally sincere to him.

The letter from Laperche reached her later than she had hoped for it, but its contents delighted her. It ran : " Come immediately. Bring luggage."

She did not look discomposed when she was

admitted to his office, but her nerves were quivering. She understood by the tone of his first words that this time she was received, not by a friend of her mother's, but by the chief of the detective force.

"Good-morning, mademoiselle. Sit down. You stated that you lived many years in England. Could you pass for an English girl?"

"Oh yes," she said. "It's French I am a little lame in. Not the pronunciation, of course, but an idiom now and then."

"Say that in English quickly. . . . Well, I do not understand all the words, but you have no accent. A chance has occurred for me to try you. I consent reluctantly, but I consent. Do you remember the affair in the rue Mozart?"

"I remember reading something about it. A woman was drugged, and had her jewelry and a lot of money stolen. The child's governess was suspected. Did she do it?"

"I wish for information about an Englishman, a bank clerk in Paris. His name is Marriott. He has just gone, most discreetly, to a cheap boarding-house at Versailles for his summer holiday. You will go and stay in the house. Your business is to discover if he has money to burn. You are, on no account, to attempt to

o

shadow him—beginners always bungle that. What are your tactics ? "

" I am a Miss . . . Vernon," she said, " a typist out of a job——"

" Can you use a typewriter ? "

" Yes. My parents used to be well off, and——"

" And your only relative is an aunt of no importance."

" And I find poverty hard. I have no friends here. I know very little French, and that makes a job frightfully difficult to find in Paris. I am sad. My business is to interest him in me."

There was approval in Laperche's eyes. " Bien. Here is the address. There are vacant rooms. Go now and inquire if there *is* one. Arrange to enter to-morrow afternoon. You sleep to-night at the Hôtel Terminus, the one next to the Gare Saint Lazare. Where's your luggage ? "

He gave her further instructions and a thousand francs on account of expenses, and she found her luggage, labelled Vernon, at the hotel when she went there after making arrangements at the boarding-house.

The next afternoon she was the new boarder. Though she sat in the little salon, with an English book, and strolled in the garden, she could see nothing of the pensionnaires till the hour of the evening meal. Then she found the fat, vulgar proprietress, madame Jobard, dispensing a ragoût among a few persons of no interest. There was a melancholy gentleman, with long white whiskers, and there was a middle-aged widow, swathed in crape; and opposite sat an ancient, mumbling dame whose artificial teeth slipped so low when she ate that they seemed likely to fall into her plate. The bank clerk came in only when his portion of the ragoût must have been half cold. He looked more French than English, and the girl was momentarily uncertain whether it was he, but the accent of his " Pardon, madame," was sufficient to identify him. Mademoiselle Vernet saw his eyes brighten to behold a new-comer who was young. The next moment he gave all his attention to his food, and she decorously regarded her own. For some time nobody uttered a word. The only sounds were those of mastication, and the scraping of knives on the crockery.

At last, however, the proprietress addressed her, inquiring if she had been in France long. She answered in English, and corrected herself haltingly. The man looked at her again. He had a pleasant face.

And when dinner is over? she wondered.

When dinner was over the lady with the teeth that didn't fit retired to her bedroom, and the melancholy old gentleman went upstairs as well. The proprietress and the widow proceeded to the salon, and she followed them. After waiting to see whether she went in, the man followed, too.

The women played draughts, and exchanged a few words with him. Madame Jobard observed, by way of introduction, that the young lady was also English. " And I wish I spoke French ! " said mademoiselle Vernet to the man.

" Yes, it must be slow for you, not talking French," he said, drawing nearer. " Not that you'd find the company here very exhilarating if you did ! Is this the first time you've been to Versailles ? "

" Yes. Am I going to be disappointed ? "

" Well, it's a paradise inside the park gates, and a hole outside them. You'll find the Trianons all right—except for the English trippers. They swarm here at this time of the year. Oh, and you can go and see the fountains play, if you're here on the first Sunday of the month. Are you staying long ? "

" I don't know," she said. " It depends. No, I hope to be back in Paris again soon. I hope so."

" Are you so fond of it ? "

" Oh, I didn't mean that," she said hesitatingly.
" Well, do tell me more about Versailles ! "
The note of anxiety in her voice had been just
marked enough to be engaging.

He stayed, talking to her, for about a quarter
of an hour, and then went upstairs, saying he
had work to do. She asked herself why work
should occupy a bank clerk on his holiday.

" He's agreeable, the new gentleman," said
the widow in French to the proprietress. " Does
he intend to remain long ? "

" Who knows ? He has plenty of luggage—
very smart. And he has taken a double room—
the big room that madame Fauchon and her
daughter used to have. It's evident he's not
without a copper, that gentleman ! "

So he had smart luggage, and could pay for a
double room ? Behind her book, mademoiselle
Vernet listened intently. Well, that was something learnt !

She was up early next day, and sat with the
book in the garden. Through an open window
the tapping of a typewriter reached her, and she
assumed it was his. She moved her chair to a
spot where she might be seen from the window,
but, though the tapping was often suspended

for a few minutes, and her hopes rose each time,
the man didn't come out.   She sat there alone,
till the gong for déjeuner was beaten.   At
déjeuner and in the evening she talked with him
again.

On four days she talked with him at déjeuner
and in the evening.   And on four mornings she
rose early and sat in the garden without result.

On the fifth morning he came sauntering up
the path and joined her.   " We progress,"
reflected mademoiselle Vernet.

She was too intelligent not to know she would
bore a man by talking of herself before he had
begun to take an interest in her—too intelligent
not to know she would flatter him by doing it
when once he had; and this morning Mr.
Marriott heard a little of her assumed position.

" I'm sorry," he said.   " Wouldn't it be easier
to find something if you were in Paris ? "

" I can answer advertisements just as well here
as there.   Not being able to take down letters in
French, of course, is the worst drawback—there
aren't many jobs in Paris for a shorthand-typist
who only knows English."

" I wonder you don't go to England."

The comment discomfited her.   She hadn't
been prepared for it.

" Perhaps I shall.   Yes, I think I'm homesick.
Are *you*? "

" Well, I *am* half French; it's different for me.
I've an accent, but I talk without any trouble.   I
don't say much in this place because there's no
one to talk to.   What a collection!   It was a
festive house to have come to on one's holiday.
You were a burst of sunshine when you arrived."

" Well, but you aren't on a holiday—you seem
to be always busy."

" I meant a holiday from the bank; I'm in a
bank in Paris.   What I'm busy on here has
nothing to do with that.   Yes, it's a cheerful
establishment.   Fancy having to live in it for
good!   One or two of them have been here for
years, I gather."

" I daresay you could find a better pension in
Versailles if you looked around."

" I don't want to move now, Miss Vernon,
thank you!   Besides, I'm bound to stop here for
the present.   Well, did you go to the Orangerie
as I told you to? "

" I set out for it, but I couldn't find it.   I shall
try again one day."

" If you don't make haste, the wistaria will be
over.   Will you come this afternoon, if you've
nothing to do? "

"You've your 'holiday work,'" she smiled.

"No; I always go for a walk in the afternoon. Do come. Will you?"

"If you're sure you can spare the time," she said.

And in her second report to Laperche she wrote, "We take a walk together every day. He has told me nothing of value. Am I being too slow for you?"

Laperche replied, "You are doing well. I shall be content if you can report anything of value in a fortnight."

It was to the Orangerie that they generally went. Often they sat among the scents of the exquisite garden, talking, for a couple of hours. There were even moments when she recognised with dismay that she had been forgetting her motive for encouraging him to talk. Then he would ask her, "What's the matter, what are you looking like that for?" And her reply would be constrained. There were times, too, when the man seemed uneasy in his mind. Once she thought a confidence was coming: "I'm worried about something!" But that was all. He seemed to regret having said as much as that. She questioned afterwards if she had been adroit enough in her response.

It was when his holiday was nearly ended that he dropped the first words she found significant. She had been reflecting that soon she wouldn't be seeing him and her attempt would have failed; and she said, " I don't suppose you'll be sorry to leave this house ? "

" I'm not going to leave," he told her.   " I see there are trains that would do me very well. Let's go and have some tea." They were approaching the Trianon Palace Hotel, and, to her surprise, he turned into the drive.

" In here ? " she exclaimed.

" It'll be nicer than a shop."

" You're very extravagant ! I don't think I will, thanks."

" You needn't be afraid; I can afford to buy a cup of tea."

" I wish I were a clerk in a bank," she laughed.

" Oh, the bank be—— I've done something lately that paid me a lot better than the bank does ! "

The chance should have been seized on the instant, but she missed it.   " Something that paid me a lot better than the bank does " ?   It might simply mean that he had backed a horse—or it might mean that he was the thief. Laperche would be interested in the words.   The thought filled her mind. It obsessed her, and made her wish she were alone. But it did not excite her pleasurably, as it ought to have done. She knew, with consternation, that it depressed and frightened her, and that she was feeling sick.

Well, the real test of her ability had begun ! Huddled in the armchair of her room by and by, mademoiselle Vernet pondered. This was the cue for her to take the course she had foreseen at the start, to incite the man to spend money till she discovered whether his means were incriminating. " Paid me a lot better than the bank does " ? What did it imply ? It would have paid him a lot better than the bank did, no doubt, if he had won a few thousand francs one week ! She wondered how much importance Laperche would attach to the phrase. . . .

She must ascertain whether his funds enabled Mr. Marriott to invite her to expensive restaurants . . . to take her to theatres in the best seats. Supposing she said she would love to go, but hadn't a decent dress ? Ah no, there was a limit ! . . . The best report she could make, of course, would be gifts of jewelry. If she led him on to propose, there would be an engagement ring. It might be valuable enough to satisfy Laperche. Perhaps it would even be one of the rings that had been stolen? No, no, not that! An insult to her. Not the sort of man to do that, thief or not. . . . She did not like the course before her. A word that Laperche himself had used recurred to her, "repugnant."

A restless night, however, revealed no other course—and her duty was to swallow her repugnance.

She said, on the morrow, "I wonder how different Paris would have looked to me if I had come when my parents were alive. They were always talking about it. I used to hear of the hotel we'd stay at, and the famous restaurants we'd go to. I can't say I understand the adoration of Paris, myself."

"You haven't had a very good time there; I don't suppose you even know it as well as you think you do. It's a backward, uncomfortable, fascinating city. I'd like to take you to—— Oh, there are lots of places I'd like to take you to! Will you dine with me there one night this week? Come to dinner with me, and we'll go to the English Players afterwards. They're doing a piece that I particularly want you to see."

"Oh, that's very kind of you," she said irresolutely. "But——"

"Please, no 'buts'!"

" I don't go out in the evening."

" We could make it a luncheon and a matinée. Only, I'd so much like to take you to a certain place to dinner! Miss Vernon? You know, you're very—er—complicated."

" Complicated?" The sigh was genuine. " Am I? No, I didn't know that."

" You *are*. You say good-night like a pal, and you say good-morning across a wall of formality sometimes. It hurts. There are more things than one that hurt. Of course, I know that—— Well, I can't say all I want to yet, I'm in a mess just now, but I'm hoping our meeting here won't be the end of it all."

Her brows had contracted slightly. She didn't speak.

" We've both got worries. But don't you think it'd do us both good to forget them for an evening? I don't go about asking for everybody's friendship. As a matter of fact, even the people I've liked best have generally wanted me more than I wanted them. Now it's the other way round."

Still words didn't come to her. The elation she had once expected wasn't there.

" You might say something."

" I don't know what you want me to say."

" I want you to say—— Well, it's difficult!

I want you to say you'll come to dinner.   Hold
on.   Will you say you'll be glad if our friendship
goes on after we've left here ? "

" It'd 've been very dull here without you,"
she stammered.

" And you'll dine with me ?   Please.   To-
morrow ? "

" Perhaps," she said wretchedly.

But she woke with an ache in her body and a
queer feeling in her head—and while she was
dressing she turned giddy, and had to lie down
again.   And, at the back of her mind, she knew
she wasn't regretful that the doctor who was
called in spoke of " la grippe " and told her to
stop in bed.   She had to pretend to be unable to
understand much that he said, and madame
Jobard was begged to interpret.   Madame
Jobard returned some hours later bearing a
basket of flowers, which " monsieur Marriott sent
to mademoiselle with his sympathy."   The girl
viewed it sombre-eyed.   The next morning it
was copies of the *Sketch*, and the *Tatler*, and the
Bystander that were brought with his sympathy.
And daily other things appeared, without a message—things edible that she knew madame
Jobard could never have prepared.   The patient
did not enjoy them.

As she ate his jelly, as she stared at his roses,

she scorned herself—by turns, for her duplicity, and for her weakness in abominating it. In every hour she reflected that she might exaggerate her illness and make it a pretext for resigning the work, and in every hour she was wrung by the ignominy of such a thought.

She was out in the garden again before long, but her convalescence was so slow that one day the doctor advised her to go to the sea for a week or two. Marriott heard of the advice from the widow, who had been interpreting on that occasion, and at the first opportunity he referred to it.

" They tell me the doctor says you ought to go to Dieppe. Are you going ? "

" No. I don't want to. I'm never well at the sea. I should hate to go. It's the last thing I want to do."

" Other people think you ought to go—everybody in the house."

" Madame Jobard doesn't."

" Madame Jobard doesn't count—you wouldn't be paying her if you were away. But you'd find Dieppe much dearer than this show; it's expensive in the season at the decent hotels. I want you to do me a big favour, an honour. Let me lend you the money to go with."

She had felt the offer coming, and she knew guiltily that she had tried to stop it.

"I can spare it all right," he urged; "I'm not hard up, I'm rolling in money just now."

She did not thank him, she didn't see him. She didn't see the garden, or the wall in front of her. She was seeing Laperche at his desk as he said, "Your business is to discover if he has money to burn." She must be disloyal to Laperche, or she must send a man who was fond of her to prison!

"You're not annoyed?"

The voice she dragged out was no more than a whisper. "Oh, I wish you wouldn't!"

"What?"

"Keep talking about money. . . . Oh, I know— I don't sound grateful. I'm sorry. Thank you very much. But it's impossible."

"That's that. I'm sorry to have upset you— damned sorry! . . . You want to be by yourself, don't you?"

"I've got a splitting headache," she said irritably. "I think I'll go upstairs and get some aspirin."

To send him to prison!—a man who was fond of her, a man she—— Yes, she *was*. It was hideous, but it couldn't be helped. To send him to prison—unless the suspicion proved to be wildly wrong! And even if it did, the shock, the horror to him! Through *her*. Through his having liked her, and been good to her, and believed she was worth it. How he would loathe and despise her when he knew!

She remained upstairs till he had left for the bank next morning, and she returned to her room before he came home. Incessantly, for more than twenty hours, she had been asking herself what she meant to do; and she lay tortured by the question during most of the second night.

Late in the morning, when she slept, there came a rapping at the door. " Mademoiselle was wanted on the telephone."

It was a message from Laperche. She was to be at his office at one o'clock.

On her frightened way to the station she said she must decide at once—and she said so unavailingly again in the slow train that took her towards the interview so much too fast. At the terminus she was afraid of meeting Marriott, for it was Saturday, and hundreds of people were pouring back to the suburbs. She hurried across the salle des pas perdus, and down the steps, as fast as the incoming crowds would let her, and, dreading in every moment to hear his voice, got

quickly into the first vacant taxi she could see.
When it reached the place, her mind was quailing
before the question still. To send him to prison,
or to deceive Laperche?

The formidable figure bent absorbed at the
desk. Nearly a minute went by while she stood
waiting.

He looked up, and spoke brusquely.

" Bonjour, mademoiselle. Your affair drags
on too long. What is the obstacle? "

" I wrote you," she faltered. " I have been ill,
and——"

" Understood. You were ill for a week.
It's now three weeks since you were better.
You're not ordered to shadow the man—your
state of health is no drawback to your working
in the house. Anything further to report? "

The muffled answer came late:

" No."

" It's clear you're no good at the work," said
Laperche harshly. " While you, who have had
every opportunity, show no results, others get
the evidence."

" You've discovered he's guilty? " she gasped.

An accusing arm shot out at her. " More! "
He made a long, terrible pause. It was extended
unendurably. She felt that his eyes were piercing

P

to every thought in her brain. "I have discovered you learnt enough to justify his arrest,
and withheld the information. The officer who
is false to her trust is herself a criminal. Your
attempt to shield your lover has failed. He's
here."

He spoke through the telephone. "Now!"

She had dropped on to a chair; and as she
watched for the door to open, she saw mentally
beyond it—to a haggard man's approach between
police agents.

The door opened, and Marriott came in alone.

"I'm sorry to have kept you waiting," said
Laperche. "Sit down." He went on, "Mademoiselle, as chief of the detective force I advise
you of the fact that the offence you have committed would, in the ordinary way, be disastrous
to you. As a friend of your dear, dead mother's
I advise you of my satisfaction that you have
perceived your unfitness for the career you were
bent on. Monsieur Marriott is a bank clerk
who does not interest me in my investigations.
He is my nephew and, so far as I am aware,
guilty of nothing worse than writing plays in a
language I do not understand. He consented to
play a part in the present comedy to help me show
you your mistake." He gave a half smile to

them both. " Officially I am not concerned with
your sentiments for each other. I counsel you
to go away and talk about them together."

After the first startled turn of her head she had
sat motionless, intent. Marriott went to her
impetuously, but her gesture checked him. The
tears running down her face were at variance with
the haughtiness of her tone.

" Mr. Marriott," she said, " your plot with
your uncle to make me treacherous to him has
been most successful. But you have told me lies
from the hour I met you, and when I had given
you my friendship you weren't above inventing
more, so that I should be unhappier still. Your
part was played well—it has made me suffer
frightfully. You have behaved to me like a cad."

" Will you hear me for a minute ? " he cried.
" I hated the job. When I told you I was in a
mess, I meant the mess of having promised him
to go through with it. I knew what you thought,
of course, but it was true when I said I'd done
something that had paid me better than the
bank did—it was the play I wanted to take you
to. It was true when I told you I wanted to go
on seeing you. Oh, Miss Vernon, Miss Vernet,
do believe me ! Forgive me. I love you."

" Ah, listen," exclaimed Laperche, " my office

is not a matrimonial bureau!" He went over to the girl, and drew her to her feet, and kissed her very gently on the brow. "False little detective, go and talk of love somewhere else. The sun is shining—the Garden of the Luxembourg will be pleasant this morning; and I recall a seat that faces the Médicis Fountain."

O N the 29th of January '24 the aspect of a miracle transfigured Paris. Some hundreds of taxi-cab drivers were on strike. In the extraordinary quietude couples on the side-walks could actually have conversed in undertones, though, being French, they still shouted. The young stared at their tranquil city as at an unimagined world. The old reviewed days when the capital that has become a pandemonium on tyres, wherein it is a perilous adventure to take a walk, was called the " Paradise of the Lounger." People who wanted taxi-cabs said it was a confounded nuisance.

One of these people was a little notary who had paused in the Avenue de Friedland, on the spot where the Chambre de Commerce now stands, with a large bouquet in his hand. Monsieur Gosselin desired to present the bouquet at Passy in person, and was much averse from exposing it to damage on the way. He made the gentle clicks with his tongue by which he habitually expressed hot annoyance—and went by the Métro, carrying the flowers as carefully as he could.

For reasons unrelated to the firm, Gosselin was deeply interested in madame Balbi. In lay terms, he was head over heels in love with her. But he was not sanguine of his chances, though he had had moments of confidence before she made the acquaintance of monsieur Champeroux. Monsieur Champeroux was connected with a financial paper to which nobody paid any attention, but in his time he had been something of a *viveur*, and shot tame pigeons, and fought tame duels, and he had an air of assurance that made the little notary look very insignificant. Gosselin was abashed by Champeroux, and angry at being so. He would often prepare small talk and resolve to assert himself on the next occasion, but when the occasion came he could never find any openings for the small talk. It was additionally galling to perceive that Champeroux recognised his rivalry with something like amusement.

As for the lady, it may be said that she admired Champeroux for his authoritative bearing, and approved Gosselin for his sympathetic nature, which the law had failed to sour. In other words, she had still to make up her mind, such as it was.

Though this was not one of the rush hours, the train was uncomfortably crowded. All the twenty-one passengers that the carriage was designed to contain seated were there, and all the forty-six passengers that it was designed to contain standing were there. As he clung to a handrail, Gosselin wished he had had the forethought to dispatch the flowers in the morning by a messenger, and make the journey unencumbered. Then, as the train jerked from Kléber, someone swayed against him with so much weight that only a feat of lightning speed saved the bouquet from destruction.

Making the clicks with his tongue, Gosselin saw, dismayed, that the offender was Champeroux.

" Pardon," said Champeroux, trying to lift his hand to his hat.

" Don't mention it," returned Gosselin with a scowl. He did not attempt to raise his own hat, since neither of his hands was free.

" We haven't too much room, hein ? " remarked Champeroux. There was a tinge of raillery in his gaze, as he noted the bouquet. " I wonder if we have the same objective ? "

" I much fear there is no doubt about it," thought Gosselin. And he answered coldly, " I go to pay my compliments to madame Balbi. It is her fête day."

" I, too," said the other. It was evident by

his composure that his own token of regard had preceded him, and Gosselin felt more inferior still. The zest with which he had anticipated the visit was gone. He regretted that he hadn't come earlier, or later; almost he regretted that he had come at all. He longed to be rid of Champeroux, but without an exhibition of the rankest jealousy, it was impossible to ignore him as they swayed shoulder to shoulder, and then alighted at the same moment, bound for the same spot.

They climbed from the station side by side; Champeroux elegant with a slim umbrella, and Gosselin stiffly guarding the bouquet.

"Ah, how good you are! It is delicious. But it is ravishing!" cried the lady, in tones of extreme surprise, when the pair had kissed her hand and congratulated her. And, having naturally expected it, she did not have to wait for a vase or water. "It makes my poor room enchanting, n'est-ce-pas?" she cooed.

To Champeroux' discomfiture, however, she made no mention of a basket of expensive roses that he had paid for, nor could his furtive glances discover it embellishing any of the furniture. Doubts assailed him. And when the meeting in the train had been explained to her, and coffee and cakes were circulating, and still she omitted to give him any thanks, the awkwardness of the situation compelled him to put a tentative inquiry. Whereupon it transpired that the basket hadn't come.

For once the advantage was with Gosselin. He could scarcely hide his elation.

"But it is outrageous!" exclaimed Champeroux, pale with chagrin. "It should have been here by ten o'clock. By ten o'clock, without fail. I stressed the point repeatedly. No, no, it will *not* be just as good by and by; I wished you to receive it when you woke. Such negligence is unpardonable; they promised me faithfully it should be delivered by ten. Mon Dieu! they shall not forget this affair in a hurry."

"Most irritating," murmured Gosselin, crossing his legs complacently.

But his superiority was short-lived. The next minute there was the sound of the bell, and the maid entered with a floral offering so impressive that he felt as if he were shrinking in his clothes. His own gift was unquestionably eclipsed; his rival was dominant once more. The notary sat humbled, and to his sensitive ear it seemed that their hostess's transports of delight had a sincerer ring now. The more tactfully she mingled her raptures with praises of his bouquet, the more bitterly he felt she must be thinking that it had cost a lot less than the basket.

" How everybody spoils me! What a lucky woman I am to have such friends," she said gaily. " Let me advise you both to try the St.-Honoré—it comes from the right place. Well, then, some bonbons? Alors, tell me things! What is the latest scandal? "

" Ma foi, that there is a cab strike just when my car is under repair! " said Champeroux. " Paris grows insufferable. I have been bored to tears. It is for you, dear lady, to furnish information. I come to hear how you have passed your fête day."

" You want to know? Well, I have been having my blood curdled," she said. " I have been hearing of a haunted house."

" Good. I am fond of ghosts—or should be fond of them if there were any."

" This is a fact, though, really! Nobody will live in it. It is just vacant again—and the people only went in last month."

" It should be obtainable at a reduced rent," remarked Gosselin, glad to find something to say.

" It is a villa, somewhere at Saint-Cloud. Nothing seems to happen except in one of the rooms upstairs. But at night, in that room, there are—footsteps."

" Echoes," opined Champeroux.

" That is what those people had said—but they have fled, like everybody else. They kept the room locked up, but it got to be too much for them, all the same. They had spent money on the house, but they told a cousin of the woman from whom I had the story, that they wouldn't remain in it for anything on earth. All night long, sometimes, those footsteps can be heard. Quite loud. They say you could swear some heavy creature was moving about there."

" A ghost in shoes," scoffed Champeroux. " However, if anyone goes in, nothing is visible, hein ? "

" Something *is* visible," said madame Balbi gravely. " That is certain."

" What is it ? "

" I have been wondering. I have heard of only one person who could say. There was a surgeon that had the house, and they made the room his study. *They* said ' echoes,' too. They were all very hale and hearty materialists, and said it would take more than echoes to drive *them* out. They said it was ' considerate of the ghost not to use the room till late.' The man used to work in it sometimes after supper. One morning they couldn't find him anywhere, so his wife went up to the room to see if he was there. He was on the floor, unconscious. After he had been brought to, he insisted on their all getting out of the house the same day. And he would never tell what he had seen! He said *there were things that should not be spoken of.*"

"Yes. I have heard other tales of the kind," said Champeroux, "but they are never to be authenticated. I would wager that one could spend a night in the room with no other sensation than ennui. I would spend a night in it myself, to satisfy you on the point."

"You are not serious?" asked madame Balbi, startled.

"But certainly I am serious," he affirmed, recognising the impression he had made. "I have been up against worse dangers than footsteps in my life," he added, with a humorous grimace. "Indeed, 'ennui' is going too far; before I had a night's sound sleep it would amuse me to form an opinion of those 'footsteps.' I beg you to do me the favour to ascertain the exact whereabouts of the mysterious abode—if it exists at all."

"You must have nerves of steel," she said,

with veneration. She turned to Gosselin. "Mustn't he have nerves of steel?"

Now, Gosselin, who had a marked aversion from the supernatural, had been unpleasantly affected by the narrative, and there was nothing he would have liked less than to spend a night in the sinister room. But Champeroux' bravery was clearly thrilling her, and, in the circumstances, it seemed essential to lie.

"To tell the truth," he said, "I am of the same mind as monsieur Champeroux. The footsteps are fascinating. I should be interested to go myself."

"Capital," said Champeroux, who didn't believe him for a moment. "We might go together some time, if it can be arranged."

"I think you are both marvellous," breathed the lady. "But I decline to provide that address. What misgivings I should suffer all night!"

Both men gazed at her with adoring and intrepid smiles—and Gosselin was infinitely relieved by her reply.

It was on the third subsequent Saturday, when he was congratulating himself on being her only visitor, that she staggered him by recurring to the villa. It appeared that, in spite of her laudable assertion, she had given the address to

Champeroux some days before, and that he was proposing to get busy. Gosselin's interior turned a somersault as he heard that his rival courteously inquired which night would be convenient to him, if he still wished to share the treat.

Desperately he deplored his unfortunate boast. But how could he take it back? How could he show the white feather, and let Champeroux sport all the laurels?

" One night would suit me as well as another," he managed to say; " I will speak to him about it." And when she went on, " I wish I hadn't mentioned the address—I didn't mean to," he had a leaping hope she was going to persuade him not to go.

To his consternation, she added, " Though I think it is gorgeous of you both to face it! I would give worlds to have the courage to go, too."

With a view to awakening her to the proper course for her to take he said emphatically, " Ah, that you should never do by *my* consent! No doubt, if we men were prudent we should abstain from going ourselves; one has heard of these adventures proving fatal. If, by some occult force, we should expire there we should not be the first corpses to be found in a haunted house."

"I blame myself for having talked about it," she sighed; "I feel responsible towards you both."

He wished to goodness she would omit the word "both" from her self-reproaches.

"As for that, I am not so keen on it but what I could bear to miss the experience," he told her; "personally, I would sacrifice my desire rather than you should suffer disquietude. But I can hardly let monsieur Champeroux down; I cannot leave monsieur Champeroux to go alone." He regarded her with a silent prayer that she would say that he could.

But she only said idiotically, "Well, it is ever so sporting of you both! No, of course you are right. It is certainly better there should be two of you."

Gosselin drew nearer to her emotionally. She wasn't so divine in his eyes during this scene as hitherto—in fact, she was exasperating him; but she was very, very pretty, and, wisely or the reverse, he was in love with her. If she were to accept him at once there wouldn't be any need to flaunt his temerity! He could say grandly that, as her future husband, he took no chances.

"Listen," he exclaimed. "I embark on this diversion with tremendous zest; to investigate a haunted house has always been an ambition of mine. Nevertheless, I recognise that there is an element of peril—one would be foolish to ignore it. It is possible I may not escape alive. While I am still with you there is something I must say. I love you. Ah, you cannot have been blind to my devotion—you cannot have failed to see what your beauty and your charm have done to me. I am no longer the same man; the dry-as-dust notary is transformed. I think of you constantly. The thought of you comes between me and cases till the practice suffers. Have pity! I beseech you to be my wife."

" My friend," she murmured, moved. " How shall I answer? I have the warmest regard for you, the greatest esteem—never, indeed, have I respected you so highly as now, when I find that you are fearless—but . . . I am not sure. Perhaps, one day. . . . Give me time to reflect."

That was just what he couldn't afford to give her.

" It is that Champeroux who has come between us," he burst out resentfully, "—the man I am going to protect! Before you knew him there was a chance for me."

" I have not said but what there is a chance still," she replied with dignity.

" You are all my world. Your decision means more to me than you know ! "

" I entreat you give me time," she pleaded.

It was a good thing the day was Saturday, for there was no room in his mind for clients when he left her. He had strong need of sustenance, and he dined at a noted restaurant that, as yet, had not deteriorated under the influence of the English and Americans, who showed their unconsciousness of perfect cooking by pouring clouds of tobacco smoke over all the food. He must communicate with Champeroux ! It couldn't be avoided. Of course he could pretend to have understood that it was Champeroux who was to suggest the appointment, and might seem very cross that he hadn't done so, but—would she credit the defence ? He thought not. It was painfully thin. And even if she did, Champeroux would have all the glory. . . . The dinner didn't do much for him.

He did not rush to communicate, on that day, or the next; but in his little salon, when Augustine, his bonne, had done creaking to pull the curtains straighter, and to fiddle with the lamps, he went to the telephone at last. And he hoped that Champeroux was out.

" Allô, allô ! Monsieur Gosselin speaking.

Q

... Ah, it is you, monsieur! I ring up to thank you for your amiable message. It is perfect."

"I shall arrange with the agent to lend me the key of the house," boomed Champeroux' tones. "And he must supply a chair or two. What night shall we decide on?"

"Ah, but any night you please," said Gosselin, wet with perspiration.

"It is a little difficult just now," said Champeroux; "I am overwhelmed with work. One moment! I will have a look at my diary. . . . Are you there? Shall we say some night the week after next?"

It was a respite! "One can wait till then," assented Gosselin.

"Let us say Saturday then. Does that suit you?"

"Quite." If the conversation lasted long, he feared his voice would fail him.

"Bien. By the way, he will have to give us a fire, too. Come, the thing may not be uninteresting, hein?"

"I confess I am hopeful," responded Gosselin.

"Well, we will settle everything later on. I shall speak to him in good time. A bientôt, monsieur."

" A bientôt," panted Gosselin, laying his head on the table.

Champeroux replaced the receiver with sharp annoyance. He had not really wanted to learn the address, nor, when it was told to him, had he meant to do more than make an elaborate note of it in madame Balbi's presence. To find his facetious invitation to Gosselin accepted took him wholly aback. It was distinctly vexatious. It threatened to commit him to a course that would be repellent, to say the least of it; a bare room that had been long unoccupied would be a damp and damnable place to spend a winter's night in ! He wished that he had refrained from the flourish of inquiring whether the notary still sought to go. He wished, too, that he had not insisted so much on his own eagerness to examine the room. . . . This fellow's butting in made the situation very awkward !

The more he thought of it, the less it appealed to him; and he thought of it frequently as the days went by, though he neglected to approach the agent. He was incensed against madame Balbi for having put him in the pass. Her folly was thrusting him into acute discomfort—and possibly into something worse. He had no definite belief in ghosts, but, after all, there might be such things ! If her fascinations had been a shade less potent, he would have expressed his disapproval of her action in the most practical way. Certainly, after they were married, he would read her a lecture !

She need never have known whether he had gone, or not, if it had not been for this intrusive Gosselin !—it would not have been difficult to *say* he had gone. He was continuously amazed that the fellow's desire to show off had strung him to such a pitch; and as the formidable Saturday drew nearer, he began to wonder uneasily whether he could scare him into backing out. At any rate, the experiment was worth trying !

Meanwhile the lady looked forward, with the keenest curiosity, to their reporting what happened on Saturday. And Gosselin had begun to derive some hope from the long silence. When Champeroux' masterful voice boomed over the line again, asking him to call, the disappointment was deep. He was an abstemious man, but he absorbed brandy bountifully before he went.

" Well, I have good news for you," said Champeroux cheerily. " We shall not be risking pneumonia in that room for nothing.' I hear it is mildewed, by the way. I have been inquiring into the matter, and there is no doubt that something very weird goes on there."

"So?" said Gosselin, clenching his teeth, in case they chattered.

"I discover I was wrong in mocking at that story of the surgeon; it is established that there *was* such a tenant. It appears that he never rallied from the shock. He was removed to an asylum. Not that I anticipate that's happening to *us*," he added, with a laugh; "we are not nervous subjects. All the same, it seems certain we shall have a view of something out of the ordinary to compensate for the pneumonia."

Gosselin felt desperately in need of a cigarette, but his hands were trembling so much that he was ashamed to take them out of his pockets. In spite of his funk, and the brandy, though, he was not wholly befuddled, and he questioned why Champeroux should relate the loathly details to him with such gusto. Whether they were true, or false, his legal intelligence found the gusto suspicious. He said in his own mind, "Your aim is to frighten me out, and have all the kudos yourself, rascal! The dodge won't work." And aloud he said:

"Fine! Besides, with luck, we may escape the pneumonia."

"Parfaitement. The right spirit!" cried Champeroux heartily. And he reflected, "You are shaking in your shoes, you humbug. Wait! I shall see you turn tail yet."

"You have made all arrangements with the agent?" asked Gosselin.

"So far, no—I have not had the time," replied Champeroux a little irritably; "I mean to do so to-morrow. I will let you hear. Yes, my inquiries have been encouraging; all that was told to us has been fully substantiated. The villa is shunned, absolutely. Ma foi! it is astounding. All my life I have denied the supernatural—and I find it manifested at Saint-Cloud! I ask myself continually what it can be, this phenomenon that comes into the room from—who knows where? A creature that is not of this world, but that has footsteps that can be heard, and hands that are—— Ah, you do not know about the hands! That reminds me; I am taking my revolver; I counsel you to take yours. Figure yourself that, long before the tragedy of the surgeon—— You care to hear?"

By dint of will-power Gosselin nodded: to say "yes" was more than he could do.

"Long before the surgeon had been driven insane, there was some morbid individual that took the Villa Fernande specially to investigate the mystery. He was a bachelor, and an orphan, and had no one to consider but himself, and he had his bed put in the room. He slept in it once only. When the femme de ménage went in with his coffee next day she fell over his body, lying broken behind the door—he had evidently been trying to get out. The contusions on the body indicated that it had been gripped by something that had fingers, of human shape, eleven inches long."

Gosselin was livid. "It is incredible," he gasped.

"Ah," rejoined Champeroux wildly, "do I not say so, myself, in moments? I say to myself, 'It is beyond belief that such things can be!' But—what will you? We cannot ignore the evidence of the body! However, nothing that I have learnt suggests that the man was provided with a pistol; he foresaw a ghost, not a monster. Since the creature is tangible, it can be shot."

Mentally he exclaimed, "Good business! I bet I shall hear from you to-morrow that you have changed your mind. And on Sunday I shall tell her that I went alone."

Intensely Gosselin wanted to change his mind. But jealousy forbade him to do it. And when

Champeroux telephoned, in high hopes, to say that arrangements were progressing, he found the message met with feigned composure.

" Ah, it goes too far," raged Champeroux, banging the receiver back. " He forces me really to approach the agent now—I shall actually have to take chances in the cursed room ! "

Nevertheless, when he rang up again on Friday, hope was still lingering in his breast.

" Alors, I have talked twice with the agent over the 'phone to-day," he announced. " All is well. I am promised chairs, and that there shall be a fire, of sorts. I suggest we should arrive to-morrow at midnight; I shall call for you about eleven-thirty. We shall go in my car, of course."

" That will be delightful," quavered Gosselin, perhaps a second late.

Champeroux made a furious and insulting gesture. He went on, less buoyantly, " By the by, the agency seems to be within a stone's throw of your own apartment—it is in the rue Balzac. I wonder if it would trouble you to look in there and take the keys ? The name is Besier."

" With pleasure," said Gosselin; " I pass that agency twice a day."

" Trop aimable. There should be two—the keys of the door, and the garden gate."

" Depend upon me."

" At eleven-thirty then ? "

" At eleven-thirty."

" Bien.   Do not omit to bring your revolver. Well, my friend—till to-morrow ! "

" Till to-morrow, my friend ! "

They turned from their telephones, hating each other.

Gosselin knew no sleep that night.   He was temperamentally unfit to monkey with the supernatural, and, when he rose in the morning, he was as pale as a ghost himself.   He thought he could read grave misgivings in the agent's face, when the dreadful keys were passed across the counter; and as the day developed, the poor man's stomach became so much disordered that only brandy would stay down.

By the afternoon, the wobbling of his knees threatened collapse before midnight.   And as the evening lengthened, the sudden bellow of any passing car set him dithering with the fear that he had been fetched too soon.   Only love, and pride, and brandy restrained him from giving in now.   No lie within the scope of human ingenuity could disguise the fact that he had been afraid !   How Champeroux would swank, and She would freeze !

" Ah, mon Dieu, mon Dieu," he wailed, " I should be throwing her into his arms ! "

The thought nerved him to a fresh display of courage. By a supreme effort Gosselin raised his head firmly and resolved to see the thing through. Then he grabbed his overcoat, jammed on his hat, and thrust the keys in the servant's hands. " A gentleman is coming. Give him these ! " he gibbered. " Say I regret I had to go out."

He was disgraced ! The night air cooled his heated brow, but it did nothing for his hot shame. His shame was as deep as his relief, as he slunk along the side-walks till, feeling too weak to walk, he dropped on to a café chair, and sat cowering before the abasement of the morrow. When he realised that a waiter was standing patiently before him, he asked for coffee. Then, remembering that he had eaten nothing all day, he ordered a sandwich too. But the coffee was cold before he thought to sip it, and the sandwich lay unbitten when the noise of the orchestra drove him distractedly away.

He longed to be in bed, but he could not conquer the misgiving that, if he didn't stay out for a long while, he might find Champeroux waiting for him when he went back. So he crawled about the streets till his protesting legs compelled him to put in time on the terrace of another café. And there, too, he sat bowed before the vision of madame Balbi's face when his cowardice was known to her. Tears sprang to his eyes, in imagining the icy tones in which she would address him. And worse! If something disastrous should happen in that room to-night? She would accuse him of having " deserted " Champeroux! No doubt she would wildly employ the term " desert "!

At last, by two o'clock, he felt it must be safe to return, and, immersed in misery, he dropped into bed without having cleaned his teeth, or wound his watch. But his apprehensions kept him awake for hours, and it was broad daylight before nightmares came to him.

Augustine with his breakfast tray brought him back to hideous realities. He eyed her haggardly, as she creaked to the window and let the feeble sunshine in.

" What did the gentleman say? " he groaned.

" Quoi? " she asked.

" What did the gentleman say when you gave him the keys? "

" Nobody came," said Augustine stolidly. " There is a letter for monsieur on the tray."

A full minute passed before his startled gaze

was withdrawn from the window—he lay motionless, with his mouth open. Then, turning his head, as in a trance, he saw that the name of Champeroux' financial rag was printed on the envelope. He snatched it. The letter was brief :

" A thousand apologies for my non-appearance. I am suddenly detained. Between ourselves, the depreciation of the franc threatens a crisis in the Chambre, and Poincaré 'phones asking to confer with me. This is strictly confidential. I am profoundly grieved to miss our excursion, but the sacrifice must be made. My paramount duty is to France."

Gosselin drew a long, slow breath, and lay staring into vacancy again. Champeroux had been afraid ! All the time Champeroux had been afraid, too ! The intensity of the little man's relief was equalled by the violence of his resentment. He thought of his long, terrified anticipation, of the agonies of yesterday, the tortures of last night. And it had all been needless. Champeroux had never meant to go. All the time Champeroux had been bluffing him. Were they merely to cry quits now ? No !

He replied by a pencilled scrawl :

" I survive ! I rejoice, for your sake, that

Poincaré withheld you. The horrors I have looked upon surpassed our worst imaginings."

Champeroux threw the note into the waste-paper basket. "You have got the best of it," he said savagely. "But nothing would ever persuade me that you went."

Madame Balbi took an unfavourable view of his defection, saying that, in any case, Poincaré could very well have waited for a day. And when Gosselin described to her his lonely entrance into the forbidding room, and frankly admitted he had been nervous, all her woman's heart went out to him.

"And what is the secret of the footsteps?" she whispered, awestruck in his arms.

"Dearest," said Gosselin solemnly, "that you must never ask me! Help me to forget. The surgeon was right—*there are things that should not be spoken of.*"

A CURE FOR DYSPEPSIA

I HAD found the comedian at a lodging-house in Bootle. We talked in the twilight. The mantelpiece was decorated with photographs of all the landlady's relations, and a half-sheet of notepaper, framed under glass; its cryptic message I couldn't guess at from my chair. I said, " I thought you'd be a West-End star by now." And Copas, pointing to the puzzle on the mantelpiece, replied, " The thing that wrecked my life was—that ! "

He wiped away a tear. I was moved. I faltered, " Don't cry."

" I'm not—in the sense you mean," he said; " it's chronic. I'm in high spirits. You mayn't think so, watching me weep, but I'm in high spirits at seeing you again. It was this way. I had been in the profession so long that I had given up putting my age back; people could count. I had been getting big notices and small salaries for donkeys' years, but never been able to get a chance in London. Well, I swore to save enough money to keep body and soul together for twelve months, and then to live on porridge in London till I did get a footing there. When I say ' porridge ' it's a figure of speech, because porridge isn't easy to digest, and I was bothered with dyspepsia.   I had tried all sorts of things for it; bicarbonate of soda was the only one that did any good, and that didn't do much. Happen to have a cigarette on you ?

" It was uphill work, the saving; as soon as I was making any progress, a tour would come to an end, and there'd be weeks or months before I got into anything else; but I scraped the money together by the time I was sweet-and-forty.   And then a complication had occurred.   I'm not going to say she was the only girl I have ever loved, but she was the only girl I ever wanted to marry.   I don't mind telling you I'd have scrapped my schedule and married her right away if she had agreed.   But she was a chum.   ' Not much,' she said.   ' You'll go to London just as you meant to do, and if the try turns out well, I'll marry you then—and if it *doesn't* turn out well, I'll marry you then.   But I'm not such a sentimental idiot as to spoil a plan you've been building on for years.'   Level-headed.   Had a mind of her own."

" Nice girl," I remarked.

"Her name was Evelyn," he said, as if that accounted for it. "Well, I resigned from the tour we were out with, and started for the lights o' London on a Saturday night after the show. She came to the station to see me off. I promised I'd write to her every day. We weren't to be apart for long, because the tour was finishing soon, and her home was in London, but I felt a bit like the hero of the old, old story: I loved, and was loved—and I was going to London town to seek my fortune.

"Yep. . . . Well, I did the usual things for a month or so without getting any forrader, and then something extraordinary happened. In the Strand, one day, I saw Gorringe coming along. I had created a part in a play of his in the Pudston Repertory, but that was two or three years before; I hardly expected him to remember me, especially as he had got on since. Imagine my surprise! He exclaimed, 'What, Copas! You're the very man I've been thinking of. Are you free for the spring?'—and he said that, personally, he'd like to have me for the next production at the Colonnade!"

"Do you mean the Gorringe that wrote *The Blue Canary*?" I inquired.

Copas nodded. "It was *The Blue Canary* he

was talking about.   I pulled myself together, and
did hearken unto him.   He couldn't say anything
definite, but he offered to read the piece to me if
I went to his flat next day—and I didn't forget
to go.   I can't say the piece struck me as a
winner, but the part was big.   My only fear was
that he wouldn't have weight enough with the
management to get me in.   Gorringe thought it
would be all right if I took low terms.   He said
he had spoken to them about me already, and
he made an appointment for me to go and see
them.

"A walk-over!   They settled with me for
fifteen pounds a week.   The part was worth
sixty, but they were giving me the chance of my
life, as they didn't omit to mention.   I had had
to wait for it till I was forty, but my chance had
come; in my middle-age the tide had turned at
last!   I rushed to a post-office to wire to Evelyn.
Wedding bells were pealing in my brain.   Celes-
tial hands showered rice and confetti.   It *wasn't*
a post-office; it was Elysium with a Beauty
Chorus.

"I didn't wire her after all; the news was too
splendiferous for a wire.   The company was at
Derby, and I made a sprint for a toothbrush, and
went down to her.   See the conquering hero

R

comes! Got in about tea-time. Took a cab to her diggings. Found her washing her hair. Dripped all down my neck as I told her. Glorious moment, glorious afternoon. Inclined to say it was the happiest afternoon I ever had. I told her the piece was expected to go into rehearsal in about three months' time, and she said she'd marry me a fortnight after the production if it was a success. I wasn't keen on the ' if,' but she said if it was a frost I shouldn't have done myself much good by the engagement. She wanted to hear all about the part. So did the boys at the theatre afterwards. They couldn't help showing they were jealous, but it takes a mighty great actor to dissemble jealousy. That Derby trip was fine; and I went back to London a proud man, and had more to eat now—and more dyspepsia.

" The dyspepsia was a nuisance, and on the strength of my prospects, I thought I'd treat myself to a first-class doctor. I had been to one chap already about it, and this time I made up my mind to go to the best physician I could hear of. I wrote to Ovid-Meanwell. To receive an answer on such distinguished stationery was an event in my lowly life, and when the stately butler ushered me into the high-toned waiting-room, I felt I had gone into Society. I was half sorry when my cue came.

"Meanwell was sitting at his table, opposite the door. Taking smile. Beautifully dressed. Steady, observant eyes. His eyes seemed to have diagnosed me before I reached the chair. It'd be a grand make-up for the part of physician; I couldn't improve on it. I liked him immensely; we had quite a friendly chat—and it was nice to think of the smart people in the other room waiting their turn and cursing me. But after he had put a lot of questions, and examined my tummy, he told me he wasn't sanguine of pills and potions doing the trick. He said that perhaps I ought to wear glasses.

"'Glasses?' I said. 'What for? My sight is my strong suit. I haven't any trouble with my sight, I'm happy to say!'

"'You may have astigmatism without knowing it,' he said; 'astigmatism would explain your dyspepsia. I can't find any local reason for it. What I should like you to do is, to see an eye man. You can try this prescription first if you like, but the best thing would be for you to go and see Superman. If Superman puts you into glasses, you can be very sure you need them—and you'll say good-bye to your dyspepsia.'

"Well, it was a blow to find I had got to pay an oculist too—but Meanwell was so strong on the point, and so jolly sincere that I said I'd go.

"'What is your fee?' I asked.

"'Two guineas,' he said briskly. Which was very decent of him, for his fee was really three. Gimme another cigarette.

"Superman was on his feet, restlessly, when I was shown in. A very rapid gentleman. Had a cut-it-short, time-is-money manner. Gave me the feeling it was intrusive of me to consult him. He hustled me into a chair—told me to look through some contraption, with himself at the other end; said the cause of my dyspepsia was astigmatism—and darted to his desk to prescribe three pairs of glasses before I could say 'Hell!'

"'Distance, close work, and bifocals,' he gabbled. 'You know what they are? You can write, and look across at—er—— You'll find them a convenience when you're writing cheques.'

"I said, 'I don't write any.'

"'Constant use. Never be without them—one pair or another. That'll be the end of your dyspepsia.'

"'I can't wear glasses on the stage,' I told him.

"'Well, put them on again directly you come off it. They'll make a different man of you.

You'll have more vigour, be in better spirits. You'll work better, sleep better, jump out of bed in the morning feeling twenty years younger. You've been fighting to correct your astigmatism unconsciously. Strain on the nervous system. Half the things people have got the matter with them are due to astigmatism, if they only knew it. They go to doctors. That's no good; drugs won't cure them. What they need is the right glasses. Scores of my patients tell me life wasn't worth living before they came to me. Take this to Swank's.'

" I said humbly, ' I can't afford a fashion-able——'

" ' No place like Swank's,' he insisted, ' fine work. I'm giving you fused lenses in the bifocals. They cost more, but the others get dirt in the join —black line across the eyes. There ! ' He scrawled something on the envelope. ' They'll know what that means. That's a private mark— they won't ruin you.'

" ' What is your fee ? ' I asked.

" ' To *you* two guineas. My fee is three,' he declaimed. And I half expected to hear him call ' Next please ! '

" I had left my umbrella in the waiting-room, and when I went in for it I heard one woman say to another mordantly, ' That's two in ten minutes ! '

" Well, I'm bound to admit Swank's took no end of pains making the things fit me—and the cases they put 'em in were ravishing. But, great Scot ! they knew how to charge, private mark or not. O, the wild charge they made ! I don't know if all the world wondered, but *I* wondered what Superman's share in the business was. The place was humming with his patients whenever I went. At every age—from the cradle to the grave. All sent to buy glasses at Swank's ! . . .

" Yep. My seeing a posh physician had let me in for about six times as much as I expected. Still, with fifteen quid a week coming along directly I bore up. I found my new possessions made my eyes tired, but I wrote a glowing account to Evelyn of the wonders they were to do. Her answer disappointed me; she didn't seem to see what a wise step I had taken. She said, ' Wouldn't glasses make me look much older, and be a drawback professionally ?—and she didn't think the dyspepsia had been very bad.' Silly thing to say. Whose stomach was it ?

" Well, as I tell you, I had never known what it was to have my eyes worry me before, but soon they were most uncomfortable. Tired, and wet too. Tears trickled down my cheeks. It was misery to try to read the newspaper. I shuddered to think the costly cure might be the reason, but there didn't seem to be anything else to explain it. I had to go back to Superman. I said, 'D'ye know, I—I'm not sure these glasses suit me.'

" I was rather afraid he might be offended, but he was only dryly amused. Told me they had nothing to do with it at all. 'Pure coincidence,' he said, and prescribed a lotion. 'Soon put you right. Fine stuff. Dyspepsia better?'

" 'Not any better yet,' I said.

" 'It wouldn't be,' he said. 'You won't know yourself in another month. *Live* in your glasses. Remember they're doing you good every minute. They do the work, and your nervous system is taking a rest—that's the idea. There was a lady in here this morning; she used to be a neurasthenic wreck; she was telling me she goes about the house singing before breakfast now. Use the lotion regularly. To *you* two guineas.'

" I used it regularly, and got worse. The tears had more vigour, if *I* hadn't. I had thought it as well not to mention the coincidence to Evelyn; but I'd become a bit slack in my correspondence

with her—it's not easy to be a copious corre-
spondent if you have to stop every other minute
to mop your eyes, and wipe the drops off your
specs—and she got the notion that my love for
her was waning. Very painful. Of course I
explained then. And, sure enough, she wrote,
'Didn't the *strange coincidence* seem all the more
reason for giving the wretched things up?' As
I said to her, when she came back to London the
next week, she had taken an unreasoning prejudice
against them from the first. I said, 'Surely you
must see for yourself it would be presumption for
you or me to question the pronouncements of the
famous Superman? Scores of his patients used
to wish themselves dead before his science made
their lives worth living. For heaven's sake,'
I said, ' don't let my cure become a bone of con-
tention between us, Evelyn; do not let his glasses
blind us to the joy of our meeting! They may
not have improved my appearance——'

" ' Have they improved *anything?* ' she asked.

" ' But they are not prescribed as an ornament,'
I went on patiently; ' they are prescribed as an
infallible cure for my dyspepsia. By a marvellous
oculist, admired by Ovid-Meanwell. I'm told I
shan't know myself in another month.'

" ' *I* hardly know you now,' she said. ' It's

awful. How in the world do you think you're going to rehearse like that? Why, you won't be able to see to read the part!'

"Well, that was just what was putting the wind up me—and I went to Superman again. On this occasion he found he had 'made a slight mistake in one of the lenses.' 'You understand how it happened?' he asked. I understood damned well how it happened—he had been in too much hurry; but I just said 'Yes,' and it seemed to satisfy him. Anyhow, I was no better off with the new lens than the old one. The only difference it made was to increase the expenses. And the date for the rehearsals to start drew nearer and nearer.

"I was in a panic. I went to Meanwell's, without an appointment. Stately butler, very dubious. Meanwell, very human. I told him I couldn't go on with the infernal things—said I had consulted him for my stomach, not my eyes. Bit hysterical. Strode about his important room as if it had been my lodging in Camberwell; and he let me do it—and then didn't take a fee. But he swore by Superman. And he said if I gave the glasses up now, I might have cataract.

"That stopped me striding. 'What?' I gasped.

"'Yes,' he said. 'Stick to them! I'm

advising you to do just what I should do myself. My dear fellow, put your faith in Superman.'

"There I was : Meanwell urging one course, and Evelyn urging the other—an altercation every time we met !—and the first rehearsal only a week ahead. The day that I had looked forward to for half a lifetime, the day that was to be the—the harbinger of my London reputation, of my marriage, had become a menace, a spectre of foreboding ! I was physically unfit now—and I quailed. Why don't you leave your cigarette-case on the table ? . . .

"Yep . . . the stage was pretty dark, and the first morning they didn't notice anything when I went in. And I took care not to be prominent before I was obliged to. But, what with the darkness, and a couple of ponds in my eyes, and the rotten typewriting, I was well up against it when I did have to go on—even before the first tears rolled. I flicked away a few debonairly with my fingers, but soon my handkerchief was indispensable, and I felt the management begin to fidget.

"'Had to take to glasses, I see, Copas,' said Gorringe later on.

"'What ?' I said. 'Glasses ? Oh, I wear them for dyspepsia. Touch of astigmatism;

dyspepsia is often due to astigmatism, if people only knew. They ought to go and see Superman about their eyes.'

" ' Yours are watering very badly, aren't they ? ' he said.

" ' Oh, that ? ' I said. ' That's nothing—nothing at all. Caught a slight cold in them, I fancy—motoring. That'll pass in a day or two.'

" To avoid the struggle to read much on the stage next day, I sat up all night studying the part —in fact, I sat up for three nights. But how much studying was to be done in three nights when I was busy with the handkerchief most of the time ? I practised with it in front of a mirror at home, so as to get easier at the rehearsals. The drill was : 1, Withdraw handkerchief. 2, Remove glasses. 3, Wipe eyes. 4, Wipe glasses. 5, Resume glasses. 6, Restore handkerchief. It all had to be done while I was holding the part open, and I required a third hand. I crashed before I was proficient. The management and Gorringe were ' very sorry, but the unfortunate state of my eyes—— They must get someone else to play the part.' I couldn't blame them; they wanted a comedian, not a juggler."

Copas paused. I made a compassionate noise. He stared at the hieroglyphics in the frame, and the cigarette burnt itself out between his fingers. He took another.

"Looking back," he groaned, "I can't reproach her; but there was a noticeable reserve in Evelyn's sympathy. Mark you, it wasn't only that I had lost the engagement at the Colonnade; it wasn't only that my hope of getting married directly was a vanished dream. There was the question how I was to rehearse for *any* part in the state I was in! I couldn't expect an engagement at all—unless they cast me for Niobe, or 'Voices off.' It couldn't be helped—I had to spend two guineas more and go to Superman for another lotion!

"This time he discovered that my eyes watered because 'my lachrymal ducts were congested.' I thought he might have made the discovery sooner, but he was so triumphant about it that I was glad I had gone. He said he'd open them for me if I went again on Thursday, and it bucked me to such an extent to think I should be able to earn my living again that I made the mistake of telling Evelyn.

"I might have known! She kept begging me to see some other oculist instead. We had very sharp words.

"I found it was to be no joke, when I went on Thursday. Superman was dressed up in white, and there was a nurse in the room. He took a pair of scissors, and snipped bits off the corners of my eyes, and then he stuffed long metal things, as thick as the handle of my safety razor, down the ducts. 'Styles' he called them. My face felt as if it would burst when he had jammed them down. And he told me they had got to stop in for three months !

" ' What do I owe you ? ' I moaned.

" ' Well, if you were Vanderbilt I should charge you fifty guineas for that operation,' he said; ' but as it is, suppose we say five guineas each eye ? '

" The shock, on top of the pain, nearly made me lose my senses. But not quite. I said, ' Suppose we say five guineas both eyes ! '

" What he *hadn't* told me was, that my eyes would water more still till the styles were taken out. No words, nothing that could be uttered, could give you the faintest notion of what I went through for three months. What with the blasted glasses *and* the bulging styles I was nearly blind. The only thing I even *tried* to read, during three months, was a notice of *The Blue Canary*— and it didn't cheer me up to see I had missed being in a big success !

" I'll be candid : I was not the perfect lover. When Evelyn called me bad-tempered I wasn't 'falsely accused.' We didn't meet so often now —and when we did meet, there was generally a dispute about Superman. I can't say I found the long days any longer when she went on the road again, though my only occupation was to pray for the end of the three months.

"I felt an old man by the time it came. He took the styles out, and said proudly, 'Now you'll find your eyes will be all right!' But I didn't. They remained just as wet as they had been when he put the things in. My fund was sinking fast, but—what was I to do?—I went to him for one lotion after another at two guineas a visit. And always I asked, distracted and dyspeptic, if the glasses weren't to blame—and always he smiled his pre-eminent smile at the foolishness of my question.

"I had written to Evelyn on the subject— sketchily, with the best intentions; and, in the epoch of the fourth lotion, she wrote that she was afraid we should never be happy together, and broke our engagement off. To tell you the truth, I don't know that I felt it so much then as I have done since. Anyhow, there was nothing for me to say. . . . Soon afterwards I became a pensioner on charity. *The Blue Canary* was still running— like my eyes.

"Yep . . . I threw the glasses away a little later

on, by other oculists' advice—and the downpour slackened, and I went back to the road. But my eyes will never be quite right any more—I wore the things too long for that. I'm told, too, that the operation to put a stop to the harm the glasses were doing, did more harm still. And Evelyn is married now; and I hear he ill-treats her. And it's too late for me to save enough money again to try my luck in London." He rose, his brooding gaze fixed upon the paper on the mantelpiece. " Those glasses," he said shakily, " lost me the girl I wanted for my wife; they wiped out my savings; they deprived me of ten months' engagement at fifteen pounds a week—and they've queered my career for the rest of my days! So I put the prescription for them in a frame—when you've paid as much as all that for anything, you ought to take care of it. In the first year alone, the pecuniary cost of that cure for dyspepsia was six hundred and eighty-seven pounds—and its cost will go on mounting till I die. The only solace in my life is—this ! "

I saw, with horror, a sinister-looking white powder in his hand.

" My God ! " I panted. " Not cocaine ? "

" No," he said; " bicarbonate of soda for the dyspepsia."

W H E N two young men, called Tricotrin and Pitou, lived in Paris, and they had gone to bed one December night, there came a peremptory pealing at the street door bell.

" Get up ! I think the house must be on fire ! " said the composer.

" What of it ?   I am only a lodger," yawned the poet.

" Don't plagiarise," said Pitou sharply; " great minds are original even in conflagrations.   Now, what the devil is it all about ? "   And opening the window, he looked out into a snowstorm.

" Allô ! Is that you, Pitou ? " inquired a figure from the pavement.   " It's I, Lajeunie."

" I might have known it," complained Pitou, withdrawing his head.   And he shouted : " This reminds me : I have often meant to inquire into your preference for discharging your social obligations in the middle of the night.   What is the true inwardness of it ?   Haven't you heard that visits are permissible at other hours ? "

"I came on impulse," called the novelist apologetically; "I am very much affected by something that has happened. Make haste and let me in—I'm getting frozen here."

"Can you tell me the right time?"

"Time? I don't know. Two o'clock. Hurry up!"

"It's not as if I hadn't heard your spirited solo on a door-bell at two o'clock in the morning before," continued the composer. "What piques my curiosity is your habitual choice of such an hour for calling on your friends. Is it that you're reluctant to interrupt their work by coming before they have gone to sleep? Let us discuss the matter fully."

"Open the door!" thundered the novelist. "Mon Dieu! do you wish me to get pneumonia?"

He climbed to the attic presently, a rivulet running from his hat. And Tricotrin said politely, "Good-morning, Lajeunie. Is it a fine day? Take a seat, and cheer us up. Your arrival is most opportune, for we always wonder what to do with ourselves about this time."

"I am not in a mood for your archaic humour," said Lajeunie, shaking his hat over the bed. "And if I know anything about you, you will

s

be no less touched than *I* am. I have wept this evening ! "

The pair regarded him more seriously.

" Our hearts are in their normal condition," affirmed Pitou. " What's up, cocky ? "

Lajeunie helped himself to the last of the poet's cigarettes. " You may remember that I once presented you to a former actor called Papa Tripier ? "

" I entertain a vast respect for him," said Tricotrin. " A sprightly octogenarian who resides in a boarding-house and has three meals every day. Does he still recount the latest news of Louis-Philippe ? "

" He scarcely mentions Louis-Philippe any more; he is much changed since you met him. I was at the boarding-house to see him this evening, and my heart bled for him. They ill-treat him there."

" What's that ? " cried the young men, shocked.

" It's quite true. They ill-treat him. That is to say, they insult him; they pick out the worst bits on the dishes for him; recently they have put him into a bedroom that used to be frankly a cellar. He suffers from rheumatism—and wall-paper and linoleum don't alter the fact that the walls are damp and the floor is stone. It's piteous. I could hardly control my indignation.

And if you knew how good he has been to the
wretches in his time! He was the friend of the
family in the days when he got big salaries.
The gifts that he used to make them! It was
because they were his friends that he gave up
his little flat and went to board with them; old
people in France do not care to live alone, of
course—they are generally murdered. He tells
me that butter would not melt in their mouths
at the beginning, but when they felt sure of
him, they took more and more advantage."

"But, good heavens! why stop there? There
are other boarding-houses."

"There are others, but he is too old to look
for one; at eighty years of age, more or less, one
is not adventurous. Also it is not so simple a
matter as it sounds for him to make a change;
you may be sure I put the point to him. I was
bound to admit that there were difficulties. The
pictures, and even the furniture in the cellar are
his own—relics of his flat, and his career; his
head swims at the thought of such a wholesale
removal. To-day, too, he has only just enough
to keep him, and he is, somehow, in arrears with
his payments; before he could go he would have
to settle up. He said to me: 'It is the cellar
I shall live and die in—unless I draw a prize in

the Lottery! There is nothing but that to set
me free.' That is his dream—that one day he
may draw a prize in the Lottery. He denies himself tobacco, and washes his linen in the basin
that he may buy a ticket sometimes. The woman
taunted him with it in my presence; 'He is a
laundress,' she jeered. 'Monsieur Tripier is a
laundress now! Well, have you won a million
in the Lottery, monsieur Tripier? That's why
he looks so joyful—he has won the first prize.'
And then to her daughter, in a voice that all
the boarders could hear, 'Dotard!' The daughter, giggling at these pleasantries, had on a gold
bracelet that had been a present from the old
man she mocked."

"The beasts! I begin to understand what
you want of us," exclaimed Tricotrin. "You
did well to come. Papa Tripier must be rescued
from this den. Eh, Pitou?"

"You bet!" said Pitou, who was pale with
sympathy. "How much does he owe the
hogs?"

"I understand that it is about two hundred
francs," said the novelist deprecatingly. "Personally I could contribute thirty. But you realise
that we shall have more to do than raise the
money—it's up to us to find a suitable place for

him, and face the rumpus that the devil will make when she hears she is to lose him. She is a violent woman, and Papa himself is far too unnerved to defy her. My own idea was that the best plan would be for us to get him quietly out of the house without letting her suspect he wasn't coming back."

"And his goods and chattels?" asked Tricotrin.

"When he had gone, we could return with a van and remove them."

"Not bad. The first thing, though, is to find out whether he has enough pluck left to be amenable; as a student of humanity, I may tell you that an ancient with a cowed spirit is an awkward victim to liberate. It horrifies me to hear of the change in him; when I saw him he was as mischievous as a monkey. Listen! If we called on him together? He would not resent our interest—we are all artists? Where is the dungeon situated?"

"It is run by a madame Louchart, in Grisy-sur-Marne. I missed the last tram back, and was obliged to foot it; that was what made me so late. Yes, we might all go out and lunch at the house—I suppose, if we get there early, she can raise enough food. What do you say?"

" As we have only work to do, I say there's nothing to prevent us. You had better stop here to-night," said Tricotrin. " I shall be glad to renew my acquaintance with the gentleman."

He was so small, so quaint, so unassuming a person, Papa Tripier, in his little skull-cap, that it was difficult to understand how anyone could be cruel to him. But his sufferings in that house, where he had been induced to instal himself by protestations of affection, were far bitterer than the young men knew. The details of his gradual descent there, from an honoured figure and a benefactor, to a martyr and a butt, would have made a long and painful history. Madame Louchart had in her nature no more gratitude than a cat. It was not that, like most people, she could ignore services rendered in years gone by—she ignored services rendered yesterday. She would embrace a boarder, with tears, for granting her a loan, and scream abuse at him a morning after the loan was granted. They who had the energy speedily forsook her, and those who remained were either too timid or too poor to incense her by taking Papa's part. At an age when one needs friends most, he was alone. And nobody divined how furious a resentment glowed under his meek exterior. Nobody suspected how hotly the submissive old man, dumbly enduring a dozen insults daily, burned to revenge himself.

"If only I could draw the big prize!" It was his obsession. In warm weather he would make his slow way to the little park and sit there picturing, for hours together, the great scene in which he proclaimed his sudden wealth to the Loucharts. It absorbed him to imagine the passion of their self-reproach for having used him ill, their desperate efforts to reinstate themselves in his good graces before he departed grandly for a smart hotel. He dwelt upon their punishment when he had gone—their hourly, festering thought of the benefits they knew would have accrued to them but for their heartlessness. To indulge in the folly of such fancies was his solitary pastime. He would grow cheerful while they lasted and forget he wasn't able to leave at all.

When the three young men arrived to acquaint him with their project, it took a long while to persuade him it might be practicable, but, convinced at last, he embraced them again and again. His smiles and tears were touching to see. "What can I say to young fellows who busy

themselves with saving an old chap like me?
It is a situation from the theatre. Sapristi! it
is of the epoch of Louis-Philippe."

"Except," said Tricotrin facetiously, "that in
the halcyon days of Louis-Philippe there were no
women like madame Louchart?"

"Listen: I will admit privately that, even
then, there were women who weren't perfect.
All the same, you are quite correct—there was
none as bad as *she* is. Ah! I envy you the
sight of her chagrin when she hears I have gone.
Without giving her a month's notice, too! It
is sublime. My little bit all the year round is
worth having, you know—especially for a cellar;
and as a rule I pay promptly. You haven't a
camera, any of you, to take a snapshot of her
consternation? I would hang it among the por-
traits of me in my favourite parts." At the
prospect of escape, his face had flushed, his eyes
twinkled; he grew so animated that it was a
shock to the trio to see the relapse he suffered at
the summons of the gong. As he entered the
dining-room, with his ingratiating "Bonjour,
madame; bonjour, mesdames et messieurs," he
seemed to shrivel.

Madame Louchart stood at the head of the
table, carving a sanguinary leg of mutton in
thin slices. A corpulent woman with purple

cheeks. She made no answer to his greeting.
The miserable boarders murmured "Bonjour,
monsieur" mechanically.

"Please seat yourselves, gentlemen," she said
to the strangers; and the young men unfolded
their napkins, and ate as many of the radishes as
they could collect. The boarders recognised by
the cloud on her brow that she was in a stormy
mood, and they hoped the bonne would do nothing
clumsy to provoke her. Lajeunie and Pitou exchanged sidelong glances, and Tricotrin muttered,
"Gay!"

It was after the woman had sat down, and the
bright red mutton was circulating that some un-
pleasantness occurred. Papa Tripier, though a
Frenchman, did not like mutton underdone, and
formerly there had always been an omelette provided for him, as a substitute, on the leg-of-
mutton days. Such privileges as that he had long
ceased to expect; but he believed himself at
liberty to decline the mutton. To-day it proved
that he was mistaken.

"Louise," said madame Louchart sharply to
the servant, "why have you not served monsieur
Tripier?"

"Monsieur does not wish for any," said the girl.

"*Comment?* You do not take mutton, monsieur? Why not?"

" I have no appetite," murmured Papa deprecatingly.

" It is a defect that I have never remarked.
What is there to complain of about the mutton ? "

" Permettez ! I do not complain ; I have said
nothing."

" You do not complain, but you turn up your
nose. There is a way of saying nothing that is
insolent. I do not allow such audacities at my
table. Old age has not all the prerogatives ; there
are more people to be considered than yourself.
You have to understand that you may not go on
here in a manner that is disagreeable to the rest,
voyons ! "

" Madame, permettez——"

" Enough ! You will behave yourself ! "

It needed all their discretion to restrain the
young men from an outbreak for which he would
have had to pay dearly when they had gone.
The melancholy meal was no sooner over than
they surrounded him, raging. " We shall move
heaven and earth," they vowed. " A month at
most should see you out of it." And that he
might have some bright moments in the meantime, they undertook to report progress by letter
once a week.

The first week was long to him, and the confidence they had inspired in him diminished, but

after that, he used to re-read each letter every day
till the next one came—and his paces to the park
grew brisker, and sometimes he would rub his
hands and chuckle.

And week by week the plan developed, until
the great news came that all the money had been
subscribed, and a suitable room found at last.
He read excitedly : " We shall be with you on
Wednesday morning at nine sharp. You will go
out with us to ' take a little walk '—and never go
back. Pitou conducts you to the new place, and
Tricotrin and I return to the harridan's to pay
what is due, less the lump in lieu of notice, and
remove your traps. Do all the secret packing
that you can ; if we meet with violence, the fewer
things we have to wrestle for, the better. But
don't fash ; we shall leave nothing behind—not a
shoe-button."

It was pathetic, and not without humour, the
scene in which he cautiously pulled forth his luggage and, fearful lest he should be overheard,
stole from the wardrobe to the trunk with collars
and socks. Madame Louchart and her daughter
clattered past the door twenty times, on the way
to the cour, and as their feet smote the passage
he stood motionless, holding his breath. Once,
angered by the sense of his own indignity, he
stood upright, shaking his fist in the air—and

then he might have been again on the stage, so dramatic was his gesture of hate.

At last all the preparations that he dared to make were made. He looked trembling at his pictures, at his furniture; he could imagine the angry woman trying to pull each piece from his saviours' hands. What an undertaking, to remove like this! Again he thought, "If only I had drawn the big prize!"

A craving for a cigarette seized him, and for months he had discarded tobacco. It had been foolish perhaps to deny himself the solace, in order to buy lottery tickets that yielded nothing but false hopes? In any case, the circumstances to-day justified an extravagance. He would go out and get a packet of Marylands!

As he made his way down the cobbled street, a newsvendor was coming up it, bawling an issue of the official list of prizes that had been won in the latest drawing, and Papa Tripier listened to the shouts wistfully. Chance had exalted some paupers to independence. How sensational if, at such an hour, it had come to *him!* What a different departure for him then! Glorious, spectacular—the Loucharts at his feet. "If life were a comedy, I should have won a million in this situation," thought the old actor. And the shouts grew louder, and, quivering, he took a copy of the list from the vendor's hand.

He did not buy it in hopes of affluence, for he held no ticket this time. He bought it quivering because of an audacious idea that had thrilled him. What if he fooled the Loucharts? He might avenge himself by a lie!

But was he capable of it? Had he still the strength for such a tour de force? Yes, he felt that his resentment would lend him strength. One hour of rapture in the house where he had suffered for so long! And afterwards, daily, in every hour that he might live, the jovial knowledge that remorse was gnawing at them!

After he had procured the cigarettes, Papa gave himself a still rarer treat: he sat musing at his ease in a café. And before he rose he penned a few lines to the young men. He wrote, "On your arrival, my beloved boys, you will hear that I am out. Listen for my return, and do not be misled by what I say when I enter. You are to have an opportunity of witnessing my last performance."

When he went back, the copy of the list was hidden in his pocket.

" Well, have you won a fortune yet? " madame

Louchart asked him coarsely at the evening meal.
" I see there has been another drawing."

" Is it so ? " faltered Papa. " Yes, yes, to be
sure !—I had forgotten the date. Ah ! Now I
shall have to wait till to-morrow."

" What a catastrophe ! " she jeered. And, to
the company at large, she said, " He has got so
half-witted that he cannot even remember the
dates of the drawings on which he wastes his
money."

At the street door there was an ancient bell-
pull, which he had always pulled diffidently;
and at about ten o'clock next morning Papa
Tripier tugged at it with a force that startled the
household, and brought the wrathful proprietress
herself from the kitchen. " You ? " she exclaimed, too astounded to say more at the moment.

Then she realised that he could not speak—he
did not speak to his three visitors, who had
hastened into the passage at the clamour of the bell;
he couldn't articulate. His jaw and head were
frantic with the effort, and now he jerked a paper
from his coat, but the only sound that came from
him was his heavy panting. He seemed to be on
the verge of a fit.

" My God," she screamed, " he has drawn a
prize ! "

He answered with wild nods. He broke into shrill laughter that quavered into sobbing. " I am rich ! " he gasped, and tumbled unconscious into Tricotrin's arms—where he winked slyly.

When he decided to come to, he was on the sofa in the salon, and madame Louchart fanned him with *Le Journal*, while her daughter held a liqueur of their best brandy to his lips.

" Ah, he revives. Thank Heaven ! " said the woman piously. " Drink it, drink it, monsieur Tripier. Ah, what a fright you gave us ! I thought it was all over with you. Look how I am trembling."

" Pardon, pardon," he murmured. His weak smile was apologetic. " I am all right again."

" I do not doubt that that brandy saved your life," said she. " N'est-ce-pas, messieurs ? He would have been gone but for the brandy. No, no, do not try to get up yet—keep still awhile."

" I am all right," he repeated feebly. " Gentlemen, I have been a bad host, but—que voulez-vous ? I do not gain a fortune every day—it took me unawares."

" Our fervent congratulations," cried the young men.

" And mine, God knows ! " said madame Louchart.

" And mine, monsieur," said her daughter winningly, pressing him to finish the liqueur.

"Rich, rich! A miracle!"

"It is the big prize?" asked madame Louchart with avidity.

"I am not so greedy," he laughed. "It is more, far more than I know how to spend."

The thought uppermost in her mind burst from her. "We shall not lose you because you are wealthy now? Where else would you be so much at home? Listen, there is the large room overlooking the garden. You would be like a prince in it."

"I am still confused. . . . It is long since I have lived in Paris," he said musingly. "A sojourn in Paris would be pleasant—say, at the Ritz. And, when I touch the money, perhaps a trip to the Midi till the winter is over! By the way, if an impulse should seize me to spread my old wings in a hurry, you would have a legal claim to a month's rent, and that would embarrass me at the moment."

"Ah, monsieur Tripier!" Her protest was vehement. "Shall we talk of 'legal claims' after all these years? You hurt me. One does not mix business with matters of affection. I have a heart. I may be irritable sometimes, but I have a heart. It is your home here—you come and go when you please. But I advise you, do nothing hastily! To speak as a friend, you would find a journey to the Midi very exhausting."

"I have a fancy to gamble at Monte Carlo for once," he said; "I have never done it."

"What a madness!" she shrieked. "To lose your good money as soon as you get it?"

"When one can afford to lose, one wins. And if I did lose fifty, or a hundred thousand francs, what would it matter now? But, after all, I do not know—I might prefer Algiers. Yes, Algiers would be more amusing perhaps."

"Listen," she said, "you have been knocked off your legs to-day, your nerves are all upset—do not expose yourself to still more excitement! The best advice anyone could give you is to keep quiet for the present. Remain where you are till you have had time to turn things over in your mind. . . . Alors, I go to arrange a special déjeuner in honour of the event. Something chic—with such a wine as you will not get at the Ritz. I know where to find it." She turned to the visitors. "I may have the pleasure of your company, gentlemen?"

"I am afraid," said Lajeunie, with sincere regret, "that an urgent matter stands in the way."

"We shall partake of the chic déjeuner first,"

T

declared Papa, rubbing his hands. " I foresee a spread from the charcuterie."

And it was not until her hospitality had been lavishly dispensed that he staggered her by a sudden whim to remove to the Ritz at once. " They will find my ticket good security," he chuckled.

" To-day ? " she cried, aghast. " *Mais!* Ah, no, you will not desert us like that ? Let us rejoice with you for a few weeks first, at any rate. Listen, if it were newly papered the large room would be superb. I saw a wallpaper yesterday in the rue Hoche that is marvellous. You will not leave us at a moment's notice ? The house would be like a tomb when you had gone. Look at the child—she is half crying already ! "

" I did not divine that I was so dear to you both," he said pointedly.

" What ? " she cried, wounded to the core. " If you are dear to me ? I did not love my father better, God rest his soul. Will they nurse you at the Ritz, if you are sick ? Will they look after you there as *we* should do ? . . . Enfin, after the Ritz—you come back to us ? It is understood ? We shall guard your furniture for you religiously."

" Ah, it is of no value to me," said Papa, with a shrug. " The pictures, yes, but the furniture has seen its best days. I shall give it away. When they find time, my friends will have it removed."

"*Removed?*" she echoed heavily. "*Removed?* It would be like making a clean sweep of us all, hein?"

"Oh, monsieur Tripier," pleaded her daughter, bending an artless gaze, "we should feel as if we had lost you for good if you took your lovely furniture away!"

"We'll have it removed this afternoon, if you like," suggested Lajeunie with great good-will. "A pleasure to us, eh, boys?"

"We shall enjoy the job," assented Tricotrin and Pitou, helping themselves to more foie gras.

When he entered upon his new abode, the furniture had not arrived, nor had the expected fuel been delivered, and the old man sat on a campstool in a naked attic, before an empty grate. But he sat smiling blissfully. He was seeing the look in the Loucharts' eyes as they watched him go. He contemplated the torments the pair would suffer, and his benign face could have been no more radiant if the fiction that he told them had been true. The luxury of revenge was sweeter to him than that of the Ritz—the glow of his triumph warmer than the sunshine of Algiers.

He rose and capered, in sheer ecstasy.

A T a date when Parisians had good bread and manners, and there were still artists in Montmartre, a young man sat dining in the Café of the Heavenly Cook; and he called to the waitress, " Bring me a word, please."

" A—what, monsieur ? " said she.

" I want a monosyllable to rhyme with ' rose ' and mean ' after hesitation, but tenderly,' " he told her, impatient at her delay.

She neglected his order, but he found merit in the waitress.

The incident blossomed to acquaintance—and ripened to romantic passion, on the young man's side. Henceforth he went often to the little restaurant, begging of the dainty waitress another monosyllable that he never got. While not averse from compliments and odes, Clémentine, who was the daughter of the proprietress, knew her worth too well to say yes to an unfledged poet. Especially as, when he did get a slim volume out at last, he was as hard up as ever, and the publishers repented their pluck.

Now, soon afterwards, the unavoidable necessity for paying his way compelled the suitor, whose
name was Archambaud Blicq, to forsake poesy in
Paris for employment in Rennes, where he had a
cousin prospering with a department store; and
our knowledge of the world would have led us to
say that his exit from the scene would be the end
of the matter. But it was not. For once we
should have erred. Strange to relate, the episode
was to bear fruit twenty-five years later.

Twenty-five years later, an elderly gentleman,
sauntering in the sunshine of the quays, chanced
to pick from a box of dilapidated books, marked
" 4 sous each," a slender, soiled volume, with a
broken back, " By Archambaud Blicq," which
was not distasteful to him in parts. Being an
eminent journalist, with a column to write and
nothing to write about, the elderly gentleman
wrote a highly sentimental article about the
broken-backed volume—the fairness of its promise and the fustiness of its fate. " What were the
sufferings," he wondered wistfully, " of this Unknown, whose gifts, whose dreams, whose aspir-
ing mind are revealed to me by accident long after
his gallant hopes and bitter tears have——" etc.,
etc. And the praiseworthy publishers, having
refreshed their memory and ascertained there

would be no royalties to pay, took a sporting chance and advertised a new edition of the thing.

This time it let them down less harshly. In strictly limited circles people mentioned the work. Even among a few eccentrics, " Archambaud Blicq " became a transient cult. And next, an out-at-elbows hack, with vague memories of Blicq, laboured for a square meal by contriving a biographical sketch, in which he narrated intimate falsehoods of his " lost comrade." Labouring to the limit of his capabilities, he " deplored the fact that an unrequited attachment for a girl of singular beauty—the Clémentine of the odes—who had been the daughter of a widow keeping a restaurant at Montmartre, had so wrought upon his comrade's mind that the ill-starred youth had destroyed himself in the Seine."

That he had dramatically broken his heart and committed suicide delighted his admirers. The publishers were pleased with him, too. They felt that Blicq had done all he could to forward sales. And now the most ardent of the eccentrics were eager to identify the restaurant—to lunch where the lover had languished, to pose where the poet had prayed.

Meanwhile, time had been proceeding with

Clémentine. She had lost her mother, and found a husband, and content with the exchange, reigned cheerfully in the restaurant by his side. Save for her figure, she was not without some faint resemblance to the dainty waitress of long ago. What is called a " fine woman," by people who can't have too much of a good thing. Her amplitude put no restraint upon her energies, and no patronne of the quarter bustled to more purpose than madame Pidoux, or boasted a livelier turn for profits. Pidoux acted as chef. Pidoux, who was fond of profits himself, approved his wife warmly. His taste inclined to women of liberal circumference, and in his loving eyes Clémentine was no less fair than efficient. A successful marriage.

At the hour of déjeuner one morning, Clémentine, alert behind her counter of the Café of the Heavenly Cook, noted the entrance of two strange and inquisitive-looking ladies. In lieu of seeking seats, the ladies approached her, and the elder said : " Pardon, madame, if it is within your knowledge, would you be so amiable as to inform us whether this is the restaurant where monsieur Archambaud Blicq used to dine ? "

" Monsieur what ? " asked the fat matron shortly.

" We inquire about Archambaud Blicq," said the younger, in reverent tones.

" Ah, my word, how shall I say ? " returned Clémentine, her attention engrossed by the short-comings of the new waiter. " I do not hear all the clients' names. Does mademoiselle see him in the room now ? "

" See him in the room ? " gulped the pilgrim. " He has been dead for twenty-five years. I speak of the poet, Archambaud Blicq," she re-peated, still more impressively.

" Ah ! Tiens ! Archambaud Blicq. That little fellow. Well, I never ! My goodness, it was not yesterday. Ah yes, he used to come pretty well every day in my mother's time. Dead, eh ? " Her interest reverted to the waiter.

" Your mother ? " gasped the two ladies in concert. " Did you say *your* mother ? "

" Is it remarkable I should have had a mother ? "

" Oh, do not think us impertinent, madame ! May we, *may* we ask your Christian name ? "

" Mais, mon Dieu, what does it mean ? " ex-claimed the fat woman, violently agitated. " Did he leave me money ? I am Clémentine Pidoux, formerly Clémentine Bouvard."

" Clémentine ! " cried the pair fervently. " Oh, isn't it thrilling ! "

" Did he leave me money ? " panted madame Pidoux.

" No, no, madame. But to see Clémentine herself ! Is the room much changed, too ? At which table used he to sit ? "

Resentful of the " too," as well as chagrined to hear there was no money, Clémentine indicated the only table where there was space for them, and snorted, " That one ! Do the ladies desire to order lunch ? "

" The imbeciles," she said wrathfully to Pidoux, when they wrote the dinner menu and re-christened remnants of rabbit " croquettes of chicken," " the imbeciles, to raise such hopes in me for nothing ! I do not comprehend the affair. Of what consequence is it whether the little nothing-at-all ever came here or not ? What do you make of it ? "

Pidoux put a forefinger to the tip of his nose, a gesture by which a Frenchman announces that his words are weighty.

" Listen," he answered. " You tell me that this gentleman was a poet. It may be that he was illustrious before he was through—it may be that they raise monuments to him. Who knows? In such a case, it will not be half bad business that he was an habitué of the Heavenly Cook. Others besides the two ladies will be fascinated to sit at his table, others who will perhaps order champagne sometimes, and liqueurs! I counsel you to recall him well, if people question you—to have vivid remembrances of him. That will make it go better still. Did you, by chance, ever hear him say anything, apart from what he would have to eat?"

"Hear him say anything?" she laughed merrily. "I have heard him say a thousand times he could not live without me! He was crazy about me, monsieur Blicq."

"You mean it?" cried her husband. "What an ad.!"

"I assure you. He wrote poems about me. If I am not mistaken, one was even called by my name."

"Now is not that superb?" chortled Pidoux, slapping his knee. "Now it is plain why to learn your name excited them so much. One may be sure it is in the mouth of all the world—when the world says 'Blicq' it murmurs 'Clémentine.' Er—you were obdurate, my love?" he asked apprehensively.

"What?"

" The world does not say that *you* were crazy, too ? "

" But—great goose that you are ! If you were not ready to be jealous ! No, no, no, be easy in your mind, old dear. There has been none but you. I did not care a potato-peeling for the chap. My word, if you are right ! Figure to yourself the boom. All Paris will flock here— the restaurant will become a gold mine."

" As for that, it is fantastic. A dead poet is not so powerful. For that it takes a live cocotte," said Pidoux. " No, to view the matter soberly, I foresee that it will yield more distinction than cash, but it is a good egg all the same. It would not astonish me if at dinner to-night we had half a dozen of his admirers."

And though it turned out that he had been too optimistic in this respect, a further specimen appeared on the morrow.

Soon, pilgrims, intense, if not numerous, gazed raptly at the walls on most days of the week, and Clémentine replied to their tentative queries in a tone of recent bereavement. Though her reminiscences were tame before she and Pidoux had had time to invent some, their triteness was atoned for by her mournful sighs. She wore black, unrelieved. The situation gratified her, apart from its slight benefit to the till—she had sprung to novel prominence. The name of Archambaud Blicq was introduced into the menu in connection with a sauce. And as she marked the bated breath with which the devotees pronounced the honoured name, her superabundant bosom waxed with pride that one so famous had adored her. Pidoux, referring to the adoration humorously one night, was surprised to find himself rebuked.

"Mais comment donc?" he faltered. "It was salad love—he was a boy."

"He was strangely older than his years," she said with dignity. "Monsieur Blicq was not as other boys."

Needless to say, it had not occurred to her to spend money to acquire a copy of his book, but when a pilgrim lent one to her, the odes to Clémentine, or those parts of them that were intelligible to her, absorbed her so deeply that she neglected two instalments of the serial in *Le Journal*. There was even an occasion when she neglected the ledger, in re-perusing lines that described her as child, woman, goddess, mocking sprite, and transcendental mystery. "What insight!" murmured madame Pidoux, the ledger lost to view. "How great a mind!"

Though she had, of course, heard by now that he had drowned himself, she had not yet been informed that the rash deed was due to her indifference, for the delicacy of the customers had naturally made them shrink from rubbing it in; and when one, more intrusive than the rest, did allude to her responsibility, she looked at him perplexed.

"If I lament? To be sure, I lament. Everybody must lament."

"Everybody must know distress, madame," said the young littérateur heavily. "But there is only Clémentine to know remorse."

"Remorse?" she echoed. "And why remorse?"

"Since it was her coldness drove him to despair."

"*Comment?*" she screamed. "It was because of *me?* Never? You astound me. It is the first time that I hear that. It is incredible. Because of *me?* You are not mistaken?"

"It is well known, madame."

"Quelle horreur! You freeze my blood. Through me? I never dreamed it—never, I swear!"

"How ironical is life!" commented the young author, who was enjoying himself immensely. "Archambaud Blicq expires for love of Clémentine—and she learns of it from Zéphirin Coquard, after twenty-five years! Alas yes, madame; had you been kinder, the master would have been with us still."

"He had not a sou," she cried defensively. "On what should we have lived, please?"

"Ah, chère madame, do I presume to criticise? Your prudence was beyond question, and your propriety above reproach—the Philistine would applaud. Yet, the artist thinks of the divine delight that thwarted heart would have given to the world, had Clémentine been tenderer. We shall never know what we have missed. We do not even know in what ultimate revolt his message would have found freedom. We can only surmise. Only surmise," grieved the young author. "The consummation of genius—or a woman's scruples? One's ethics are entangled—the artist is torn," he said reflectively. "May I wonder if Clémentine is torn too, in looking back?"

"No, you may not wonder, and I am not torn," blared madame Pidoux. "Enough said, young man!"

But her emotion was not to be subdued as swiftly as the littérateur, and the way she went

on in the parlour nearly startled Pidoux out of
his wits.

" Be calm, be calm, chérie," he begged, fanning
her with a napkin. " You upbraid yourself
without cause."

" To perish in his youth, for *me !* A character
so fine ! I am much moved," she wailed.

" Yes, it was a silly ass thing to do, but it was
no fault of yours. Besides, how should they
know ? Very likely it was not on your account
at all. It is more than possible there was some
other reason. I dare say it was because he was
stony broke."

" Now, I should like to know how you dare
to say such a thing ! " she exclaimed, deeply
offended. " Certainly it was on my account.
C'est incontestable. I was his idol. Of course
it was on my account. The world admits it.
So noble an intellect ! I was too young to value
him. It is terrible. What misery ! Never shall
I recover from it, never in all the world ! "

" Ah, but listen," expostulated Pidoux, losing
patience. " You go out of your head. It is
enough that you mouth his verses and cast
figures wrong. If I am to watch you weep for
him as well, it is a bit too strong. I begin to
wish we had never heard of this Archambaud

Blicq. God knows, his admirers are no spend-thrifts—it appears to me I lose more on the swings than I make on the roundabouts."

And time strengthened this view. The defunct poet was not only a drawback domestically—it was evident before long that, far from being an asset, he was a commercial drawback as well. Madame's talented histrionics at the desk had rapidly become second nature to her. Her pensive attitudes, her airs of oblivion to her surroundings, might be pleasing to the penurious pilgrims, but the bulk of the daily clients, who were the backbone and sinews of the business, did not like them at all—and if Pidoux so much as hinted a remonstrance to her, she would remind him loftily of his enthusiasm at the start. Bitterly the poor man bemoaned it. More than one complaint had come to his ears. The hairdresser, monsieur Wouters himself, had now mentioned stiffly that his bow on entering was barely noted. With this, the time had come when it behoved Pidoux to rebuke his wife in no uncertain tone.

He said to her, " Ma chère, I shall commence by avowing that I made an error of judgment. It is therefore unnecessary for you to remind me again that I approved at the beginning. I speak of the affair Blicq——"

" You were not enraptured when you heard such an honour had come to us, I suppose ? " she broke in excitedly.

" My love, if you wish it, I stood on my head, and waved flags with my feet. Are you content ? My posture, however, was premature. To proceed, it can no longer be ignored that this literary distinction that has befallen the restaurant is a curse. I say nothing of your reveries in the home, though they give me the hump, but for both our sakes I must urge you to ameliorate your demeanour at the desk. You have affronted monsieur Wouters. Monsieur Wouters is a person of importance, who has lunched here regularly for years, who orders superior wines on occasion, and we cannot afford to estrange him for a bunch of Blicqs, voyons ! It is not long ago you would have been the first to recognise it. You are a woman totally changed since the disaster of literary distinction overtook us. I spit at a distinction that reduces custom ! He ruins my restaurant, your spoony poet."

" *Your* restaurant ? " she retorted heatedly. " It did not exist before I married you, hein ? "

" Mon Dieu ! " roared Pidoux, purple with pain, " she throws her inheritance in my face ! I receive the final blow. If it existed ? Yes, inso-

U

lent ingrate, it existed for strays that blew in by mischance, and were careful not to come back. You have but to turn up the books to see what it owes to my direction. If it existed! You could not have fed six clients at the same time—you would have been short of crockery. I brought to it my management, and my cuisine. Prior to my cuisine, the name of the restaurant was absurd."

" There was one client that came back," she sneered—" that came back every day ! "

" I forbid you to revive him."

" That came back every day. I ask myself what he would think now, if he were here and heard you."

" He would think he had been rash to show me his nose."

" To hear me abused by a husband of no sensibility ! Yes, it is your Clémentine herself who has come to this—it is the Clémentine you called ' mocking sprite ' ! Your sprite has had it in the neck since then. What I have lived to see ! It takes all sorts of men to make a world."

" It takes but one sort of woman to make a hell. Again, I forbid you to speak of him," bellowed Pidoux. " I forbid you to sop up his verses, I forbid you to garb yourself for a funeral and despair at the desk as if it were a tomb. It dejects monsieur Wouters—and many more. Monsieur Wouters can no longer relish his repasts."

So lost was the woman to her better self, that not even the last words had power to move her. Confronted by this, the overwhelming proof of her inconstancy, poor Pidoux' senses reeled. The sinister influence of the defunct then had been complete! Clémentine, the wary wife, the able helpmeet, was no more; her heart, erstwhile in the restaurant, was now in the sundering waters of the Seine!

All this time, Archambaud Blicq, whom we have not had the pleasure of seeing for so long, had been commending himself nicely to his cousin of the department store. He had, in fact, manifested a more marked ability for merchandise than he had shown for poetry, and by dint of putting his shoulder to the wheel, and his versifying behind him, had risen by degrees to a responsible position, and eventually been admitted into partnership. It was not to be called a coincidence that he was now a visitor in Paris—blandly unaware of the new edition—for he had returned more than once in the interval,

though never to the Montmartre district.   But
there were coincidences to come.

To begin with, at the majestic Gaumont-
Palace a wondrous film had been released, and
madame Blicq and the three little Blicqs desired
to see it.   Next, it chanced that on the day the
happy family went, the lady made a slender
luncheon, and when the matinée was over and
they had sauntered as far as the rue Lepic without finding a vacant taxi, she complained of a
" sinking."

" What will you ?   You would take no lunch !
One must eat.   It is very bad for the health,
what you do," exclaimed her husband vehemently.
He had, in middle age, developed a slight tendency
to fussiness.   " You should eat *now*.   You will
be exhausted by seven o'clock.   I tell you always
the same thing."   They were by the door of a
little restaurant, not repellent, and he caught her
by the arm.   " Why should you wait ?   We shall
dine, voyons—we shall eat here.   It will do well
enough.   Let us enter ! " he insisted.   And when
they had selected a table to their satisfaction—
there were no other customers yet—he went on,
" Come, it is clean, it is not bad !   I declare I
am peckish myself.   And you, my little ones ?
Thou art hungry, too, Isabelle, like maman ? "

As he glanced around, at the display of dessert on the counter, and the fat proprietress behind it, and polished his pince-nez to study the bill of fare, no memories of the scene stirred within him; nothing hinted to his senses that twenty-five years earlier he had besought at the fat woman's feet. And as the proprietress contemplated the party, no instinct in her whispered that the desiccated family man with a bald pate had been the passionate youth she mourned as dead.

And then suddenly monsieur Blicq was spluttering amazement. The bill of fare had blazoned to him his own name. It invited him to partake of " Cutlets with the Archambaud Blicq sauce."

" Well, I never! Here is a strange thing! Just look at that! What do you think of that! Now, is it not remarkable? " he burst out. And talking on, through madame Blicq's volubility and the youngsters' chorus of interrogation, he persisted, " But you do not realise what an extraordinary chance it is! Mine is an uncommon name. Consider: I bear an uncommon name; I enter a restaurant by accident—and I find my name on the menu! It is unique, it is veritably unique. It is an incident to recount in a newspaper. Waiter! *Sst!* Tell me. How is it derived, the name of this sauce? "

" It is very good, monsieur," said the waiter dully.

" That is not the question. I inquire how it is derived."

" It has horseradish in it, monsieur," said the waiter, doing his best.

" Ah ! " cried monsieur Blicq with exasperation, " I shall ascertain by and by." And he ordered the dinner, including the sensational sauce. " We shall inquire of the proprietress when we get up," he told his wife.

But he was too curious to be patient, and he had scarcely taken a spoonful of soup when he was dispatching the waiter to inquire at once.

" Eh bien ? You have learnt the derivation ? " he demanded when the fish appeared.

" Oui, monsieur. The patronne informs monsieur that the sauce is named after the great young poet."

Monsieur Blicq was so long before he answered that the waiter had nearly gone. " What ? " said monsieur Blicq very faintly.

" After the great young poet, monsieur. He used to dine here, monsieur, many years ago. He is dead."

" I do not know that I have heard of a poet of

that name," said madame Blicq. "Have you, my dear?"

"Ah, no—ah, never," said her husband, in trancelike tones. He was noting now the heading of the menu—the "Café of the Heavenly Cook."

"You do not enjoy your whiting. What ails you? We dine too early for you," she grieved.

"Ah, yes—ah, no; I enjoy my whiting," he murmured. And to his elder son, who kept re-iterating, "Maman, why is papa's name on the menu?" he gasped, "I entreat thee do not bombard us with imbecile questions, Alexandre! Is it astonishing that I see my name once on a menu? In a directory I may see it a hundred times."

What did it mean? On the few occasions that he had recalled his poems he had been ashamed of having perpetrated them. Whence this celebrity? Again he regarded the portly female behind the grapes and bananas, and he asked himself, "Could that ever have been the girl?" His self-esteem replied, "Ridiculous!" Curiosity twitched in him; and in his struggle to appear at ease, his whiting seemed to him of the dimensions of a whale.

When the meal concluded, and they were all in the street again, monsieur Blicq captured a taxi for his family, and at the moment when they looked for him to squeeze in after them, cast an appreciative glance at the sky. " How heavenly a night ! " he observed, bringing forth an ex- aggeratory adjective because it was running in his mind. " Upon my word, I prefer to walk ! "

He walked back to the restaurant.

And, sad to say, it is here that Archambaud Blicq disappoints us. In the streets of Paris, where he had once craved for literary reputation, the middle-aged shopkeeper stood believing him- self famous—and felt no rapture. He didn't know that he had any use for fame. His one definite impression was that, if he had not made a shocking bad contract, there would have been thousands of francs due to him in royalties now, and this thought chafed him exceedingly. His brow was glum as he saluted Clémentine.

" I return to complete an excellent dinner by a liqueur, madame." And, sipping a *fine* at the counter, he continued, " Apropos, the superb sauce that I tasted reproaches me for my ignor- ance of the poet. Now, how does his poetry sell ? You will honour me by taking a liqueur also, madame ? "

" Bien aimable, monsieur," said Clémentine. " I have not yet dined. If you insist, a tiny glass of vermouth."

"His reputation is new to me. Is he going strong, this Archambaud Blicq, your poet?"

"Alas, monsieur, he is no more."

"I refer to his works—I learned of his decease from the waiter. Are they in great demand? Approximately, how many copies would you say have been sold?"

Her shrug was disapproving. "How should I know? He left but one work—he perished very young."

"So? Of what complaint?"

"Of suicide, monsieur."

"Suicide?" ejaculated monsieur Blicq, hissing with indignation. "Ah! no! That goes too far."

"But, yes, monsieur. He died for love."

"But you make a great error, madame. May I ask if you had any personal acquaintance with him?"

"It is possible we met, since one finds me in his poems," she returned haughtily.

"Can it be?" groaned Blicq. "*You* were really Clémentine?"

"Oho! Monsieur appears to be better informed than I understood him to say? Yes, I am Clémentine—and all Paris can tell you it was because Clémentine was cold that he made a hole in the water."

" I am informed well enough to state that you deceive yourself ridiculously, madame. He made no hole in the water, and his health is A1."

She clutched at air. " Alive ? "

" And kicking—against the outrage you commit. I do not permit you to represent me to all Paris as your victim ! "

After a breathless interval she cried acridly, " Poor chap—and as a boy you were good-looking ! "

" We will not discuss the ravages time has inflicted on us," said monsieur Blicq, hiding the wound. " The point is that I refuse to be advertised as a *felo-de-se*, to tickle your vanity and boom your restaurant. I formally forbid you to flaunt me on your menu as your suicidal suitor. I shall take steps to repudiate the scandal."

" To flaunt you on our menu ? To boom our restaurant ? " she volleyed. " It is a fine boom, my word ! You are a valuable flaunt ! What do you think you draw ? You are a frost, grandpa—a bitter frost. We do you unmerited honour, for which you should blush. You do not recoup us for the horseradish in the sauce. You may take what steps your poor legs allow— we should not have to widen the door for all your admirers to march out abreast. *Sst !* A moment more, grandpa—you have forgotten to pay for the *fine* and the vermouth!"

The excellent publishers were startled next day to receive a visit from Archambaud Blicq. And when he had learned that the coarse statements of Clémentine were not destitute of foundation, when his fear of having enriched the firm had been dispelled even more conclusively than he could have desired, monsieur Blicq opened his heart to them. He said:

"In thinking it over, I am not sure I shall put myself out to deny the yarn, ludicrous as it is. The world does not associate me with the poet— why should I be bothered to vindicate him? I am now in another line—the affair would not harmonise with my occupations. Also I have sons. You can understand I do not want them to discover their father was a poet. It would be to hold up a terrible example. I project them for the business, naturally. There is more money in dry goods than in poetry, what?"

"Sure; and than in publishing too," said the firm.

"Voilà! As business men we see eye to eye. With your assent, I shall leave the young poet in his watery grave."

"Cher monsieur," responded the firm heartily,

" he is at your disposal. Depend upon it, we shall not resuscitate him against your will."

" Gentlemen, I appreciate your co-operation," said monsieur Blicq. " Au revoir. If at any time you should have occasion to make purchases in Rennes I shall be happy to offer you a special discount."

So people heard nothing of the poet's survival. Pidoux himself heard nothing of it—Clémentine did not feel communicative on the subject of a survivor who had proved so thankless to her. But what pen can paint the joy of Pidoux that eve when, ascending from the kitchen, he found his Clémentine again coquettishly attired—a weighty watch-chain on her bosom, and a red rose in her hair ! Even without her tender smile, her toilette had said all. And as the couple sat at dinner, she seized the waiter's pencil and with a queenly stroke repealed a line upon the bill of fare. " Finished," she told her husband. " 'Archambaud Blicq' is off ! "

There are no longer any pilgrims, but monsieur Wouters may still be seen there every day.

THE END

The £1000 Religious Prize Novel

THE SHIP OF TRUTH
By LETTICE ULPHA COOPER

> " Man, with his burning soul,
> Has but an hour to breathe,
> To build a Ship of Truth
> On which his soul may sail—
> Sail on the seas of death—
> For death takes toll
> Of beauty, courage, youth—
> Of all but Truth."

This is the prize novel in Hodder and Stoughton's recent religious novel £1000 prize competition. In the unanimous opinion of the judges " The Ship of Truth " outdistanced all its 400 competitors. It is distinguished by its remarkable candour, its absence of bias, and its perception and allowance for human weakness. As a novel, and as a religious novel, it rings true. The central idea is taken from the above verse of the poem " Truth," by John Masefield, and its purpose is to show that this life on earth is but a brief stage of an adventurous journey that began with God and shall end with Him. The only thing that a man can take with him into the next stage is that measure of Truth that his spirit has been able to achieve in this one. This is the story of Clement Dyson, a young clergyman in a Yorkshire parish. Happily married, keenly interested in his work and in the people under his care, he was eager to share with them the feeling of certainty that he himself felt in the orthodox beliefs in which he had been brought up. Nevertheless, watching their lives and seeing their difficulties and hardships, he found his own faith wavering; and feeling that with his loss of faith in the very existence of God he could no longer continue in the Ministry, he resigned his living. Leaving his wife and children, he went to London; but London with its many creeds and busy multitudes had neither work for his body nor peace for his soul, and it was not until he returned to the simplicities of life, to the starkness of man's fight with Nature, that he began to build again for himself a Ship of Truth which should carry him through this life to the next. His faith was born again, and, brushing aside all creeds, ritual and dogma, he got back to first beginnings and to his belief in God and in Everlasting Life.

THE SECRET OF THE CREEK
By VICTOR BRIDGES

AUTHOR OF THE MAN FROM NOWHERE, ETC.

" The Secret of the Creek " is another of those joyous tales of modern adventure which have endeared him to all lovers of a first-class thriller. The scene, as in " Green Sea Island," is laid on the East Coast, amongst the creeks and marshes of which the author is so happily at home. It is salted throughout with Mr. Bridges' characteristic humour—that rare gift with which so few writers of sensational fiction seem able to endow their plots. It is this quality that has helped to make his books as popular all over the Continent and America as they are here.

THE GOLDEN POUND

Stories by A. S. M. HUTCHINSON

AUTHOR OF IF WINTER COMES, ETC.

A. S. M. Hutchinson writes very few short stories, and this is but his second collection. Of his first *The Times Literary Supplement* was constrained to write : " The secret of Mr. Hutchinson's wizardry is his simplicity; he speaks to the common heart of all of us with words which that part of us understands "; and that same wizardry is here in " The Golden Pound " in all its compelling phases. As whimsical humour of " A.S.M.'s " own peculiar sort, the story entitled " The Girl with the Grave Nose " is sheerest delight, and there are several others in precisely the same vein. "What Shakespeare Knew " is, on the other hand, a theory of Shakespeare's genius which, though presented in story form, may well enough leave many readers, and them by no means the least thoughtful, with the serious reflection : " 'Pon my soul, I believe there is something in it ! " And the volume concludes with an allegory, " Set in Dominion," which probably no one but A. S. M. Hutchinson could have written, and which might well have been issued in separate form, so that the lesson it reads and the hope it gives could be preserved as stimulus and inspiration when life seems out of joint and how to mend it hard indeed.

MEDAL WITHOUT BAR

AN ENGLISH WAR NOVEL

By RICHARD BLAKER

Hodder and Stoughton announce the greatest and most British of all war novels. Here is no hysterical pessimism or windy optimism; no reactionary anti-patriotism and no flag-wagging; no nastiness for the sake of nastiness; no obscenity; no sentimental hero-worship and at the same time singularly little bitterness—none at all of the noisy, futile kind. On the other hand, there is here a truly remarkable mass of decent, practical, sane, British common sense. The whole massive record is clean, shrewd, balanced, honest, and, in the best sense, true. A British quality permeates the entire work, and every aspect of it. " Medal Without Bar " is something that no Latin or Teutonic writer could hope to achieve. To miss this book would be something of a disaster. Just as it is assuredly the biggest English war novel that has so far appeared, it is the best, truest, and most comprehensive. Nothing could be more British than this book.

THE LITTLE DOG LAUGHED
By LEONARD MERRICK

Under perhaps the most charming of all his titles—" The Little Dog Laughed "—Mr. Leonard Merrick gives us at length a further volume of his inimitable stories. Here again is that charm of style and brilliance of execution with which every reader of " While Paris laughed " or " A Chair on the Boulevard " is so familiar. The titles of the stories making up this volume are as follows : " The Elevation of Lulu," " Five Bells," " Little Birdie—A Christmas Idyll," " The Shoelace," " Mate," " The Vengeance of Monsieur Dutripon," " The Dovecote," " Poor Dear George," " The Crime of Olga Jibinsky," " I Recall a Seat," " The Surgeon was Right," " A Cure for Dyspepsia," " The Departure of Papa," " The Epic of the Heavenly Cook."

BLUE FLAMES
By RICHMAL CROMPTON
AUTHOR OF THE WILDINGS, ETC.

All admirers of Richmal Crompton will welcome this novel, the most recent and most typical example of her skilful craft. It exhibits to the full those characteristics which have won her well-known popularity—dealing, as it does, in observant detail with the different members of a large and widely varying family, who are drawn with masterly touch. The title is derived from the blue flames in a log fire—which, to the hero of the story, signify his boyish dreams and vague ambitions. These visions are never quite realised—whose are ?—but their charm and fascination linger with him right through life, to compensate him for the actualities of his self-sacrificing career. Readers will follow with keen interest and enjoyment the fortunes of the numerous *dramatis personæ* presented to them in " Blue Flames."

THE KNIFE BEHIND THE CURTAIN
STORIES OF THE SECRET SERVICE
By VALENTINE WILLIAMS
AUTHOR OF THE CROUCHING BEAST, ETC.

The creator of " Clubfoot " has a fine flair for the mystery and crime story, as all who read his magnificent detective novel, " The Eye in Attendance," know so well. Into this volume he has collected a baker's dozen of short stories, all dealing with mystery and crime in their various manifestations. These stories make a splendid and most exciting volume.

PRINTER'S DEVIL
By CLEMENCE DANE & HELEN SIMPSON
AUTHORS OF ENTER SIR JOHN

The entry of these two brilliant collaborators into the field of detective fiction with "Enter Sir John" was quite one of the outstanding literary events of the past year. The same qualities of brilliance and wit that characterise "Enter Sir John" characterise the mystery of the murder of a publisher, which is the central fact of "Printer's Devil," the new novel which Miss Clemence Dane and Miss Helen Simpson have written. Fond, foolish Horrie Pedlar—rejoicing in the success of her unique publishing business, "The Pedlar's Pack," and the return to England of her star author, Marmion Poole, debonair, devil-may-care, as ever; and happy in the devotion of her many friends—was found dead at the foot of the little twisted staircase that led to her flat high above the roofs of the City. Many mourned her; the newspapers published laudatory obituary notices; but, at the Coroner's inquest, a faint, sinister note was heard, particularly with regard to the disappearance of a certain MS. Rumour had it that the MS. contained many people's business, and Horrie alone, besides its author, had read it! So cleverly have the authors mixed comedy and tragedy that the ridiculous, charming little love affair of the Highbrow Gilda and the little Cockney publicity agent, Koko Fry, is inseparable from the tragedy of Horrie's death, and right to the last page readers will be quite undecided as to whether they have enjoyed a first-class comedy or a breath-taking thriller, for both are to be found in this story.

THE LAST HERO
By LESLIE CHARTERIS

Hodder and Stoughton present Leslie Charteris for the first time in their lists. His work is in fact most uncommon and most uncommonly good. There is even something very intriguing in this little paragraph which he has kindly written for us to introduce his new novel "The Last Hero." "There are gathered here," said Simon Templar, known to many as the Saint, "three somewhat shop-soiled musketeers—and a blessed angel. Barring the blessed angel, we've broken half the Commandments and most of the private laws of several countries. Fighting is our job. Battle and sudden death. In fact, we must be the last three men in the wide world who ought to be interfering with the makings of a perfectly good war. But there aren't many like us. Will you think me quite mad if I put it to you that three shabby hell-bursting outlaws might, by the grace of God . . . ?"